A fitting place for her prisoner.

She peered through the slot at him… and swallowed.

He was shirtless, his chest glistening, his muscles rippling from his broad shoulders to his ridged abdomen.

He shot her a sexy smile.

"Hello, sweetness."

She forced an end to her stare. "Up against the wall." She dragged the pulley of chains to pull his hands back against the wall. Only then did she approach. Pity. She'd fantasized of stepping too close, of him grabbing her… doing wicked things.

He tugged the chains. "Let me go, Melissa."

Her glare morphed into a cool, brittle smile. "Oh, but, Hunter, we're only just getting started."

Her triumph was short-lived when his brutal gaze raked her from head to toe. "If you still want me around after five months, maybe it's not revenge you're after."

WARRIOR UNTAMED

BY
SHANNON CURTIS

MILLS & BOON

First Published in Great Britain 2016
By Mills & Boon, an imprint of HarperCollins*Publishers*
1 London Bridge Street, London, SE1 9GF

© 2016 Shannon Curtis

ISBN: 978-0-263-92192-2

89-1216

Shannon Curtis grew up picnicking in graveyards (long story) and reading by torchlight, and has worked in various roles, such as office admin manager, logistics supervisor and betting agent, to mention a few. Her first love—after reading, and her husband—is writing, and she writes romantic suspense, paranormal and contemporary romance. From faeries to cowboys, military men to business tycoons, she loves crafting stories of thrills, chills, kills and kisses. She divides her time between being an office administrator for the Romance Writers of Australia and creating spellbinding tales of mischief, mayhem and the occasional murder. She lives in Sydney, Australia, with her best-friend husband, three children, a woolly dog and a very disdainful cat. Shannon can be found lurking on Twitter, @2BShannonCurtis, and Facebook or you can email her at contactme@shannoncurtis.com—she loves hearing from readers. Like… LOVES it. Disturbingly so.

Prologue

He heard the grate of a key in a lock, followed by the creak and clang as the gate at the far end of the corridor was slowly opened. He kept his eyes closed, bending and working the blazing colors in his mind like a fiery kaleidoscope. The warmth and light in his mind kept the dark chill at bay, the cold stone against his back and beneath his buttocks a sensation he'd learned to ignore.

He heard the whispers, the rough slide of regulation boots on stone floor, felt the faint stir in the air currents as one—no, two people made their way toward his cell. It was her scent, though, that caught his attention. Something light, floral…he could almost sense the innocence, the naïveté—the gullibility. He resisted the urge to smile. No sense in giving anything away.

The peephole in his cell door slid open, the noise an annoying squeal in the silence of the tomb—for this was a tomb. There was no other word for it. It was where they hoped he'd spend the rest of his lifetime, and the next.

"What's he doing?" He heard the woman whisper. He couldn't tell much from the soft sound, but her scent was now stronger, laced with a tired curiosity. Like a wilted frangipani.

"Dunno. Meditating. Plotting. Maybe just losing his sanity. He's like that all the time." He knew that voice, had become quite practiced at ignoring it, but this morning—or was it evening—he decided to give it his attention.

"He doesn't do anything else?" Her voice was raspy, as though even the question taxed her reserves. She sounded fatigued. Drained.

She didn't know the meaning of that word. *Drained.* But she would.

"Nope. Pretty easy duty, I must admit."

"Why is he locked all the way down here? There's nobody else in this block."

"The lights. There is no natural light in here, so it's fluorescent lighting."

He knew they couldn't see the clenching of his shoulder muscles beneath the rough fabric of his prison uniform, but he still tried to mask it with a deep inhalation. He needed something to relax him whenever he thought of his current circumstances, the weakness that even now leeched the energy from his limbs. He needed light. Or *something*. And he wasn't getting it down in the bowels of this prison, thanks largely to his sons.

White-hot rage welled inside him whenever he thought of their betrayal. Ryder, he could understand. That kid had always been ungrateful. But Hunter—his son's betrayal stung the most. Hunter had worked diligently by his side for years, just like a sheep, following his every command. Until that last night… The cold kiss of fury snaked down his back. He hadn't seen that betrayal coming. He'd always believed that if it came down to it, Hunter would choose his father over his brother, but his son had surprised him. Just like his mother.

He exhaled, expelling the tension. But he would have his due. The light, floral, stale scent of the prison guard teased his senses again. And soon.

"What do the lights have to do with anything?" he heard her whisper.

The rustle of fabric told him the guard was shrugging his shoulders. "Who the hell knows? We're just here to make sure he rots where he sits. He organized the murder of an Alpha Prime. He deserves everything coming his way."

There was a brief silence, and he found himself waiting for her response.

"I heard about that. He supposedly conspired with the Woodland Pack?"

"Yeah, with the Woodland Alpha Prime. But seeing as that was pack against pack, that case has been handed over to Alpine Pack under tribal jurisdiction."

"Well, it was their Alpha Prime who was murdered. But wasn't he murdered in some dentist's chair? Why is this guy here?"

He took another slow breath in. She was asking questions. Good. She had doubts. He was going to exploit that, and he was going to enjoy it.

"This guy organized the poison to be delivered. The dentist knew nothing about it. Get this—the dentist was his *son*."

His jaw muscles clenched. Well, Ryder had deserved it. Pulling away from the family like that, ignoring them. He'd ceased to be his son the day he started using his trust fund on his own practice—that would be in competition with the family's medical center. Hell. What did Ryder think would happen, that he'd actually give his blessing? He almost shook his head in disbelief, but kept himself still. What Ryder had done, well, it was to be expected. Hunter, though—that stung. That really, really stung. He thought he'd raised him better than that.

"But why is he *here*? He hasn't had a trial yet. I thought everyone was innocent until proven guilty?"

"Good grief, how long have you been working for Reform?" The male guard wheezed with laughter. "There's no such thing as innocence here."

"I just thought—"

"Don't. Don't think he can be saved, don't think he's decent and don't pity the bastard. Just look in on him once in a while, make sure he hasn't strung himself up with his bedsheets—or if he has, make sure he's good and dead before you call anyone."

There was a hesitation, then finally a sigh. "Sure. What else is there to do?"

"I'll show you the break room. It's going to be where you spend most of your time—the screen in there is awesome."

He heard the snick as the peephole was closed, then the soft shuffle of footsteps until they reached the gate at the end of the corridor. It wasn't until the gate had opened and closed, the keys had clinked as they turned in the lock and the scent had faded, that he let the sly smile lift his lips.

Arthur Armstrong opened his eyes slowly. They had no idea who they were dealing with.

Chapter 1

Melissa Carter tried to be patient. Really. But it wasn't her strongest personality trait. Actually, most would argue she didn't possess it at all. And she hadn't had a decent night's sleep in so long. "Anytime this century, Lexi."

Lexi glanced up and frowned. "If I have to wear this day in, day out, then I need to make sure it's *right*."

Melissa pursed her lips but refrained from comment as she let the young woman scan her rings for the fourth time. It was fine. She could handle this without screaming. She could prove her mother wrong and be *patient*.

"And it has to be a ring? Not a necklace?" Lexi asked wistfully, eyeing an intricately woven Celtic knot pendant on a stand behind the counter.

Melissa kept her expression neutral as she heard that same question for the third time. She shook her head. "No. You're likely to change a necklace depending on the outfit. Or it might get snagged—or yanked. A ring is more likely to stay on, and that's what we want for you, Lexi. Something to stay with you." Her irritation died as she remembered the reason for this, and she kept the sympathy out of her eyes, out of her voice. Lexi didn't need sympathy. There were times when she thought Lexi needed a smack upside the head, but she'd leave that to Lexi's older brother, Lance. For now, she just wanted to make Lexi safe, and if Lexi had come to her, it meant the young woman had come to the same realization—she was out of her depth and needed help. The fact she'd come to Melissa, well, perhaps *that* required some sympathy, but Melissa preferred action to the warm and fuzzies.

She leaned over the tray, and scanned through the silver jewelry. Usually she let the stones in the jewelry speak to her clients, and attract them on their own. But her bookstore was filling with customers, and Lexi suffered a lack of confidence—hence her current situation. She still couldn't quite understand that one. Lexi was beautiful. Blonde, petite, the kind of woman guys wanted to do things for, like open doors and carry bags. She sighed. She couldn't remember the last time someone offered to carry something for her. Oh, wait. Lexi's brother, Lance, had—but he'd been carrying her supplies, and it had been his job, so that didn't really count.

"How's Lance doing?" She hadn't seen him for a few weeks. She didn't get along with a lot of people, but Lance was an exception. He was the only set of fangs she allowed in her zone, with a special dispensation built within her wards to give him access. He'd worked hard, never complained—a trait she admired in her staff—and had always been punctual. Not too chatty, but decent, in a rough kind of way. She didn't make a habit of hiring ex-cons, but he'd been her exception. He'd needed a job, she'd needed someone to haul supplies—and his fangs were actually the good kind. Perfect. The fact they'd formed a strong friendship surprised them both—and probably everyone who knew her, considering her personality didn't really lend itself to making a lot of friends. After what had happened with Theo, though... she blinked. Lance had gone above and beyond the duties of a friend, then.

"Haven't heard from him in a while," Lexi said, shrugging.

Melissa frowned. She knew the kind of trouble Lance chased. Admired him for it. "You're not worried?"

Lexi looked up and blinked, her eyes taking on a blank glaze. "What? No. Everything is fine," she said in a flat voice.

Melissa's eyes narrowed. Ri-ight. Lexi definitely needed to get away from the compelling effects of her current boyfriend.

"What about this one?" She tapped at a delicate ring. Its band was intertwined silver strands, and the stone was speckled with green and black. "Green snakeskin jasper. It's a protective stone, perfectly suited to what you need, and it matches your..." She flicked her gaze up to Lexi's eyes. Oh. They were a deep blue. Melissa's eyebrows dipped briefly. She'd never noticed that. Lexi's brother had worked as a stock boy—okay, stock *man*—for her a few years ago, and his eyes were the darkest green, almost black. She'd never noticed the siblings didn't share the same eye color. Her gaze drifted downward. "Scarf. They match your scarf."

Lexi wore a bottle green-and-black scarf to go with the rest of her outfit. She frowned. "But that's just today."

"And you look fantastic, so it obviously agrees with

you. With your coloring, this ring will either comple-
ment or present a tasteful contrast with any of your other
outfits," Melissa lied quickly.

Lexi looked at it doubtfully. "Really?"

Melissa nodded as she plucked the ring from the tray.
"Yep. Trust me. Let me go enhance it for you." She
stepped into the back room behind the shop's counter—
it was basically the size of a broom closet. She placed
the ring on the midnight blue swath of velvet that lay
on a low shelf. She closed the door and pulled on the
cord. Warm light bathed the tiny space, and she stood
there for a moment. Shelves lined the space, and a spo-
radic collection of small bottles, vials and bowls were
placed in order of need around the working space. These
were only her more commonly used ingredients. Her
lips pursed. Not as many as there should be, thanks to
the pyro jerk who had torched her hidden apothecary
below her bookstore.

She was slowly renovating the space, though. It was
no secret she was a witch—a witch who sold spells,
incantations and laced trinkets. Those customers who
wanted more than books usually stepped below stairs…
but she'd learned a hard lesson five months ago. Never
trust a soul—no matter how innocent and tempting he
looked. She'd lost so much…it was taking a lot longer
to rebuild her valuable stock, damn it.

As tiny and as bare as this space was, it was fast becoming a haven for her. There were no requests from
customers, no pleading and no demands for attention in
here, just her and her magic. She eyed the ring briefly.
Green snakeskin jasper guarded against negativity and
could act as a shield against psychic attack, protecting
the wearer against harmful or destructive temptations.
Lexi had a vampire boyfriend, and Melissa could sense

the compulsions at work on the young woman. The fact Lexi was still wearing a scarf inside her store didn't escape her, either. It was cold outside, and dirty snow lined the gutters and sidewalks of Irondell as winter descended on the city, but inside the Better Read Than Dead Bookstore it was warm and cozy. Consciously or unconsciously, Lexi was hiding the bite marks and she needed a little help to withstand the mesmerizing coercions this man was exerting over her. If she didn't resist soon, she'd end up a vamp slave... Melissa shuddered. It was one thing she couldn't quite comprehend, those people who willingly surrendered their blood and actively sought to be bitten by the vamps, chasing one bite after another, after another. The life span of a vamp slave wasn't long, for obvious reasons. Why Lexi was with a bloodsucker in the first place, Melissa couldn't understand. But she could help.

She held both her hands over the ring, closed her eyes and drew on her magic. She could feel it rising to her fingertips like a warm bath of light, and she focused, chanting a protection spell to further imbue the natural qualities of the stone. She added in a little layer of confidence, as well. Lexi had to stop hanging out with the Mr. Wrongs, and start believing she was worthy of a Mr. Right—not that Melissa would ever have that kind of conversation with the woman. She soooo didn't do warm and fuzzies.

Melissa opened her eyes, and the stone in the ring glowed briefly as the spell anchored, and then the magical light slowly banked. Melissa lifted the ring, feeling the warmth and weight of its new power. She smiled with satisfaction. The ring was constructed of silver— she'd like to see Mr. Wrong try to take this off his little blood bag.

She left the broom closet—no, Power Room. She frowned. She had to come up with a better name for it. Maybe the Dark Well of Influence? She wrinkled her nose. She'd keep working on it.

She smiled brightly at Lexi and handed her the ring. "Here you go."

Lexi reached for it timidly, eyeing it before sliding it onto the middle finger of her right hand. She tilted her head, then her gaze flicked to Melissa across the counter. "I don't feel anything. Are you sure it's working?"

Melissa rolled her eyes. "These things don't come with a built-in electric shock, Lexi. Give it time. It will grow on you."

Lexi sighed, then nodded. "Okay. I hope this works." She dug her wallet out of her handbag. "How much?"

Melissa named her price, and Lexi's eyebrows rose in surprise. "Oh, cool, I thought it would be more."

Normally it would, but Lexi was Lance's sister. This was the least she could do for a friend. She didn't have many friends.

Melissa met her gaze squarely. "Stay safe, Lexi."

Lexi nodded, then fidgeted with her scarf. "You do like to crank the heat up in here, don't you, Melissa?" She loosened the scarf, and Melissa could see the edge of a dark bruise, and the open, angry bite mark.

She reached beneath the counter. "Hey, try this." She handed over a small tub of lotion. Lexi tilted her head as she read the label.

"What is it?"

"An all-over body moisturizer with a new scent I've been working on. This is a sample bottle. Let me know what you think."

Lexi flipped the cap and sniffed the contents, then

smiled. "Okay, thanks." The young woman eyed her for a moment, and her brow dipped. "You look tired."

Melissa winced. "Thanks."

"No, seriously. You look tired, and you never look tired. What gives? Is your mom giving you grief?"

Melissa's smile was brittle. It was no secret her mother always gave her grief. "I'm not sleeping well," she admitted. She wasn't in the habit of confiding with Lexi—with anyone, really, but maybe it was an indication of just how tired she was that she relaxed her usual guard with the petite blonde.

Lexi raised her eyebrows. "Is something troubling you? Bad dreams?"

That was an understatement. It was as though all her awful life moments were on auto-replay whenever she closed her eyes. Especially the day her mother told her she'd never let her daughter step in as Elder Prime... And the night her father walked out... She blinked. Yeah. Those weren't dreams. They were nightmares. And she most definitely didn't want to "share" those. Not with Lexi, not with anyone.

"I'm fine. I'll just drink some chamomile tea tonight."

Lexi shrugged, then placed her items in her tote bag. "Whatever. I have to hustle. I have a hot date tonight."

Melissa smiled, mentally batting away a tiny green flame of envy that flared within her. One, she wasn't interested in any dates, hot or otherwise, and two, Lexi was dating a shadow breed, for Pete's sake. There was nothing worthy of envy there.

"Well, that moisturizer is guaranteed to make the night interesting," she murmured, and Lexi laughed as she left the store. Melissa watched her briefly in the street. The young woman eyed up and down the street, then loosened the scarf some more so it fell open. A smile twitched at Melissa's lips as Lexi strode down the street, a confident sway to her hips catching the eye of males passing by. The ring was working. Good.

She hoped Lexi would try that "moisturizer" as soon as she got home. It was a mix laced with lavender, chamomile and a heavy dose of verbena. No vampire would want to get near her if she slathered that toxic herb all over her.

Her watch beeped, and her smile fell. Great. Time to feed the pyro jerk. She beckoned Jenna, her assistant, over.

"Can you man the cash for me? I'm going to take a quick lunch break."

Jenna nodded, stepping behind the counter.

Melissa grabbed the brown paper bag and a plastic bottle of water from the bottom shelf of the counter, and strode toward the door behind a stack of books at the back of her store. When she reached that last stack, she pulled her heavy keyring from the front pocket of her jeans, and sifted through them until she found the two keys for the double-lock system she'd asked her brother, Dave, to install on the door, and then pulled on the cord that lit the stairwell. She could use her magic to open the doors, but loved to hear the click and snick of the locks. She skipped lightly down the stairs and stopped to key in the code to unlock the next intricate lock system she'd installed on the second door.

The heavy steel door swung inward and muted lighting automatically switched on, illuminating the work areas, but leaving the rest of the area in soft shadows. She stepped inside the large room. Now it bore little resemblance to the scarred and ashen remains of five months before. They'd installed fire-retardant hardwood and plastic composite to limit the possibility of a fire occurring again. Like anything below surface, this place was off the plans, off-the-record—and not insured. She'd have her apothecary back soon, and then she'd be able to do more than just bespell jewelry and mix herbs into lotions and drinking drafts. She'd be able to do some considerable damage to the damned shadow breeds. Her eyes narrowed, and she stepped farther into her secret space.

It was the door she'd cleverly painted as an intricately carved tree trunk that she now made her way over to. This one had a series of locks, but was also warded, so she waved her hand to lift the spelled lock, then opened the door. She grabbed the large torch that she hung off a hook just behind the door, flicked it on and stepped carefully down into the dark void, her sneakers squeaking softly on the steep narrow metal steps that led down into the darkness. The light emitted was blue— something she knew her prisoner couldn't draw on.

The air down here was dank and musty. She took a deep breath. Metal. Rust. Concrete. Stone. It wasn't exactly a forgiving place, all hard surfaces and cold darkness. She thought of her prisoner, and her mouth firmed. A fitting place for the pyro jerk. Goose bumps rose on her arms as she located the trapdoor. That trapdoor was about three stories below street level, and she'd never ventured beyond it. She'd opened it once, hauled it up with the help of a crowbar. She'd been curious… but when she'd crouched at the lip of the hole, she'd paused. Listened.

Something had slithered in the darkness, something that breathed, and…*waited.* She'd leaned forward, and the shuffling noise sped up, grew louder, and she just managed to replace the lid—but not before she caught the glimpse of that pale hand with the elongated gray fingernails.

Even now, she shuddered at the memory. Creepy. She'd heard tales of Old Irondell—hell, every parent seemed to enjoy bouncing their child on their knee and freaking the crap out of them with the old stories—hers included.

But that's what they were to most people—stories. Wicked, cautionary tales to make kids toe the line and not wander off.

Only, she knew they weren't *just* stories. Old Irondell may be just a pale memory that was passed down, less and less, from one generation to the next. But there were some folks who still knew of the origins of the Reformation, of the time of The Troubles, when humanity discovered the existence of the shadow breeds: the vampires, werewolves, shifters and other creatures that were just plain weird, but who seemed to be on a mission to eat, or kill, or eat *and* kill any human they encountered. It had started a war that had lasted generations, until the time of Resolution, when all breeds gathered to negotiate a truce, which led to the Reformation, the redefining of territories and laws, and society itself. The homeless, the outcasts, those who didn't "fit" into the normal, new Reform society had migrated to dwell below Irondell, away from the light. Away from Reform law. Nobody went into Old Irondell and came out unchanged.

If they ever returned. Most didn't.

She didn't need to go into Old Irondell. She had enough problems dealing with the shadow breeds above surface.

She turned back to the door, slid the peephole open and peered through the slot. There he was. Pyro jerk.

That mean, homicidal son of a—oh. Wow. She swallowed.

He was doing a handstand. Correction, he was doing push-ups in a handstand position. He was shirtless and the jeans he wore were smeared with dirt, rust and grime. His chest glistened, his muscles rippling with each dip and raise, from the corded strength of his broad shoulders down to the ridged abdomen that showed the control and power of each move. His hair was long, touching the floor when he moved, and the beard that covered his jaw gave him a wild, untamed look. She'd made a point of providing her prisoner with a bucket of water every other day so he could wash, but she'd never seen him actually bathe, or sweat—or glisten. She swallowed again.

He pushed himself up, exhaling in a gust, then slowly lowered his feet to the ground with the grace of a gymnast. He rose from his position, his back to her, and he rolled his shoulders. There wasn't an ounce of fat on him. Sure, he'd been on a prison diet for the last five months, but still, he didn't look like he was wasting away. No. He looked....healthy. Very...healthy. The chains that connected his wrists to the bolt in the wall clanked with his movements. She stared at that glorious wall of muscle, his figure an enticing V that narrowed into lean hips and a tight, tantalizing butt. He turned his head from side to side, as though stretching out some kinks, shook out those massive arms and then paused.

His head turned slowly to his right. He didn't face her, but she could see the corner of his mouth lift up in a sexy little curl.

"Why, hello, Red."

A sneaky, traitorous warmth flared inside her at his familiarity, quickly squashed by a wave of annoyance. No warmth for him, damn it.

Chapter 2

Hunter turned to face the door, refusing to let her presence bother him. She was right on time. He wasn't sure if his captor's punctuality was something he appreciated, or whether it irritated the hell out of him. It depended on his mood. He stood there for a moment, assessing his mood, and his stomach growled. Okay, so today it was appreciation. He was hungry, and she'd brought him food.

He raised his hands to his hips and tilted his head back to meet the green-eyed gaze of the witch behind the door. She stared at him for a moment, her gaze full of suspicion and wariness. He wasn't going to try anything. He'd learned that lesson. Four times. Didn't mean he wouldn't try again, he just wasn't feeling it today.

"Back up against the wall." Her voice was low, husky and, just like yesterday, and the day before, and the day before that, the sound curled inside him, and he hated it as much as he enjoyed it. Five months he'd been trapped in this hole in the wall. Five lonely months. He'd never really been a social kind of guy, but after too many months of his own company, he was beginning to look forward to these too-brief moments of company with the bitchy witch. Crave it, even. Resented it, but craved it.

Yeah, he was a sick bastard. He backed up against the wall as instructed and folded his arms. If he didn't threaten her, his cold little captor might stay longer.

The key clanked in the lock, and then the heavy steel door swung inward. She stepped into the room, and straightaway, he could smell her, *feel* her. Cinnamon and smoke. Lazy heat. He didn't think the smoke could be blamed on him, though. He'd heard the sounds from above, the drilling, banging and clanging. They'd cleaned up that little mess he'd made. No, that scent of smoke was entirely of her own making. He was pretty sure his captor dabbled with fires of her own. As usual, she carried a torch. He hid a smile. She'd done her research. No candles, no flames, no access to sunlight, no fire of any kind…and blue light. But blue light was notoriously difficult to get hold of, so his captor had used a blue slide over the head of the torch. Sure the color of the light was blue, and gave an interesting hue to her skin, making her look otherworldly, but it was still light behind the shade. He could still use the feeble light of a torch to feed his power, if only a little. Yeah, they hadn't put *that* little tidbit in the history books. It wasn't the most efficient way for him to recharge—the light warriors had made sure to keep that one secret, too—but the glow from a torch did help. Each day, she fed him, both in food and energy.

Today she wore some sort of silky green top that flowed about her. It didn't hug her form, but just hinted at the willowy, lithe frame beneath. Her jeans were tucked into leather boots. Boots with heels he knew from experience that hurt like the dickens if she kicked him.

She crossed to the pulley of chains that hung against the wall, set the brown paper bag and bottle of water on the floor and started to drag down on a length of chain. His jaw tightened as the iron chafed against his skin, and he could feel the sting as the cuff burned him. He thought he'd get used to it—especially with the efforts he'd put into those chains recently, but he hadn't. Each contact of the metal with his body was like a hot poker to his skin.

Soon his right hand rose with each pull on the chain, and when she was satisfied with the position of his arm, she roped the chain around a hook on the wall. Then she started with the second chain. She did this every time, and he sighed. Damn her caution.

Of course, he'd given her good reason to exercise it whenever she was around him.

She left just enough give in the chain for him to have a limited range of movement with his left arm, then stooped to pick up the brown paper bag. He eyed the silky top as it gaped open with her movement, and he caught a glimpse of the creamy swell of her breasts, the scalloped pattern of black lace. He should be angry at himself. One, for being a pervert, and two, for spying on *her*. But, no. Five months. No sex. *Angry* wasn't the right word for what he was feeling.

She opened the bag and pulled out a sandwich wrapped in plastic. She unwrapped it, then tossed it to him.

He caught it easily, eyeing the distance between them. She was just outside of his reach. Pity. He had fantasies of her stepping too close, of him stepping up and grab-

bing her, of him…doing wicked things. And then he'd
call himself all sorts of a pathetic idiot for thinking anything remotely lustful about his captor and would replace
those secret fantasies with something harsher, like forcing her to set him free.

He stared at her for a moment. She had red hair that
looked like it had a life of its own, all vibrant curls and
shiny locks, and green eyes that were a vivid spark of
color, the pale complexion with a faint tinge of pink high
on the cheeks was smooth and clear. The woman had
the face of an angel, a body built for sin…and the fero-
cious temperament of a saltwater crocodile at sunset.

He looked down at the sandwich. Peanut butter and
jelly. He was heartily sick of that combination, but damn
it, he was also hungry. At least she gave him something
more substantial in the evenings. Mostly. He tried to
lower his other hand to hold the sandwich properly, but
the chain clanked against the wall, and he hissed softly
at the sting at his wrist. He covered the noise with a
tight smile.

"Come on, Red," he crooned. "How about loosening
up the other one?"

She arched an eyebrow and stepped back. "You only
need one hand to eat, jerk."

His lips pulled up at the corners. And there it was,
her regular endearment. He gestured toward her. "What,
you're not going to join me? We could swap sandwiches
and bitch about our boyfriends."

She would come, feed him, and when she was sure
he'd eaten, she'd fetch him the bottle of water so he
could wash it down. Before she left, she'd loosen the
chains enough so that hc had more slack in his restraints.
Enough for him to make use of the crude seat fashioned

on a stone ledge across the stone room he'd called home for way too long, and to walk a little around the room.

"Just eat."

He should be thankful they were now on speaking terms. For the first two months of his captivity she'd treated him to a cold silence—and a blinding headache each time he tried to talk to her.

Or attack her.

He chewed on his peanut butter and jelly sandwich, then forced the food down his throat. "You know, one day we'll have a proper meal together, Red. I'm thinking filet mignon and a glass of fine wine."

"I'm thinking I'd rather hang myself up by hooks in my eyelids than spend one evening with you," she said, folding her arms and leaning back against the stone wall. He watched as she crossed one long, slender leg over the other. Again, something curled inside him, something he resented, but couldn't fight. Yeah. Five months, no sex. It screwed with your brain, making the most unsuitable woman seem compellingly attractive. Desirable. Sweet. He met those frosty green eyes again. Maybe not *that* sweet.

He needed to get out of here. He wanted to get back to work. Being alone with his thoughts was depressing. Too much time to think, to remember. To grieve…to regret. *Ugh*. He needed to work, otherwise he just sat here in this cold, dank little hole with only his memories and Steve to keep him company. At the thought of the rat he'd befriended, he broke off a portion of his sandwich and tucked it into his jeans pocket for later. She watched his movements, but just like every other day, didn't query him. Probably thought he was squirreling away afternoon tea. He almost laughed at the suggestion of decorum and propriety in this misery. He took another bite of the sandwich, and chewed slowly, drawing their time together out. She glanced pointedly at her watch, and he grinned.

"If this cuts into your day, Red, you could always release me," he suggested smoothly. "Just think—you wouldn't have to spend so much of your culinary talents on me, such as they are. You wouldn't have to stand and wait, watching me chew every bite…wouldn't have to watch your back every second you're down here. Set me free, Red."

She rolled her eyes. "Don't you ever get tired of this conversation?"

He shrugged. "I'm afraid I'm not much of a conversationalist after being in the dark for so many months."

Her gaze flicked around the cell. "You brought this on yourself."

His gaze dropped. Yes, well, he couldn't argue with that. "Why don't we start over?" He smiled, calling on his customary charm he knew worked so well with the ladies.

Her eyes narrowed, and she straightened from the wall. "You tried to kill me. There's no starting over."

Except for this lady.

He sighed. "How long can you hold a grudge?" he asked, tilting his head to the side. "Aren't you bored with this yet? Isn't it exhausting, keeping me fed and watered, dreaming up new tortures? All that effort…"

She smiled, but it wasn't a warm, friendly smile, and she stepped closer. "Oh, I still post hate mail to my first ex. That's since second grade."

He eyed her. He couldn't tell if she was joking or not.

"Look, I'm sorry. How many times do I have to say it?"

"If you mean it, only once." The remark was quietly

spoken, and gave him pause. Her green gaze was blazingly direct. He ate the rest of his sandwich, forcing the gooey mess down his throat. Her gaze dipped to his throat, then lower, before it flickered away. Not quick enough that he didn't notice it, though—or the faint bloom of color in her cheeks.

Interesting.

He lifted his hand to indicate the gloomy room. "Trust me, I'm sorry."

She nodded. "Yeah. You're sorry you're stuck here. That's what you're sorry for." She turned back to the door, halted, then faced him. "You tried to kill me," she said, her voice low and shaking with anger.

He held up a finger. "No, I just wanted to destroy your shop," he corrected her.

Her eyes rounded. "With me in it."

He winced. "Yeah, well, that was my bad." He did feel guilty over that. Just a little. Not that he'd let her know.

Her lips firmed, and he focused on her mouth, those full, pouty lips that were pressed together so tightly. "You torched my apothecary. Do you have any idea what you've cost me? Or my clients? I have had to turn away people in need because of you."

He snorted. "Please. You create more damage than you know with your little witchy-woo spells and potions. I spend half my time cleaning up your messes."

She tilted her head back, her vibrant red curls a blaze of color in the gloomy, torchlit cell. "Oh, that's right. You're *their* doctor."

He'd have to be blind and deaf to miss her contempt, particularly when she talked about the shadow breeds like some stinky mess she'd stepped in and needed to wipe off her shoe. He smiled dryly. "I'm getting this vibe that you're not really into the shadow breeds."

Her smile was brittle and tight, and she stepped away from the wall, strolling slowly toward him. "Were-wolves, vampires, shifters…your kind," she said, casually lifting a hand to indicate him, "you all deserve to die." She said it so matter-of-factly, he almost didn't take offense. "You consume humans, with little or no regard for our lives. You all behave as though we are of no consequence, and yet you think the problem is ours when we arm ourselves against you." She shook her head. "Hypocrite."

His eyebrows rose. "*I'm* the hypocrite? You talk as though we're the only ones capable of evil, yet you create the cruelest weapons for your precious humans to use against the breeds. Do you have any idea what your wolfsbane tisanes do to the intestines, to the stomach or throat? You think *we* are cruel, yet slipping a toxic corrosive to a living being is all in a day's work for you." As a shadow breed healer he'd seen the horrors humans had subjected the shadow breeds to, and had made it his mission to help them. "You've held me here for months, *starving* me of light. That's the cruelest torture for one of my kind, yet you stand here and spout righteous indignation when you are guilty of doing the same yourself."

"You are so deluded. You are here because you tried to *incinerate* me."

"You're fine," he retorted. He still couldn't figure out how that had happened. "I didn't even singe you."

"Only because I had defenses, not because that was your intention," she snapped, stepping closer. This close, he could see the rosy bloom of anger high on her cheeks.

"And I've been paying for it ever since. Let me go. Let me get back to my life, to my work." Hell, what had happened to his clinic in all this time? Had his brother, Ryder, stepped in? Or did it lie in ruins? Despite what everyone thought, he did care about the business, about what they did. Well, what he did. He had been surprised to discover what his father had been doing... His work was the only good thing about him. If he didn't have his work, then he really was the selfish, destructive bastard everyone claimed him to be.

He'd be just like his father.

Damn it, he'd been confined in this prison for long enough.

First there'd been the spiders, then the rats. She'd even covered the floor with snakes once. Sure, it had been an illusion, a spell, but he'd still felt trapped, and the hallucinations had been terrifying.

Never piss off a witch.

"And you'll be paying for it for a long time to come," she said fiercely.

"If you hate me so much, why don't you kill me?" he challenged her in frustration. "Just end this. Let me go, or kill me."

Because if she didn't, he'd go mad. He was sure of it.

"Come on, set me free. You can trust me. I'm a doctor." He flashed her his most charming smile.

She rolled her eyes.

"Let me go, or end this," he urged her.

Her gaze flickered, then she masked her expression behind a cool, brittle smile. "Oh, but we're only just getting started."

"Red, if you still want me around after five months, maybe it's not revenge you're after," he said softly, suggestively. He knew he was poking the bear, but she started it.

"You think I won't hurt you?" She shook her head as she stepped even closer, and he measured the decreasing distance between them.

"Oh, I think you could," he said, leaning forward ever so slightly. "But I don't think you'll kill me." The realization hit him like a spark of lightning, and he wondered why the hell he hadn't figured that out much earlier. "You've had five months to do it—but you haven't." He tilted his head. "I wonder why not?"

Something flickered in her gaze, and her lips tightened. He'd hit a nerve. Triumph washed over him. God, he'd finally found a crack, a weakness. "You. Can't. Kill me." He drew the words out slowly. "Am I paying for your daddy issues, little girl?"

Her eyes narrowed, and that was all the warning he got—it was all the warning he needed. She swung at him. He caught her wrist, pulling her around with one hand as he yanked at the chain tethering his other.

There was a loud crack. Bricks crashed to the floor as the old pulley tore away from the ceiling, and then he had her back pressed up against him.

"Tut-tut, Red. You got too close."

Chapter 3

Melissa didn't quite know how he did it, but the bastard broke his chain. Just one, but it was enough to give him dangerous freedom. With one arm around her neck and the other wrapped around her waist and trapping her arms, he lifted her clear off the floor. She experienced a brief flare of panic. She tried to kick, tried to dig her heel into his instep, but he dodged her easily.

"Let's end this now, Red. One way or another. Let me go, or I'll snap your pretty little neck."

"Let me go," she gasped past the press of his arm against her throat.

"What? You don't like to be held against your will? Try it for *five months*," he muttered, his lips near her ear, then grunted as she lashed out with her foot. She made contact, but her kick had no force behind it.

The strength in his arms was frightening, yet he just held her. The breadth of his shoulders easily bracketed her own body, and she could feel his muscles bunch as he bore her weight. He could crush her. He could easily do as he threatened and snap her neck—but he didn't. He held her. Then he did something that shocked her.

He leaned forward and rubbed his chin against her neck. His beard brushed against her sensitive skin, at once soft yet prickly, and the rough sensation set her trembling. "Come on, Red. You know you don't hate me."

Her breath hitched, and her nipples peaked at the tingles that spread down her neck, bringing a warm flush along with it. His naked chest was a wall of heat against her back, and his hips cradled her butt. Awareness, sharp and consuming, swept over her. She could feel him against her, every ridge of muscle against her back, the strength of his thighs and something that throbbed and moved against her, which created an answering pulse deep in her core. Her breasts swelled. *No.* She wasn't— she couldn't—*no.*

She stiffened in his arms. "No, I *loathe* you," she said through gritted teeth. She twisted her wrist until her palm could make contact with his muscular forearm, and she latched on, pouring every inch of her resentment into that contact. She whispered a spell. Heat seared between them, and she tightened her grip. He grunted. Hissed. His arm moved slightly, and she managed to move her other arm until her hand could press against the outside of his thigh, and she clutched him, focusing her power on those two points of contact. The heat increased. She could feel his skin blistering under her hand, smell the fabric of his jeans burning.

His breath hitched, then he let her go, pushing her away. She whirled, hands raised, and an invisible force threw him against the wall behind him, holding him against the brick surface.

"Argh!" He tried to pull away, tried to reach for her, and she curled her fingers until he threw his head back in pain. "Stop it!"

She'd captured him initially with the help of her brother—and that was only after Hunter had exhausted himself in a battle first against his brother, and then his Warrior Prime of a father. Keeping the pyro jerk imprisoned on her own was proving a challenge. If it wasn't for the iron cuffs he wore that bound his light warrior magic, he would have already overpowered her.

Melissa retreated and didn't let up on the force she was directing against him until she reached the door. She clenched her hands and shoved her fists in a downward motion, and her prisoner collapsed to the floor. He moaned as he clasped his head, curling up into the fetal position, and she stormed out into the tunnel. With a flick of her fingers, the door slammed behind her, the lock sliding home. She strode up the corridor, fuming.

She'd gotten too close. She should have known better. He was like a viper, waiting for you to get within striking distance. Five months ago she'd been tempted by him, by his devilish smile and wicked brown-eyed gaze when he'd walked into her store. He'd been so confident, so darn cocky, saying he'd heard she was the best witch in Irondell with the best supplies, best spells, best concoctions—and the best strain of wolfsbane, and she'd swallowed his flattery, hook, line and sinker. She'd taken him into her apothecary, just like he'd taken her in with his false compliments.

She'd been thinking how gorgeous he was, and was even returning the flirty banter as she'd opened up her order book. Then her world had exploded. Fire, heat, and those brown eyes shot with burning flecks of red amber as he'd cast his flames throughout her little store. Then he'd backed out and closed the door, closing her inside her inferno.

He'd used her. She'd found out later he'd been trying to turn to ash any evidence of his brother's involvement in a murder. He'd smiled at her. Teased her. Tempted her.

Torched her.

She pulled herself up the steep staircase that led back to her apothecary, trying to shoot strength into her shaking arms. That comment, though…the one about her father…that was—weird. For the past few weeks she'd been dreaming of the night he'd left—and other nightmares. She hesitated. Could he…? She shook her head. She didn't know that anyone could do *that*. She closed the door behind her, engaging all the locks and wards, and then sagged against its surface, craving the unmovable support.

Tears burned beneath her eyelids. For a moment, ever so brief…she shook her head. No. Not *that* guy. Not ever.

"You look like you've seen a ghost," a woman's voice murmured from the gloom.

Melissa startled, then peered across the room. A figure moved away from the wall, stepping into the soft pool of light. Melissa closed her eyes briefly. She wasn't in the mood for this.

"Mother," she greeted the woman with resignation. "What are you doing here?"

"I came to see how your…" Her mother hesitated briefly, then continued "…project was coming along."

For a moment, Melissa thought her mother was talking about the renovation. Then almost laughed. Right. The last time her mother had shown any interest in her life was five months ago, when they'd had a terrible argument.

Over the pyro jerk downstairs.

"Well, as you can see, the apothecary is coming along nicely," Melissa said, deliberately taking the obvious direction for conversation.

Her mother's green eyes flared briefly. "I meant our little light warrior," her mother stated succinctly, folding her arms.

Melissa glared at her. "He's not *our* little light warrior, Mother. He's mine." She frowned at the possessive phrasing, realizing it probably sounded completely different than the way she intended. "And he's not so little."

She closed her eyes. And yep, that could be taken out of context, too. Her heart still pumped at being held against that large body, so much stronger than her own. She told herself the elevated heart rate, the sensitive... she folded her arms over her chest. Adrenaline. That's all it was, adrenaline.

"Please tell me he's still alive," Eleanor Carter didn't bother to hide her exasperation.

Melissa faced her mother reluctantly. "What if he's not, Mother? What if he's dead? How would that make you feel?"

"Do not play with me, Melissa," Eleanor snapped. "He is a light warrior, for heaven's sake. Do you know how rare that is?"

"With the way they make enemies? Trust me, Mother, it's as much a surprise to me as it is to you this one has survived as long as he has." She walked across the room to the door and the stairwell that would lead to her shop.

"He would make a useful ally, Melissa. He's in our debt. Use it to your advantage—and for God's sake, don't screw it up," her mother ordered as she followed closely. "You know we have to nurture this relationship."

Melissa halted at the door. "That is so ironic—you talking about nurturing." She bit off a brittle laugh.

"Melissa! You never stand back to look at the big picture. He is valuable."

Melissa whirled. "What about me, Mother? What value do you have for *me*?" Anger flared to encapsulate her hurt. "He tried to kill me, Mother, and all you can talk about is creating an alliance with the pyromaniac psychopath. What about *me*? Don't I matter in this? Why aren't you angry that he tried to kill your daughter? And if not your daughter, at the very least one of your coven. Why aren't you knocking down that door to tear his heart out?" *Why won't you fight for me?* She turned and stomped up the stairs.

The door at the head of the stairs slammed shut, and Melissa halted, pursing her lips. This is how her mother had dealt with conversations when she was a teen, for Pete's sake. She turned around to face her mother, arms folded.

Eleanor Carter slowly walked up the stairs until they were on the same tread and they could meet each other's gaze on an equal level. "Do not lecture me on defending my coven, Melissa," her mother stated in a cold tone, and Melissa realized she was no longer talking to her parent. "You may be my daughter and a Coven Scion, but you are still only a second-degree witch, and I am your Elder Prime. Do not presume to discipline *me* on coven matters." Eleanor lifted her chin. "You are popular with the humans, and you are gifted, but you still behave like a liability, whereas that light warrior is an asset. *That* is why I'm not tearing his heart out."

Eleanor flicked her fingers, and the door opened.

She walked into the bookstore, chin up and shoulders back, looking every inch the coven regent she was. Melissa stayed in the stairwell for a moment, blinking back the burn. God, she was so pathetic, always hoping her mother would for once put her daughter before her coven.

Should have known better.

She stomped up the steps and slammed the door shut behind her, closing off all thoughts of the "asset" downstairs, and the humiliating pain that her mother valued the man who'd tried to kill her more than her own daughter.

Hunter held out the remains of his sandwich to the rat. "You better fill up while you can, Steve. Might be a while before we get another feed."

He winced as he shuffled back against the wall. His body ached. Everywhere. His burns were almost healed, though. It had taken him a few hours longer than usual to mend—a sign of his low reserves. He grimaced. "Mental note—knock her out, next time. She hits like a…witch." He tilted his head back against the brick behind him. She hadn't brought down the evening meal. He supposed he deserved that. He hadn't intended to start anything with her today. It had just…happened.

He frowned. Things just happened a lot around him. She'd been right. Her surviving their meeting in her apothecary was purely based on her luck, not his design. He'd had one thought—protect his brother. He hadn't spared the witch any consideration when he'd obliterated all records of her orders.

He and Ryder hadn't been on speaking terms when Jared Gray, Alpha Prime to the Alpine Pack, had died in his brother's surgery, poisoned by wolfsbane. His first instinct was to slap some sense into his brother for committing a crime that could be so easily traced back to him. His second instinct was to hide any evidence connected to the case. If they couldn't prove his guilt, they couldn't convict his brother.

How was he supposed to know his brother wasn't the coldhearted murderer Hunter thought he was? Okay, so it didn't help that his brother had thought the same thing about him. Turns out, they were both wrong. Their father, on the other hand, could account for at least two murders. Hunter didn't want to think about the probability that there were more. He eyed Steve. The rat held the morsel of the sandwich in his front paws, nibbling at it delicately.

"Such petite table manners, Steve. You know, I think folks underestimate you rats." He shifted again, getting a little more comfortable in his stone-and-brick cell. He forced himself to relax. It was night. He wasn't quite sure what time, but he could sense the sun had set. Over the last few weeks he'd gone dreamwalking. He'd learned quite a lot about his temperamental prison warden as she'd slept. He'd managed to crack the locks on some of the memories she'd tried to shield. She'd been happy, once. A red-haired sprite with a cheeky sense of humor. That had changed, though, the night her father had left. He'd played that one over a few times, just to try to understand it, but it was a garbled mess in there. Her emotions were too jumbled to get much of a read.

Perhaps tonight he could find out why she hated the shadow breeds so much? If he could find that key, he could use it to his advantage.

Closing his eyes, he regulated his breathing, allowing himself to slip into slumber, his consciousness drifting away from his body as he started his dreamwalk. It didn't take long to find her subconscious—he'd made the trip enough times he could find her easily enough.

Melissa carefully picked her way down the steps into the grand ballroom. Oh, wow. She hadn't been to a Reform society debutante ball since, well, since Theo. Couldn't quite figure out why she was at one, now. Where was Theo? There was something bothering her, but she couldn't quite put her finger on it. She tried to remember how this had come to be, but each time she tried to recall how she got here, her thoughts danced and flitted, and she couldn't follow anything down to its source. She sighed. She felt like she should be worried, perhaps even alarmed, but even those thoughts zipped away, as though dancing with the wind.

She glanced around the opulent ballroom. As a teen, she'd thought it was a romantic event, magical even—a sign of maturity and acceptance. Then she'd discovered what a tedious torture they were, with all the Scions of the Prime classes gathered in some sort of archaic custom of forging alliances among the Reform elite.

She tripped, bracing a hand against a nearby wall to catch herself. She glanced down. What the...? She gaped. She was wearing an emerald green gown, with a strapless beaded bodice and flowing skirt. She couldn't see her shoes, and her hair was such a heavy weight on her head, she didn't want to bend over too much in case she overbalanced. But she could look down enough to see her outfit. She was wearing a bodice that seemed to cover only half her chest. Oh. My. God. She straightened to prevent displaying her full assets. She wasn't wearing a bra, but the bodice support was gravity-defying.

She fingered the satin of the skirt. It was quite simply the most beautiful thing she'd ever worn. And the most feminine. She wished Theo could see her in it. But he wouldn't. Regret bloomed, stiff and uncomfortable. Why wouldn't he? Again, the flutter of something at the edge of her consciousness teased her. She blinked, and her eyelashes brushed a solid edge. She raised her hands to touch her face. She was wearing a mask. She had no idea what it looked like, but she could feel the crystals on the surface. Her wrist caught her eye. Where was her tattoo? Two years ago her brother had etched it into her skin—painstakingly and way too gleefully, she'd thought at the time. But now, the inside skin of her wrist was smooth and unmarked. Confusion and concern for the missing mark teased at her, like the gossamer wings of a dragonfly, before fluttering away.

She stepped farther into the ballroom, her gaze flickering from one elegant sight to the next. Waiters bearing crystal flutes filled with champagne—or blood for the vampires. Her lips tightened. She could see them, despite their masks, their alabaster skin a dead giveaway. The lycans, too, were easy to spot, with their longer, thicker hair, the rebellious attitude they all seemed born with—and their obvious antipathy toward the vamps.

Her fingers curled as she raised them, and she startled when a waiter stepped in front of her, offering her a glass of blush pink champagne. She accepted it, sighing brusquely. Her mother would not like it if she used magic against a fellow Scion. It was encouraged for the offspring of the Prime leaders to get along—at least at the ball. She glanced around the room. An elegant cage full of monsters.

"What are you looking for?" a deep voice murmured above her right ear. She managed not to flinch, although she couldn't quite hide the shiver that tingled down her back at the low masculine voice so close to her ear, the whisper of breath across her collarbone.

"An escape, perhaps?" she commented casually as she slowly turned, raising the glass of champagne to her lips. When she faced him, she forgot to drink.

He was tall, his black jacket perfectly tailored for his broad shoulders and muscular arms. The dark vest he wore over the white dress shirt emphasized his narrow waist and lean hips, and the black bow tie highlighted the strong column of his throat. He looked like a tall drink of handsome, barely contained strength poured into a dark suit. The mask concealed the upper half of his face, but the strong jawline and sculpted lips she could see were tantalizing, attractive, with an inherent pout that was undeniably sexy—and frustratingly familiar. Recognition—just like the memories of how she wound up here tonight—dipped and danced out of reach. Her gaze lifted. His dark hair was cut short, but still long enough for her to play with—if she'd just reach up and…

Her fingers tightened around the stem of her glass. If he was at the ball, he was a Scion. She didn't play with Scions. That would delight her mother and she made a practice of not delighting her mother. She refused to participate in the woman's political power plays.

The dark eyes behind the mask turned assessing, and he tilted his head. "They all seem nice enough," he commented, inclining his head to the crowd behind her.

She stared at him. His skin was tanned, a healthy complexion that didn't suit a vampire, and he didn't give off a lycan vibe. She was curious, but that in itself was enough of a warning for her. She hadn't been curious about a guy since Theo. Wasn't ready to be curious about a guy. Not now, and hopefully not ever. She glanced around the room. Where was Theo? She wanted to go home.

"It's just not my kind of scene," she murmured, and sipped from her glass.

His gaze flicked to the open French doors and he smiled. "Then why don't we change the scene?" he suggested, lifting his hand to indicate the terrace outside in a graceful gesture. For a moment she stared at his hand. Long fingers that looked courtly in their gesture, yet masculine, and a steady palm that showed a solid, stable strength. The hands of a musician with the strength of a warrior. The thought came out of nowhere, distracting and disturbing, and she shook it off. She was the Scion of the White Oak Coven; she could more than handle herself with any man in this room.

She clutched her skirt, lifting it slightly to step outside without falling flat on her face. The night air was warm, with a slight breeze that was like a sensual trail of ethereal fingers across the skin. Her brows dipped. Surprisingly balmy for December—but Reform balls were always held in October. She was sure it was snowing outside…again, something fluttered in her mind, easily ignored. Small starbursts of color bloomed in the pots evenly spaced along the balustrade, white roses unfurling under the stars.

She stepped out of the light of the doorway to face the stranger. "So tell me, which Prime family are you associated with?"

He shrugged. "Does it matter?" He grinned, and she stared at the sexy tilt of his lips, the flash of white teeth. "Honestly, I never really got into these events. Always thought they were too pompous. Didn't realize the company could be so beautiful."

Her cheeks warmed as his dark eyes flared with a

heated appreciation that was hard to miss, despite the mask. An appreciation that was returned. Despite her champagne, her mouth felt dry, and something lazy and sensual uncurled deep within her.

"So, you're not really a fan, huh?" she whispered, intrigued someone else viewed the marriage mart and alliance negotiations with as much disdain as she did. Intrigued by a man who seemed neither vampire nor lycan—or any of the other shifter breeds.

He took the glass from her hand and placed it on the ledge of the stone balustrade that bordered the terrace, his gaze dropping to focus on the cleavage revealed by her low-cut bodice. His lips curled higher, his gaze grew hotter and her heart thumped in her chest. "I could be changing my mind about that," he whispered, raising his hands to cradle her face, turning her until the base of her spine pressed against the balustrade. Her heart thumped a little faster. She didn't feel physically threatened, but something whispered to her, something full of warning and wickedness, and yet it didn't frighten her. It excited her.

His scent, something wicked and musky, with patchouli and a faint undertone of amber, enveloped her, entrancing her, and she slowly raised her hands to his broad shoulders—not sure yet whether she was pushing him away or drawing him closer.

Then he lowered his lips to hers.

There was no soft teasing or gentle awakening, Melissa realized. His mouth demanded, and she delivered, parting her lips as his tongue swept in to rub against hers. His hands delved into the intricate curls on top of her head, angling her head so he could deepen the kiss. Over and over, his mouth moved against hers. Her pulse began to throb in her ears as a sensual warmth swept over her. He pressed against her, and she could feel the breadth of his shoulders, the strength in the biceps that bunched as he pulled her closer, ever closer. She moaned softly, tilting her head back as he explored her mouth, her heart thumping in her chest, her breasts swelling as arousal, hot and hungry, flared within her.

He bent down, his hands sliding over the back of her skirts, and she felt the earth shift as he lifted her up and settled her on the balustrade. His lips left hers to trail a hot caress down the side of her neck, and moist heat gathered between her legs as she tried to wrap her thighs around his waist, the cumbersome skirts an aggravating barrier between their bodies. Cool air teased against the moist trail, and her nipples tightened at the sensation. He pressed his hips against hers, and damp heat flared between her thighs. She tilted her head back as he rubbed himself against her in a carnal dance that had her aching for more. *Now.*

The erotic heat spread from her chest to her thighs, and she writhed against him, craving skin-on-skin contact and deliciously frustrated by their clothing. He nipped, his teeth sharp but delicate, causing the pinpricks of sensation to dart down to her nipples and farther. He licked his way across the swell of her breasts to the edge of her beaded bodice, hot licks that had her trembling, her breasts swelling even further at the attention. Desire, arousal, a deep yearning couched in hot hunger flooded through her, hot and demanding.

Her eyes opened, and she glanced down as her nipples tightened, craving his touch—any touch. His dark hair was so stark against her pale skin, like some carnal demon having his wicked way with a virgin.

She smiled. Only she wasn't a virgin. Her hands slid

to his hair and she tugged, tilting his head up and claiming his lips with a hunger that rivaled his. Their tongues tangled, dueling for domination. This…this was heady, wanton… She'd never felt this free, this shameless, with anyone. Not even Theo.

Theo. The last time she'd been to a ball, she'd been with Theo.

But this wasn't Theo.

She tore her mouth from his, panting as she stared at the handsome face, his lips wet from her kisses. She knew those lips.

"No," she gasped.

Chapter 4

Melissa jolted awake, her body tight with need, craving a satisfaction she'd just denied herself. She rolled over in her lonely bed, groaning with frustration.

Her heart pounded, her nipples were tight and longing for the touch of a man's hands and her thighs were damp. She sat up in bed, her eyes wide as her chest rose and fell with her pants. What. The. *Hell?*

Realization dawned, and she dived out of the bed, stomping out of her bedroom and through her small apartment above the bookstore. That bastard. She didn't know how he'd done it, but he'd taken one of her memories and twisted it. She remembered that night, damn it, and she sure as hell hadn't been out on the balcony kissing an anonymous stranger. She flung her front door open, then slammed it shut behind her. That... *jerk*. The relief at realizing she wasn't willingly fantasizing about her prisoner was quickly consumed by rage. She ran barefoot down the stairwell to the corridor that led to the external street access, her pink nightgown streaming, the silk unfurling in her wake as though caught in an invisible tempest. Two steps down the hall was the internal security door to her store. She didn't bother to manually key in the code. She snapped her fingers. The door swung open. She stormed through her bookstore, disregarding the books flying off the shelves and falling to the floor behind her as her power raged around her. Anger poured through her, and she could feel her power building within her. She should scale it back, temper it a little, but she just wanted to let loose.

She swept through the door at the back of the store, chanting as she scampered down the stairs. The door to her apothecary burst open before her and she stalked across the underground room. The cupboard hiding her fire hose reel caught her eye, and she halted, seething.

Yep, this would do the trick. She yanked open the doors and pulled on the head of the hose, flicking the lever at the base of the hose reel. She turned to face the mural. A flick of her hand, a quick, fiercely muttered incantation, and she unlocked her wards. The painted door flung open. She didn't stop for the torch. She climbed down the stairwell, tugging the hose along with her. The bare concrete floor felt cold beneath her feet, but she didn't pause until she came up to the steel door. She used her power to slide the lock and thrust the door open. It made a resounding clang as it snapped back to the wall.

Her prisoner jolted awake, blinking as he pushed himself up from the floor where he lay.

"You need to cool down," she snapped, and yanked the lever on the hose.

Ice-cold water shot across the room, pummeling the man on the floor. He roared, trying to gain his feet, but she kept the hose trained on him. He slipped, tried to rise again, but the force of the water was too powerful, and he fell back against the wall.

He bellowed as he tried to twist away from the high-pressure blast of water, but she didn't give him any relief. After a long moment, she shut the hose off.

"Stay the hell out of my head," she yelled, and whirled around, the door slamming shut behind her, the lock sliding home.

Anger was good. Anger she could hold on to, anger she could use. She pulled it around her like a cloak. Because if she didn't have anger, all that would be left would be guilt at the fantasy that betrayed her fiancé's memory, and the shame of betrayal, of giving in to temptation from one of *them*. She climbed the stairs and locked up, but paused when she entered the bookstore. It looked like a mini-tornado had whirled through, leaving devastation in its wake.

Just like pyro jerk. That dream, that wicked kiss— that had devastated her. She had to get control. Of herself, of her powers...of her reaction to him. She would not give in.

Sniffing, she knelt down to start picking up the scattered items throughout the store, restoring order to the shelves as she calmly restored order to her thoughts.

Hunter shook the water out of his eyes, then glared at the door as he leaned back against the wall. That cold shower had cooled his desire for the damn woman. He made a fist and hit the floor beside him, and a spray of water hit him in the face. Damn it.

Arousal, tight and unrelenting, gripped his cock, stirred his pulse. He hadn't expected that. Hadn't planned it. His lips tightened as he rubbed at the hard ache. That cold shower had been painful, like ice bullets against his ardor. He swore. He'd meant to lurk, that was all, let her lead the way. He'd sent her a subliminal suggestion. Why did she hate the shadow breeds?

He hadn't expected her to take him to a Reform society ball. He'd given her a gown straight out of his imagination, one that hugged that siren figure yet had hidden her secrets. Classical yet incredibly sexy. That had *not* been his intention. Usually he just contented himself with being a mere witness to memories—like the dreams he'd previously walked through as Melissa had slept. His father had often played with suggestion, as had Hunter when first learning his dreamwalking skill. But what had just happened—that wasn't normal. He couldn't tell if that scene on the balcony was driven by his subconscious or hers. Whose suppressed desire had shanghaied that dream? Goose bumps rose on his skin as the chill night air caressed the icy water that drenched him, leeching at his desire. She'd surprised him, though. When he'd asked her subconscious to reveal the source of her hatred for shadow breeds, she'd shown him a scene of society's civility, and instead of following that clue, he'd been distracted. The muscles in his jaw felt so tight he had to consciously relax them. He wished he could blame it on the icy drenching, but he practiced deluding others, not himself. He was painfully horny, damn it. For the bitchy witch.

He shook his head, droplets of water flicking off his head like a shaggy dog. A damn Reform ball.

He'd heard all about them, but had never attended one. He should have—he was the eldest son of a Warrior Prime, and the ball was a social event to gather all the Scions of each Prime family in one spot, as a celebration of Reformation Day. It was also where connections were made, alliances were forged and some strategic pairings were made among the sons and daughters of the Primes. As a Warrior Scion, he had a right to attend. As a light warrior, a shadow breed that kept its very existence secret, though, there was no way his family would ever participate in such an event.

They had other ways of making alliances and wielding power, and it was far more delicate and discreet than the obnoxious gatherings of the Reform elite.

He rubbed his bare arms. He was chilled now. His lips curled. And yet, he was also energized. Strange. Usually when he dreamwalked, it was to find out secrets and implant suggestions, or fake memories—even make people forget... He'd never once thought to use it to entice, to seduce. Light warriors drew energy and power from all sources of light, except for created fluorescence. They were also able to pull power from sexual energy and emotions. He'd always believed there needed to be a physical proximity for that to work, though, not something that could be accomplished through an unconscious connection. Apparently he was wrong.

He'd connected with the witch, and with just one dreamy kiss she'd revitalized some of his stores. Totally worth a cold shower. He idly wondered what a real kiss with the woman would be like, then shook his head. He didn't think her reaction would stop at just an uncomfortable, near-Arctic dousing.

Two days later, Melissa stared at her pale features in the mirror of the store's bathroom. She pinched her cheeks, blinking her eyes open wide as she tried to wake up. She glanced at her watch. One hour. One hour before she could close the shop. Part of her wanted to curl up under the counter and sleep for a hundred years. Another part of her wanted to inject caffeine and never close her eyes again.

She was going to kill him. Sure, her mother would be disappointed, but she'd be able to *sleep*, damn it. He was tormenting her, and no matter what spell she conjured up, he managed to get past her defenses and dance through her dreamscapes.

She turned the tap and splashed cold water on her face. Last night had been bad. Over and over again, she'd relived the night her father had left. She eyed herself in the mirror, the haunted memories surfacing so easily now, as though her mind no longer obeyed her command to bury it.

She and her brother, Dave, had crept out from their rooms, eyeing each other warily in the darkened upstairs hallway as their parents had argued downstairs. It was the eve of Melissa's sixteenth birthday, when she would graduate from adolescent to Initiate and attend her first Reform ball.

"She's too young, Eleanor, and you know it."

"She's the Daughter-Scion, Phillip, and she has to start behaving like one."

"She's *sixteen*. She's our daughter. You can't marry her off, not yet."

"She doesn't have the luxury of just being our daughter, and you know it. We have to form that alliance. I don't want to be at the mercy of the Armstrongs, or the Marchettas, or any other Reform family. We need to ensure our witches have strong representation within the Senate, and this merger will ensure that. You know we can't use David, but we can at least use Melissa as an asset."

David pulled her away from the banister and tried to drag her back into her bedroom, but she shook her brother off, her blood chilling at the argument down-stairs as she returned to the railing. An asset? That's how her mother saw her?

Their parents were in the living room, oblivious to the listening ears upstairs.

"Why the Hawthorns?" Her father's question was laced with frustration and exasperation.

Melissa's eyes rounded, and she glanced up at her brother. The Hawthorns? They were known to dabble in blood magic. Hadn't one of their ancestors given in to the blood-craze? She shook her head. No, surely not. Surely her mother wouldn't ally the House of White Oak with the House of Hawthorn...she turned toward the head of the stairs, but Dave yanked her back, lifting his finger to his lips in caution.

"The Hawthorns are strong, Phillip, and because of their—proclivities—they count some vampire colonies among their allies." Her mother's answer was haughty, as though offended she had to explain herself.

"Do you hear yourself? Vampires? We don't want to align with the bloodsuckers, Eleanor."

"Why? Are you afraid of them?"

Melissa frowned at the blatant scorn in her mother's tone.

"I am wary of them. I don't trust them, and neither should you. Anyone slave to the blood thirst will always be an enemy to the humans and witches, Eleanor, and you know it."

"Well, I'm not scared of them, Phillip. It's done. I've already discussed it with Marcus Hawthorn. He is willing to formally introduce his son to Melissa at the ball tomorrow night."

"So, you've gone ahead and done it without discussing it with me." Her father's tone brought tears to Melissa's eyes. It was so brittle, so cold.

"I do not need, nor seek, your permission, Phillip. I am the Coven Elder, and in this my authority is absolute. Deal with it."

"I won't stand for this, Eleanor."

Her mother laughed, a cold little tinkle that sounded like broken glass cascading over stone. "There is nothing you can do, Phillip. It's already arranged."

"I won't stand by your side and watch this. You've gone too far—you should have discussed this with me. We could have come up with an alternative."

"You're my Consort, Phillip, not my confidant."

Melissa flinched at the sound of breaking glass, and then her father stormed out of the living room and into the front foyer.

"Well, you won't have to worry about that anymore, Eleanor. I'm renouncing this farce of a marriage. Do as you will—you always have." He gave a sharp, cruel bark of laughter. "You're so worried about your standing among the society, I'm almost interested to see the spin you'll put on that, but I find I really couldn't care less."

Her father yanked his coat down from the hook behind the door. Melissa broke away from David, tears streaming down her face as she started to walk down the stairs.

"Daddy, please don't go."

Phillip Carter turned around, and she could see his struggle to contain his anger in front of his children. Finally, he smiled sadly and shrugged as she approached him. "Sorry, poppet. I just can't do this anymore."

He gave her a hug, then gazed up at David. Father and son looked at each other for a long moment, and then Phillip finally nodded, as though there was some meaningful, silent exchange.

And then her father left.

When Melissa turned away from the open front door, she saw him, a shadow in the corner of the foyer, his brown eyes watching the scene intently. He hadn't been there at the time, but he was there, inside her memory, replaying it for her again and again. There was something predatory about his gaze that suggested his name was more than just something handed down to him at birth, but more a characteristic of his personality.

Damn pyro jerk. Just for that, she'd cast an elemental spell and had made it snow in his cell for the rest of the night. He was still shivering when she'd tossed him his sandwich at lunchtime.

Melissa looked away from the mirror and grabbed the hand towel hanging from a loop attached to the wall. She dabbed her face dry, her teeth clenched, that last image of her father storming off into the night haunting her. Neither she nor Dave had seen him since. She wasn't going to cry. Not again. She'd wasted too many tears, remembering that night.

She fluffed her hair, pasted a fake smile on her face, then turned to the door that led out to her store. She had a client coming in to pick up a hex pouch, and another one due for an extremely diluted solution of wolfsbane. It wasn't enough to kill a lycan, but it was enough to make the man's abusive werewolf wife feel poorly enough to leave him alone.

Her hand rested on the doorknob. That night memories of her father weren't the only dreams she was having. She frowned. She'd have to do something about her prisoner. She didn't want these dreams, didn't want these painful memories resurfacing at his whim, not hers. She didn't think she could let him go, though. Who knew what chaos he would wreak on the unsuspecting and vulnerable if let out. He showed no real remorse for his actions, no consideration for others, but continued to push his own agenda. She wasn't allowed to kill him, but she had wanted to teach him a lesson. Her shoulders sagged. Perhaps he was unredeemable.

Right now, though, she was too tired to care.

Straightening her shoulders, she swept into her store, a fake smile on her face as she greeted her customers.

A while later, after the two customers had left, she was almost deliriously happy to shut her front door, swinging the sign to Closed. She switched the light off over the display window and rubbed the back of her neck as she walked down the aisle toward the internal door that opened near the stairs that led to her apartment.

A furious tapping on the door at the front of the store had her turning, her brows dipping as the tapping became thumping. She walked back toward the store entrance, then started running when she caught a good look at one person propped up against her store window and another person struggling to keep him up. Melissa unlocked the door, and Lexi sobbed, nearly hysterical as she draped her brother's arm over her shoulders.

"Please, Melissa. We need your help. Lance is hurt—bad."

Chapter 5

Hunter hugged himself. The snow flurries had melted within his cell, but there was still a leftover chill from the witch's retaliatory snowstorm. How apt that she took an icy approach. She probably thought he'd been replaying that particular memory out of spite, but he wasn't.

Okay, so maybe there was a tiny bit of spite in there, but he'd really wanted to find out more about his captor. She'd been so young in that memory, not even an Initiate—untried and untested with her powers. He'd seen her hurt flare when her mother discussed her as no more than a resource for the coven, sensed her fear and anxiety at being married off, seen her blanch at the mention of the Hawthorns. The White Oak Coven… He racked his brain, trying to remember what he knew of the family. He knew of no current alliance between the Hawthorns and the White Oaks, and managing and orchestrating alliances and enmities were part of a light warrior's toolbox, as his manipulative father had taught him. Arthur Armstrong had made it his business to understand, and even to influence, the partnerships and negotiations within Reform society.

When he saw Melissa's dream of the ball, though, she'd been close enough to her current age—definitely an adult, and not some sixteen-year-old on her first introduction into Reform society. What had happened with the Hawthorns? He knew enough of Eleanor Carter's reputation to know the Coven Elder was politically savvy and extremely powerful. What had happened to Melissa's arranged marriage? It was an archaic custom, and one that couldn't be enforced. If the Scion didn't wish to be married off, there were opportunities to withdraw without causing insult, but he couldn't remember hearing of anything involving the White Oak Coven. Hell. It wasn't like Melissa was the kind of woman who could be discreet and diplomatic in that kind of situation, so surely he would have heard of some shock or scandal…?

Every time he learned something of his captor, it just raised more questions. Not that a broken engagement was any help to him getting out of his prison… He was just…curious.

He settled himself back against the wall. She was tired. His dreamwalking was disturbing her sleep. He regretted that. Her face had been pale and drawn when he'd caught a brief glimpse of her as she'd tossed him his lunch. If she wasn't craving a nap, she'd be going to bed early tonight. He frowned. Goose bumps rose on his arms. He realized there was a chill in the air, but he also knew excitement when he felt it—and he was strangely excited by the prospect of seeing her in her dreams. She was unguarded there, and hadn't quite figured out how to block him, yet—although he'd had to exercise more effort last night, so she was getting there. He saw her in all her vulnerable, awkward and naive glory. So far, though, he still couldn't understand why she was such a hard-ass when it came to the shadow breeds. To be fair, he'd behaved badly toward her, and all thoughts of protecting his brother aside, he should have factored her into his firestorm, and was ashamed he hadn't. She had a right to be angry with him, but he sensed there was more to the anger than just him nearly killing her—although some might think that was enough of a reason.

No, he sensed there was more behind that anger, a bitter sense of betrayal he just didn't understand—and now he couldn't use it to get the hell out of here.

He closed his eyes. She might be avoiding him, tossing him his food from the door, and not speaking to him at all, but she couldn't avoid him in her unconsciousness—and he'd be ready and waiting for her tonight.

Melissa grimaced as she and Lexi struggled to carry Lance's massive form over to the bed in her spare bedroom. It had been quite the challenge for both her and Lexi to get him up the stairs from the bookstore in his semiconscious state, but she had no place to lie him down in the store.

God, the blood. There was so much blood. Lance's complexion was almost gray, and his eyelids kept fluttering, as though he was struggling against a tide of unconsciousness that threatened to claim him.

"I haven't seen him in ages, and for some reason, I just felt this need to touch base with him," Lexi said between ragged breaths, her words stumbling over each other. "I found him like this—" Lexi shook her head, unable to continue.

"Get his legs up," Melissa instructed as she lowered

him onto the bed. She glanced at the young woman. Apparently the ring was doing its job. "There are towels in the bathroom and a bucket under the sink. Fill it up with water—don't worry, it's clean, and then bring it all in here."

Lexi's hands were shaking as she hoisted her brother's feet up onto the bed, and Melissa touched her shoulder. The young woman turned to her, her blue eyes glistening with tears and bright with fear.

"It's okay, Lexi. You did good, bringing him here. How did it happen?"

Lexi shrugged. "I don't know. I was on the way to his place, and found him in the park down on Addison Road. You were the first person I thought of for help."

Melissa patted her shoulder reassuringly. "He'll be fine."

Lexi nodded, took a deep breath, then hurried to the bathroom down the hall.

Melissa opened Lance's leather jacket and sucked in her breath. His shirtfront was dark and shiny with blood, so much that she couldn't rip the damp material, and had to slide the buttons out of holes to peel back the fabric. His chest rose and fell rapidly, as though he couldn't quite fill his lungs, and his body was bathed in a cool perspiration.

She gently rolled him onto his side, wincing as he groaned. There was blood on his back, as well.

Her mouth dried when she saw the extent of his injuries, and her gaze flicked up to Lance's face. He stared at her, his green eyes dull with pain and sadness, a weary acceptance stamped on his features.

"It's fine, Mel. I know."

Melissa shook her head, blinking back the tears. "Don't say that, Lance. You're going to be fine. We'll fix you." This man had worked quietly and diligently in her store, had listened to her rants about her mother, had gotten drunk with her and her brother on the odd occasion, and had been there when Theo had died in a way no other could have been. "You're going to be fine," she repeated in a whisper, gazing at the cuts on his chest, and the hole that looked too close to his heart.

It took an effort, but Lance covered her hand with his bloodstained fingers, and she flinched at the cool touch. "I've been shot, Mel. I'm dying. You can't fix this."

Lexi entered the room with a bucket of water and towels, and Melissa lifted her chin toward the bedside table. "Good woman. Now, there is a cupboard at the end of the hall, with a basket on the bottom shelf. Go get it for me quickly." Lexi jogged out of the room, and Melissa turned to her friend.

"Who did this to you, Lance? Who did this?" She hissed the words at him softly, conscious of Lexi just down the hall.

Lance smiled weakly. "It doesn't matter."

Melissa's eyes narrowed. "Oh, it does, because we are going to deliver a whole world of hurt on them." She dipped a hand towel into the bucket, squeezed it, then started to clean his chest. She needed to see exactly what she was dealing with here.

Lance's smile fell, and he shook his head, just once. "No, stay out of it, Mel. Look after Lexi for me."

Her gaze flicked up to meet his. She wasn't ready for this, wasn't ready to say goodbye to one of her best friends, wasn't ready to take on his burdens. "Oh, no you don't," she whispered harshly. "You don't get to dump that high-maintenance chick on me. *You* can clean up her messes." She wiped away most of the blood, although it still pulsed, slowly, from some of his wounds, so red—unnaturally so. The lacerations were deep, but it was the hole near his heart that most concerned her. A bullet wound, through and through, with an exit wound in his back. Lance was a dhampir, with a metabolism that aided self-healing, but the fact that he was healing so slowly suggested he was, indeed, gravely injured.

She brushed his dark blond hair back from his forehead. "But for now, you need to sleep." She whispered a sleep spell, and his eyelids drifted shut, his dark lashes forming crescents against his cheeks.

Lexi ran back into the room, and halted when she saw her brother. "Oh, God, is he—?"

"No, he isn't, and he won't, not if I've got anything to do with it." She took the basket from Lexi and opened it up. Inside were her essentials—her emergency magic kit. This wasn't the first time an injured person was brought to her. "Round up as many candles as you can and bring them here. You'll find them everywhere throughout the apartment."

Elements helped her focus her magic, and as she wasn't near a watercourse or a garden, and she didn't want to subject Lance to a gale, not in his state, then fire was her go-to element.

She worked quietly, cutting Lance's bloodstained clothing away from his body, and Lexi helped her clean him up. She frowned. His cuts weren't healing. As a dhampir, Lance had the ability to heal fast—which wasn't happening.

"Help me place the candles around him," she told Lexi. Using the furniture setup of the room, she and Lexi placed the candles on the surfaces so that they formed a rough circle around the bed. With a flick of her fingers, all the wicks of the candles lit up, and Lexi turned off the overhead light so that candlelight was the only illumination within the room.

"Sit over there," Melissa instructed, pointing to the chair in the corner, and Lexi hurried over, her face pale and anxious as she watched her brother on the bed. Melissa climbed up near the head of the bed, gently lifting Lance's limp head and resting it on her knees. Closing her eyes, she took a deep breath, calming her heart, evening out her breathing and summoning her powers. Placing her fingers at Lance's temples, she let her magic flow over him.

She frowned. She could sense something inside him, something small, but sharp, with a shadow that was slowly spreading. Whatever it was, it wasn't letting him heal. She tried to battle it, tried to conquer it, then tried to confine it, but she could sense it diffusing through his system.

She didn't know how long they remained like that—Lexi sitting quietly on her chair in the corner, Lance breathing harshly into the silence and Melissa holding on to her friend, trying desperately to pull him back from the brink of death. She poured her own strength, her essence, into helping him. It slowed down the creeping shadow, but it didn't stop it. This was some sort of natural poison that she couldn't halt. She focused on that small, sharp object, the source of the toxin. It was so close to his heart. She tried to draw it out of him, using her magic like a magnet, but Lance moaned softly with pain. Melissa felt the raw edge of agony stiffen his muscles. She was only hurting him further.

She sagged back against the head of the bed and opened her eyes. The room was almost dark. She'd burned through many of the candles, and only a couple still flickered with light. Her legs felt numb. She must have been sitting there for hours. Lexi was staring at her, her expression of anxiety and hope like a suffocating weight on Melissa's chest.

"I can't do this," she whispered brokenly, shame and desolation washing over her as she stared at her friend's sister. "It's not—it's not responding to my magic." Admitting that she couldn't help her friend felt like a betrayal, an abandonment. "He needs medical help."

Lexi stared down at her brother in confusion. "What?"

"He's a dhampir, Lexi. In some ways, he's the strongest being I know. In this, though, he is as weak and vulnerable as the rest of us humans. He's got a bullet fragment inside him, and I can't get it out."

"No." Lexi shook her head, tears streaming down her face as she rose from her chair. "There has to be something you can do, Mel. Please. Whatever it is—I'll pay."

Briefly, anger flared within her at the suggestion she would receive payment for helping a friend, but she quashed that anger. Lexi loved her brother and was desperate. She'd do anything to save him, and Melissa could relate to that—she'd do anything to save her own brother as well as her close friend. No, it was better to save her anger for those responsible for this—whoever shot Lance. But they weren't going to be able to wreak any vengeance if they didn't know who pulled the trigger, and in order for that to happen, Lance *must* survive. Only, she couldn't help him.

Her gaze drifted down to the man lying on the bed, his features so still. She knew someone who could, though, and the very thought of asking him for help burned like acid in her stomach. The thought, though, that Lance would die was even worse.

Melissa dredged up her remaining stores of magic. The work she'd already done on Lance had been draining. She pressed gently against his temple and whispered a dormancy spell. It wasn't quite as effective as a suspension spell, but putting the half-human Lance into a suspended state would halt his heartbeat, and a continuance spell may not work without that vital pulse. A dormancy spell allowed his body and mind to go into a state of hibernation, still sustaining life, but limiting the spread of that toxin, whatever it was.

"I, uh, I need to step out," she said, her voice husky with strain. She blinked. Her vision was blurry and gray. Dormancy spells weren't easy, and they took a toll. "Stay with him. Talk to him, Lexi. I've put him in a coma, to stop…it." Death. She'd put him in a coma to stop death. Her mother would freak if she found her playing with the natural order of things. Magic could be used, but once you used it against nature's course there were consequences. Melissa mentally defended herself against the imaginary conversation with her Coven Elder. She'd delayed death, not contravened it.

She knew one person, though, who could prevent it—and he was currently shivering in a cell in her basement.

With each step she took down to his prison, she argued with herself. Was there another option? Could anyone else help? What about Dave? No. He'd encounter the same issue she did. Lance needed medical help, not magical. How long could she keep Lance dormant? Perhaps she could wait just a little longer, until someone more suitable could be reached? The stairs leading from her store down to her apothecary spun for a moment, and she clutched the wall for support until her vision settled and she could enter her secret store.

A dormancy spell worked differently to most. For it to continue its effect, it had to siphon energy from her own reserves, and she'd drained most in her efforts to heal

Lance and to halt the toxin. It was almost too much effort to despell the wards on the mural door. She reached for the torch and carefully made her way down the steep stairs, clinging to the railing as she went.

She halted before the dark door and took a deep breath, composing her features. She hated this. *Hated* it. She swung open the door and the torch cut a swathe of light through the darkness.

Her prisoner sat on the floor, his back to the wall, and he lifted his head. His lips curled in a wicked smile.

"Hello, Red. Come to make a deal with the devil?"

Chapter 6

Hunter eyed the witch, his eyebrows dipping slightly. She looked like hell. He saw the blood on her shirt, saw her sway, and he rose to his feet. He had one only cuff that was anchored, but if she collapsed, he wouldn't be able to reach her. "Are you okay?" He gestured to her shirt. He didn't know who was more surprised by his concern, the witch or him.

The witch looked down at herself. "Uh, yeah, I'm—I'm—it's not mine." Her voice was huskier than usual, a slight rasp that was like velvet against skin.

She stepped inside the room and rubbed absently at her forehead. He masked his concern with expectation. He'd seen her angry, mildly curious, angry, exasperated, angry, wary, more angry...he'd never seen her so... flustered. Yeah, flustered.

She put her hands on her hips and looked down at her

boots—those same killer heels—then looked up at him. "I need your help."

His eyebrows rose. Okay. That was unexpected. She looked so damn uncomfortable, he almost laughed, yet her obvious exhaustion, the blood...she wasn't here to ask him to stop dreamwalking, as he'd thought, as he'd hoped. His intention had been to wear her out so that she would be begging him to leave. "What kind of help?" he inquired smoothly.

She moved her arms, halted, then folded them against her body, as though unsure what to do with her limbs. "I, uh, I need a doctor."

His heart thudded in his chest, and he stepped closer. "Why? What's wrong with you?" He looked her up and down. She was a mess. Her hair was tangled, and dark shadows rested beneath her eyes. Her lips were tightly pursed, and her shirt...all that blood. He wanted to check her, make sure she really was all right. The instinct surprised him. He told himself it was his medical training taking over...although he wasn't really the nurturing type.

"Uh, not for me. For a friend. I need your help for a friend." She couldn't quite meet his gaze.

He raised an eyebrow. "Really? You have a friend?" Melissa Carter, bitchy witch, had a friend. He'd have to see it to believe it. "You?"

She frowned. "Yes, *me*," she said through gritted teeth. "I have a friend, and he needs help."

He. Her *male* friend needed help. His concern shrank, swallowed by a darker emotion. He shrugged. "Then take him to a hospital."

"There's no time, and the transfer could kill him," she said quietly, at last meeting his gaze directly.

His eyes narrowed. "So...you *need* me." He leaned

back against the wall. Hmm. She was in a position of demand, and he was in a position of supply. He liked where this conversation was going. "What exactly do you *need* from me?"

"You have a reputation for being good at what you do," she said brusquely, although her tone suggested she found it hard to believe. "I want you to fix him. Heal my friend."

"And what do I get in return?" he asked her, a smile teasing at his lips. She was direct. He'd give her that.

"What do you want?" she asked, shrugging.

He blinked. She was asking him to name his price? He tilted his head. "This friend must mean a lot to you." She struck him as being so prickly, so quick-tempered, it was fascinating to see this side of her, this loyal, protective side.

She tilted her head back, and he watched her red hair slide over her shoulder. "I'm too tired for games, Hunter. What do you want in return for healing my friend?"

Hunter. Not pyro jerk or any of the other monikers she'd given him. It was the first time she'd used his name. Things were serious. He rubbed his chin, the remaining chain clinking with his movements. "I want you to release me," he said simply.

Those green eyes flared with anger, and he met her gaze intently. Did she care more for this friend, or for her own revenge? Her lips tightened, then she dipped her head. Once.

"Fine. You heal my friend, and you can walk away."

"And then you and I are done, right? No more snakes or snow or spiders?"

She nodded. "No more snakes or snow or spiders."

His eyes narrowed. Yeah, she wasn't the first witch he'd ever dealt with. "Or any other form of revenge or retribution from you for what I did. It was wrong, I'm sorry, we're moving on."

Her pouty lips tightened even further, and he saw the anger, the reluctance to let go of her punishment. She nodded. "You do this, and we're done. Moving on."

It was so obvious she hated this whole discussion. His curiosity deepened. Who was this friend, and why was he so damn important to this witch? Not that he cared, it would just be nice to know what reasoning had bought his freedom. He held up the chained cuff.

"Release me," he said softly.

She stepped closer, and her eyes narrowed. "The deal is you heal him. If he dies, or if you kill him—"

"I'm not in the habit of killing folks," he interrupted in exasperation.

"You tried to kill me," she pointed out, and he grimaced.

"Okay, so just that one time…"

"You've attacked me five times."

"Nobody's perfect."

"You don't get to leave until my friend is well," she snapped. "If he dies, you die."

He stared at her for a moment, reading in her eyes the worry she tried to hide. He tried to think of someone who would do this for him, sacrifice their own vengeance for his well-being. Sadly, no name came to mind. "If he has a pulse, he'll live." His reputation was understated. He wasn't just good, he was the best.

Her eyes narrowed. "You sound cocky."

"Oh, you have no idea. Now, if you want me to save your friend, I suggest we stop flirting and you release me," he said, taking extra care to pronounce his last two words clearly as he jangled the chain.

She raised a finger, then paused. "If you try to attack

me, or harm me or my friends, whatever you try to do will be visited a hundredfold back on you."

"You have my word as a gentleman," he promised, bowing. He kept the triumph out of his voice, his expression. He was getting the hell out of here.

"You're not a gentleman."

He raised his hand, parting his fingers. "Scout's honor."

"That's not a scout's—"

"I promise," he growled, then sighed. He dipped his head to meet her gaze directly. "I promise to heal your friend," he told her, all attempts at levity gone. "You'll have to trust me." He waggled his eyebrows. "I am a doctor, after all."

Her gaze flickered away, and it was so clear she didn't trust him. He straightened. He guessed he deserved that. "What else can you do for your friend?" He knew already she couldn't do anything else, because sure as hell, he would have been her last resort.

She blinked and looked away. Were those—were those tears? She really was worried about this guy. This time it was Hunter who looked away, unprepared for the spark of envy for a dying man.

"Do we have a deal?" he asked roughly. "I don't hurt you, you don't hurt me, your friend lives and we go our separate ways?"

She nodded. "We have a deal."

"For this to work, you'll need to do as I say. You'll need to be my—nurse." He smiled. "See, we get to play doctors and nurses."

The witch didn't crack a smile. At all. He needed her promise, though. He got the impression that promises were important to her. "Your word—I don't want to argue over treatment, I just need you to do as I say."

Her lips tightened. "Fine. With regard to Lance, I'll do as you say."

He didn't miss the qualification but didn't comment. He jangled the cuff, eyeing her suggestively. She waved her hand casually and the cuffs around his wrists snapped open and fell to the floor. She turned and led the way to the door.

He nodded as he rubbed his wrists. "Neat trick."

She didn't look over her shoulder. "Oh, you have no idea."

Melissa walked into her apartment, conscious of the man who followed behind her. Her shoulders were tense and she occasionally glanced over her shoulder warily. This man had tried to kill her, and now she was letting him into her home, her haven.

God, what the hell was she thinking? But what choice did she have? She'd understated Hunter Armstrong's reputation. No, wait, he was Hunter Galen now. She'd been hiding in the next room when he'd renounced his father's name. Hunter wasn't renowned simply for being adequate, or even good at his job. He was widely reputed to be the *best* at his job. Surgeon. General practitioner. Specialist. If anyone was to work on Lance, she'd want him to be the best.

She'd also want him not to have homicidal tendencies.

She led him into the spare bedroom, and Lexi looked up from the bed. She rose to her feet, frowning. "Who's this?"

"A friend."

"A doctor." Melissa eyed him. They'd responded simultaneously, and he'd called himself a friend. Friend? Good grief. If he thought this was friendship, she'd hate to see the man's enemies.

No, wait, they were probably all ashes, somewhere.

"This is Hunter Galen. Hunter, this is Lexi, and that's her brother, Lance," she said, indicating the bed.

Lance's chest rose and fell rapidly, and sweat gave a sheen to his body in the muted candlelight. Gauze and bandages covered his chest, and although she'd seen Lance's injuries, and had treated his wounds as best she could, the sight of his damaged body was still a shock. She glanced away. Only three candles remained burning, the rest had long since blown out or burned out.

Hunter stepped closer, his bulk casting a shadow over Lance's body. Hunter touched his patient's forehead, then raised the man's eyelids. He placed his fingers at the side of Lance's neck, as though taking a pulse, and a faint frown marred his brow.

"What is it?" Melissa whispered.

"Talk to me. Tell me what happened," he commanded.

Melissa drew in a breath. "I don't know." She glanced over to Lexi, who shrugged, her eyes wide. "This is how he was found. I asked him what had happened, but he wouldn't tell me."

"Oh, so you two are close, huh?" Hunter commented dryly.

"He doesn't want me to go after who did this," Melissa whispered, ensuring Lexi didn't hear her. Hunter's gaze met hers briefly, then flicked over to Lexi and then back to his patient.

"He's been cut. Doesn't look like claws, though. And he's been shot."

Hunter peeled the gauze off Lance's chest and grimaced. "Yikes. That's nasty."

"There's—there's something near his heart," Melissa told him, pointing to the bullet wound high on Lance's chest. "A fragment, maybe."

Hunter leaned down to peer closely, not at all bothered by the blood. "Uh-huh."

"But you can heal him, right?" Melissa stepped up to stand beside him. She'd meant it to sound like an order, not a plea. It was such a contrast, her friend, pale and sickly on the bed, and the light warrior, so damn vital and strong, next to her. Hunter flicked a quick glance toward her, and his eyes darkened as he noted the short distance between them. He finally nodded.

"I believe so."

Her shoulders sagged with relief.

Hunter frowned and placed his head on Lance's forehead. "There's something not quite right here," he muttered.

"I, uh, I think that bullet is creating more damage with every breath he takes."

Hunter raised an eyebrow at her. "Oh, so now you're a doctor, too, huh?"

She frowned. "No, but I am a witch, and I sensed something dark in there, like a shadow that is expanding inside him."

Hunter nodded. "Poison. Looks like the bullet was possibly tainted. If the bullet had just passed through him, he would have been really sick. With that bullet fragment in there, and the sustained exposure to the toxin, it's killing him. His body hasn't got a chance to rejuvenate with that thing eating at him." Hunter tilted his head. "But that's not quite what I meant. There is something…unnatural here."

"Oh, that would be me. I worked a dormancy spell." She couldn't think of anything else to do for her friend, and the knowledge of her limitations was excruciating.

She met his gaze, and was surprised by the flicker of approval she saw there.

"Smart move. It slows the spread of the toxin, but still keeps his system active." Hunter folded his arms. "A dormancy spell, huh? I'm surprised you're still standing. So, he's human, or at least part human? I mean, I have to assume that, otherwise you would have used a suspension spell, right?"

He seemed to possess an uncomfortable amount of knowledge on witchcraft. The suspension spell could be used on most of the pure-breeds, like full-blooded vampires, and those that were undead in their natural state. She nodded. "He's a dhampir."

She saw his brown eyes widen.

"A dhampir? As in, vampire hunter? But that would make him a shadow breed." Hunter's brows dipped with confusion. He'd never seen a dhampir in action before. Sure, he knew the basics; they consumed vampire blood. Their human nature still desired food and drink, but to build their strength and other enhanced physical qualities, they had to consume the blood of the undead. Nature's solution to the vampire abomination. Half human, half vampire, they became a natural-born vampire hunter. Most didn't survive to maturity, having been killed off by the vampires before they could become a true threat. Those who did survive that long spent the rest of their lives with a target on their back, hunted by the entire vampire breed. It was an interesting relationship, but one of equal footing, the hunted also becoming the hunter.

"But you hate shadow breeds, remember? You go on and on about how you wish we'd all die." He rolled his hands as he spoke. "On and on."

Melissa lifted her chin. "Dhampirs hate vampires just as much as I do. Dhampirs want vampires dead. Ergo, that makes them the good guys."

Hunter gazed absently at the wall behind her as he considered her words. "So you don't hate *all* shadow breeds, then, huh?" He leaned forward. "*Ergo*, there's hope for me yet," he whispered in her ear.

"No, there isn't." She pulled back a little, ignoring the little kick-start to her pulse. No. No way in hell would she be going there. She checked behind her to avoid stepping on Lexi. He was so big, and warm, and…cheeky, damn it. "What do you need to get started here?"

Hunter turned around the room, taking an instant visual inventory. "We're going to need more water, for starters. Towels, bandages, scissors, tweezers, needles, candles—lots of candles." He counted off the items on his fingers. "And alcohol. Bourbon, preferably." He glanced meaningfully at Lexi, who nodded and hurried out of the room.

"Bourbon?" Melissa's brow wrinkled as she tried to remember the medicinal purposes of the liquor. Maybe sterilization?

Hunter nodded. "Yeah. That'll be for me." He shrugged. "Five months…"

She folded her arms. "You can't—"

"Tut-tut. Whatever I asked, remember?"

Her eyes narrowed. She knew he was going to take advantage of the situation. She guessed she should be relieved it was just a drink or three. "Don't screw up," she warned him.

Hunter grimaced. "Can't promise that. I'm renowned for screwing up, just ask my brother."

Melissa took a deep breath, praying for patience, and he waved a hand at her. "Relax. I'll be fine. Soon."

"Soon?" Oh, hell, now what did he want? What cockamamy demand was he going to make? His words finally registered. He'd be fine *soon*. Which implied he wasn't fine *now*. Her mental alarm bells started to ring. "What do you mean?"

Hunter turned to face her. "You've kept me locked away," he said coolly, and took a step toward her. She eyed him. He was going all predator on her. She took a wary step back. Uh-oh. He wasn't chained to a wall anymore.

"Five months in the dark," he grated, and she saw the muscles in his jaw clench. He stepped closer again. Damn it. He was going to try to kill her again. This had all been a ploy for him to get out of those iron cuffs. She cast her gaze toward Lance, unconscious on the bed. He couldn't help her. Her fingers tensed.

"I'm dry," he told her, his stare intent.

She hesitated. Frowned. "Dry? What do you mean, dry?"

"I have no energy," he told her quietly. "Your friend—he's going to need some serious energy, and I don't have it at the moment because you've kept me in the dark for so long."

She blinked. "Oh." She'd researched, but there wasn't a great deal of information available about light warriors. Any records that mentioned them were notoriously sketchy. They siphoned energy from the sun, flame, some light—but they couldn't draw energy from the blue fluorescence. She backed away again, only to come up against the bedroom wall. "Uh, what—what do you need?"

"Candles," he told her, and rested his palm against the wall, right beside her head. She swallowed. He was close. Really, really close. The corded strength of his arm was right there, tendon, sinew and muscle covered in golden skin. He even smelled…clean. She guessed the fire hose and a mini-blizzard had that effect on a man.

There was no aftershave, no cultured scent, just him. He smelled pleasant, with a hint of amber and male musk.

Nope, she wasn't going to think about musk.

She snapped her attention back to the conversation. "Uh, well, Lexi will bring some in shortly."

Hunter nodded, placing his other hand on the wall on the other side of her head, effectively hemming her into a space within his reach that was growing smaller with every breath she took. She could sense the warmth of his body, so close, that naked chest just inches away from her own form. Warmth and heat. Heart pounding. Male musk. Muscles.

"Fire," he told her, his gaze on hers, and she could see the flare of heat there, too, as though he could feel the sizzle between them.

"Fire?" she repeated, then cleared her throat at the hoarse sound. "Fire?" she repeated, this time in a stronger voice. Oh, dear. That chest, those muscles, covered in that smooth, golden skin.

"I need fire," he said, and her eyes widened. Did he mean he was going to set her place on fire again?

"I need to draw energy from fire," he told her, apparently reading the concern in her gaze. He bent his elbows, drawing himself even closer, his gaze lowering to focus on her neck, her shoulders…her chest. "I'm a light warrior, Melissa. I need light to do what I do." His voice had dropped to a whisper. "Light. Warmth. Heat. I draw energy from it. It's like blood for vampires—I need it to survive."

She swallowed. Well, she could certainly help him with the heat. Her cheeks were hot, her mouth dry. "Oh. Uh, well, those candles…"

"Your friend is going to need a lot of energy, Melissa," Hunter said, and dipped his head toward her neck. She heard him inhale.

"Uh…" Good grief, he wasn't even touching her, but her nipples were tightening in reaction.

"It's going to take time for me to rejuice, heal, rejuice, heal," he told her. His chest was so close, all warmth and naked skin. If she took a deep breath, they'd be touching, breast to breast. She swallowed.

"There is a way I can get some pure energy, fast," he whispered, his breath against her neck.

She closed her eyes. "There is?" Good grief, he was so *there*, so big, so…sexy. All tall and broad shoulders, male musk and—

Something delicate and damp flicked against her neck, and her eyes sprang open. He'd licked her. He lifted his head, his gaze meeting hers.

She gasped. His eyes. They'd gone from dark brown to warm hazel, with shards of golden amber flecking his irises. Even as she watched, her gaze never leaving his, he pressed closer, his chest coming into contact with hers, separated by her cream blouse and lacy bra. His eyes brightened. Not with emotion, but actually brightened. Sparks of amber brightened to flecks of gold, and his eyes glowed.

They *glowed*. His expression looked stunned for a moment. "You're so—hot," he whispered finally, and lowered his lips to hers.

Chapter 7

This was no dream. His lips were warm and supple against hers, and she closed her eyes as he kissed her. Even with her eyes shut, though, she could sense his heat, a sensual haze creeping over her, through her. Her heart thumped in her chest, and he changed the angle, drawing back for barely a moment before pressing his mouth to hers again, his tongue darting in to tease at hers.

The sensations were at once familiar and alien. She remembered passion, she remembered arousal, desire... she just hadn't felt any of that in so long.

Her breasts swelled, and he sighed as he rubbed his chest against hers, her nipples peaking at the delicious contact. His tongue caressed hers, causing a tremble to start low in her stomach and ripple outward...down to her core and up to her breasts. His kisses were well practiced, expert—drawing a response from her, a surrender she wasn't prepared for. She was panting, trying to catch her breath, but not wanting to relinquish the sweet, hot hold of his lips. She realized her hands were pressed against the wall by her sides, as though she was trying to hold herself back.

Screw that.

She raised her arms, and his hands left the wall, his fingers intertwining with hers. He raised his head, panting, his beautiful golden eyes staring down at her. He looked like he was going to come back for round two, and then he blinked. The golden fire in his eyes banked, and the passion of his expression cooled into a remote mask.

"Thank you," he said politely, taking a step back.

She gaped at him for a moment, feeling a chill wash over her. "What for?" she whispered hoarsely, although glimpsing the glow and golden flecks of his previously dark brown eyes, she thought she knew.

"I, uh, needed that." He licked his lips and stepped back again.

"Needed what?" she asked, strength returning to her voice, her limbs. Despite the passion and excitement of a few seconds ago, she felt drained, exhausted.

"A small recharge." He indicated Lance on the bed behind him. "You know, to look after your friend."

She hid her dismay. All thoughts of Lance had fled her mind as soon as Hunter's lips had touched hers. She'd been swept away. Excited. Horny. Hell. She hadn't kissed anyone since...

She blinked once. Twice. No. She clamped her lips tight, as though they could keep her horror, her pain and her shame hidden away inside her. She'd kissed Hunter, and she'd forgotten all about Theo. She'd been totally lost to the passion—with Hunter, of all people. A light warrior—a damn shadow breed. And he'd just been using her to "recharge." Guilt hit her like a solid punch to the gut. She wasn't going to tear up, damn it. She wasn't going to give pyro jerk the satisfaction.

She took a breath, sagging back against the wall. For a moment, the room swirled, and she flattened her hands against the wall for balance.

"Melissa," Hunter spoke softly, stepping back toward her, his hand raised.

She hit it away. "Don't touch me," she rasped. "Not ever."

He halted, something flashing in those eyes that looked almost like hurt, but she ignored it. He was incapable of empathy. "You need to break the dormancy spell," he told her. "You're—drained." His gaze flicked away for a moment. "You need to break away from Lance."

She shook her head, but he nodded, his chin lifting. "You have to. I can't do what I need to do if he's dormant. Let him go."

She eyed him. If she let him go, Lance's injuries would flare up. He'd feel pain. The poison would spread. He could die.

"Trust me," he told her softly.

She blanched. After what he'd just done to her, he expected her to trust him? Anger flared, and if she'd had the energy, she would have punched him. She wanted to lash out, make him hurt as much as she did.

Hunter dipped his chin, meeting her gaze squarely. "I will heal your friend, Melissa, but you need to trust me to do it."

She fixed him with a glare, pouring as much anger and bitterness into it as she could. "If anything happens to him, I will kill you."

He nodded. "Understood. Now, let go."

She closed her eyes, her head tilting back against the wall. She was so gosh-darn tired. She didn't want to argue anymore, didn't have the energy. Summoning up the dregs of her power, she whispered an incantation that severed the magical link between her stores and Lance's life source. It was like a small burst of light disappearing into the darkness.

She opened her eyes, and startled. Hunter had stepped right up to her, his face close to hers.

"You need to rest," he whispered, touching her forehead gently. She tried to move away, to open her mouth to protest, but a warmth rolled through her mind, a comforting blanket of white that stole her consciousness, and then she knew nothing.

Hunter caught her as she started to slide to the floor, scooping her up and carrying her to the chair in the corner her friend—what was her name?—had sat in. He placed her gently in the chair, pulling up one of the cushions that had fallen to the floor and carefully placing it against the wall. He tilted Melissa's head into a comfortable position, making sure the cushion was placed to prevent a crick in the neck, and squatted there for a moment, gazing up at her.

She looked so peaceful, so damn luscious. It always surprised him how a woman with so much sass and attitude could look so angelic. He took advantage of the moment, staring at her without worrying about her hissing, spitting, kicking or smashing his head in, because he'd sensed that was where she was headed when she realized he'd used her.

His mouth pulled down at the corners. He hadn't lied to her. Light warriors needed sources of light to fill their energy stores. Sexual energy, though, was like a pure shot of adrenaline, a caffeine triple hit. It could also be draining for the source, if the light warrior was feeding and not careful. Most light warriors learned how to consume the energy without bringing their source to the brink of death, although it was possible to kill a partner if the light warrior didn't stop.

Melissa's energy was like an inferno. He wondered if that was because she was a witch. Regardless, her energy was a seduction in itself, especially with him being half-starved. With her lack of sleep, though, and the magic she'd expended on trying to heal her friend, she was dangerously low on power. It had felt so good, but despite their shared passion and it was shared—she'd reciprocated, he hadn't imagined that—he could also sense the lethargy stealing into her limbs. He'd had to pull back.

Normally he wasn't quite so—enthusiastic—in a light feed. He knew control, he knew discipline. He blamed it on subsisting on torchlight for the past few months, and not on any kind of magnetic attraction he might feel for the witch.

Her friend entered the room, carrying a bundle of towels and a bucket, steam curling up from the water. She halted when she saw Melissa sleeping in the corner. "What's wrong with her?" Her expression showed her alarm, and Hunter rose, holding his hand out in a soothing gesture.

"She's fine. She's just really tired after working on your brother." He took the towels from her. "Thanks…" He racked his brain for her name, but honestly, he'd been kind of focused on Melissa, and checking out her home, more than anything—including his new patient.

"Lexi," she supplied. She indicated the candles. Some were just hardened puddles of wax, some could be relit.

"Melissa used all of her candles earlier. Do you need me to run out and get some?"

He nodded. "Please." He was good to go, but working on Lance was going to take some time and energy, and he'd need to top up and rest. Lexi nodded, then paused, clearly hesitant to leave him alone with her brother and Melissa. "He's going to be fine," he said, hoping he was right. There was never any guarantee with a patient, there were too many variables, but he would have promised Melissa anything to get out of that cell.

"Uh, okay. Well, I'll go get some candles," Lexi murmured, backing out of the doorway. She eyed his chest for a moment, and he saw the curiosity flare in her eyes before she glanced at her brother. "I'll bring some clothes, too. For both of you."

He smiled. "Thanks." He didn't offer her any explanation for his half-naked state.

Lexi left, and he heard her light tread on the stairs. He glanced around the room. Lance was still unconscious on the bed and Melissa was sleeping deeply in the corner. The whole apartment was filled with an eerie silence. He couldn't even hear the tick of a clock. At present, he may as well have been alone.

He turned and eyed the door. He could leave. Lance was out cold, and couldn't stop him—although the guy looked massive enough to present a challenge if he'd been alert. Melissa was in a forced sleep. She would waken when she was fully rested, her energy restored.

He stepped out into the hallway, turning in a full circle. There was absolutely nothing to stop him leaving. He eyed the door at the end of the hall.

He could just up and leave. Step through that door and escape.

* * *

Melissa stirred. Her eyelids flickered. Something fluffy made her nose itchy, and she put her hand up to rub it, her eyes opening. Pale blue wool filled her vision, and she frowned. She was covered in the fringed blanket she normally draped across the back of her sofa, and it was the strips of heavy yarn that teased her face. She lowered the blanket to her waist and straightened, frowning as a cushion behind her shifted and fell into her lap. She yawned and stretched. God, she'd needed that sleep. She felt so…refreshed. Then she remembered how she'd fallen asleep. Her muscles stiffened. That rat bastard. She glanced about her.

Everything around her was cast in a golden hue. Candles sat on every surface. Many, many candles. It would almost be romantic if it wasn't for the bloodied rags she spied on the floor. Hunter stood with his back to her, his feet planted shoulder-width apart, his back all smooth and golden. He held his hands out over Lance's unconscious body, his arms and shoulders roped with muscle, and her mouth dropped.

Tendrils of light glowed and snaked from Hunter's palms to the bullet hole in Lance's chest, and she could see the radiance moving beneath his skin, as though glowworms pulsed inside his body.

She rose from the chair, the blanket falling to her feet as she stepped toward the bed. Lance's body was covered in perspiration, and he'd been stripped, cleaned and covered with a sheet. His complexion was still gray, yet his chest and limbs looked flushed. Every now and then he would groan softly, and Hunter would draw his hands away, the threads of light dimming, before continuing. She glanced at Hunter.

His eyes were closed, his face pale and perspiring,

and occasionally his brow would dip, and the stream of light would pulse beneath his palms. Melissa glanced at her watch, and her eyes widened. Four hours had passed since she'd last glanced at it. It was well past two in the morning.

Hunter was silent, his attention focused inward, and Melissa didn't want to distract him. She folded her arms and moved to stand at the foot of the bed.

She did it to watch over her friend, not to get an eyeful of Hunter's bare torso.

She focused on Lance, but every now and then her gaze would return to the light warrior, to his hands…his chest…his lips. She found herself staring at his mouth.

He'd kissed her.

She'd kissed him back.

It had felt incredible. They'd barely touched, really, but he'd managed to stir something in her, hot passion and a soft vulnerability she didn't know quite what to do with. Bury it. Showing this man a weakness like that would only lead to pain. Maybe even death.

Her lips tightened. He'd done it again, damn it.

She couldn't believe she'd allowed him to get close to her again. She'd been totally sucked into that kiss, and he'd just been using her to drain her energy and fill his own stores. She lifted her chin. Well, she knew what the jerk was capable of. She would make damn sure he never used her again, that he never fooled her again.

Lance flinched in his unconscious state, emitting a low moan, and Hunter rolled his lips in, his brows drawing into a deep V. He curled his palms, his fingers dancing as though playing an instrument, and Melissa was mesmerized by the grace and fluidity of his movements.

Lance's breathing sped up, and Melissa bit her lip. She had no idea what was going on, but it looked like

Lance was in tremendous pain. Hunter rolled his hand over, as though grabbing the tendrils of light in his fist, and raised his hand, as though pulling on a fishing line.

Lance's features contorted and his body arched off the bed. Melissa shifted, not sure what to do, and then she heard a soft, moist squish and something slid out of Lance's chest. Her eyes rounded as Lance's body subsided back on the bed, his head lolling to the side, his features relaxed once more. His eyes remained closed, but his breathing changed. No longer panting, his breaths slowed down, deepened.

Hunter's eyes opened, and the tendrils of light disappeared, winked out of existence. He reached for a clean hand towel near Lance's head and used it to pick up the bloodied bullet fragment that lay on Lance's chest, a smile of triumph curling his lips.

Melissa stepped forward, and Hunter turned, as though surprised for a moment to see her. His expression changed from triumphant to wary in the blink of an eye.

"You're awake," he noted, his voice a soft murmur in the room.

She raised an eyebrow. "I am." No thanks to him. She kept her voice and expression cool. She'd wanted to throttle him when she awoke, but watching him work had mollified her anger somewhat. She was still angry, just not violently so. Besides, revenge was a dish best served cold, right? She stepped closer toward him, eyeing the small item resting on the hand towel.

"Is that part of the bullet?" She reached out, but he pulled the hand towel out of her reach.

"Careful, it's tainted, remember." He tipped the fragment into a glass on the bedside table. "Hemlock, if I'm not mistaken."

"Easy to get your hands on," she commented. It was

one of the first toxins she'd been able to restock, although it wasn't necessarily a high-demand plant. Mainly because you could find it growing on roadsides and near water sources everywhere.

"Nasty, especially if you're dipping your weapons in it."

She nodded, making a mental note. If you wanted to kill a vampire, you dipped your weapons in verbena. If you wanted to kill a werewolf, you dipped your weapons in wolfsbane. If you wanted to kill a human—or a dhampir—you used hemlock, or any other common poison at your disposal. Lance wasn't shot by accident. Someone had wanted to hurt him, and knew what would do the trick.

"Where is Lexi?" She finally realized Lance's sister was nowhere to be seen.

"She ducked out for some supplies, but then I sent her home for a rest. She'll be back sometime in the morning."

Melissa raised her eyebrows. "I'm surprised you convinced her to leave her brother." The young woman had remained in the room when Melissa had worked her magic.

Hunter shrugged. "She needed a little convincing, but she was tired, there was nothing she could do here and, quite frankly, I don't like a cluttered workspace."

She eyed him for a moment. Needed a little convincing, huh? She wondered if light warriors possessed a talent for compulsion, like vampires did. She thought about her dreams. Maybe they had some skill with mind bending.

Another reason to hate.

Then she realized she'd been alone with Hunter—and she'd survived. No infernos, no explosions, no retribution for locking him up for five months. Not only had she survived, he was still here. She hadn't thought to put up any blocking wards to prevent him leaving.

She turned her gaze to her friend. He was breathing easier now, and although his flesh still looked damp with perspiration, color was beginning to return to his complexion. But he still looked weak and unwell. "Why isn't he waking up?"

Hunter threw the hand towel onto the soiled linen by his feet. "Because I'm a light warrior, not God." He folded his arms, staring down at his patient, and she forced herself to ignore the way the muscles in his arms and chest bunched with the movement. "He was badly hurt, Melissa. That poison has spread through his body. I've been able to remove the toxin, but traces still remain in his body. It's not going to kill him, but it's going to take time for his metabolism to burn through it, especially in his weakened state."

"So do something to speed it up," she told him.

He dipped his chin. "I'm beat."

"No." She stepped away from him. She wasn't going to go anywhere near him when he needed to "recharge." He held up his hand to halt her, correctly interpreting the reason for her retreat.

"Relax. Lance needs a break from the treatment. Too much light force too fast, and I could end up killing him. He's had enough for now, as have I. I'll start working on him again in the morning, once we've both rested." He smiled at her, and for a moment she stared. There wasn't anything wicked, or calculating. Rather, it was a tired, sincere smile, and utterly without guile. "I'd love a shower, though…?"

And there it was. A vision of him, naked, in her shower, water sluicing over those abs, droplets trailing down his body. She bent over and scooped up the linen, hiding her flushed cheeks.

"Bathroom is at the end of the hall, towels are in the cupboard underneath the sink. You can look after yourself. You're not here as a guest." She didn't look at him to see his reaction, but stalked down the hallway to the cupboard that cleverly hid her laundry. After a moment she heard him behind her, shifting aside to let him pass her to the bathroom. He carried a dark bundle of clothing, but he shut the door before she could inquire about them.

She busied herself with the laundry, determinedly shutting any vision of his wet, naked body from her mind as she heard the water turn on in the shower. She heard him moan and realized this was his first real shower since his capture. Those bucket washes had consisted of cold water and a cloth.

Her lips curled as she poured some stain remover and detergent into the machine, then switched it on. The machine shuddered, then she heard the reassuring noise of water filling the tub.

A choked cry came from behind the door, and she heard a series of thumps, as though he was recoiling against the wall. A series of curse words were bellowed, and then nothing but the fall of water in the shower.

She walked down the hallway to her bedroom, her hips swinging, and she shut the door.

Nope. Not a guest.

Chapter 8

Hunter scooped up the eggs and slid them onto the three plates on the table. He was wearing an apron he'd found in a kitchen drawer. Either Melissa or someone she knew had a sense of humor, because the apron had the words *I kiss better than I cook* across it. It was true, though. Melissa did kiss a hell of a lot better than she cooked, if her prison food was anything to go by.

Lexi poured the juice, and he was moving the plates to the set places on the tiny round kitchen table when Melissa walked into the kitchen.

He almost dropped the plate, and fumbled to catch it.

She was all sleep-tousled and rosy-cheeked, her eyes blinking as she took in the domestic scene. She wore loose-fitting slate blue cotton pants and a matching top that looked soft from many washings, and pink-and-black polka-dotted woolen socks that looked like they'd been knitted from the hair of a Persian cat, all fluffy and spiky.

She looked adorable. Before, when she'd stormed down to his cell in her silken nightie, she'd looked all womanly and sexy, like a dangerously sexy siren. This morning, she was girl-next-door, scoop-me-up-and-screw-me cute. Like a sleepy tomboy stripper. He put the plate on the table with a thud.

"What's going on?" Melissa asked, her voice all husky and soft from sleep. That voice. It still had that same effect, curling deep inside him with an insidious desire. Her brows dipped, her lips were pulled into a sexy little pout and she looked adorably grumpy.

"I noticed you had barely any food in your fridge and brought some groceries," Lexi informed her as she took a seat at the table. "Hunter cooked breakfast."

Melissa padded over to grab the coffeepot off the warmer and fill it with water. "Did he just?" she muttered as she placed the pot back on the warmer, scooped coffee into the filter and jabbed the button to turn it on.

"You're a morning person, I see," Hunter commented dryly as he lowered himself into the seat.

"I'm a coffee person," she muttered, as she sank into the remaining seat. She eyed the food on the table with suspicion. Hunter's stomach growled, but he held up his cutlery politely, waiting for the ladies to start eating.

Green eyes met his, narrowed and mistrustful. "After you," she said coolly.

He tilted his head to the side. "It's not poisoned," he told her.

Lexi laughed as she chewed on some bacon. She swallowed. "It's delicious. Besides, he's a friend—and a doctor. I'm sure he can cook something without killing us."

Hunter waggled his eyebrows. "See, Melissa. I'm a friend. And a doctor. I wouldn't hurt you."

She glared at him, and he sighed. She really didn't

trust him. "Fine." He scooped up some egg and put it in his mouth. "Hmm-mmm. Yum."

Melissa finally raised her cutlery, twirling her knife meaningfully as she met his eyes, then began to eat. He saw the soft flare of surprise in her expression as she tasted the food, and he smiled. "I didn't think you'd mind me cooking for once. I mean, I know how you love cooking for me, but I wanted to return the favor." No more peanut butter and jelly sandwiches.

Lexi's eyebrows rose. "Oh, so you two are—"

"No," Melissa interjected shaking her head.

"Not yet," Hunter stated, enjoying the flare of annoyance in her green eyes.

"Not ever."

Lexi glanced between them. "Okay," she said slowly, before focusing on her food.

Melissa rose from her seat, and Hunter watched as she crossed over to the cupboards. "Does anyone else want coffee?"

"No, thanks. I'm trying to go no-caffeine," Lexi said as she pierced some bacon with her fork and ate it.

"Yes, please," Hunter said, mostly because he'd gone five months without the stuff, but also because he knew it would annoy her, serving him. She shot him another hard stare and poured the freshly brewed coffee into two cups. She placed one in front of him with a thud. He had to move his hand to avoid the hot droplets that spilled with the movement. She gestured to the bottle of milk on the table and the pot of sugar.

"Help yourself," she told him sweetly, then resumed her seat. She sipped from her cup, eyeing him over the rim. Her gaze drifted down to his clothes, and he straightened his shoulders, then almost laughed at himself, puffing up his chest like a courting parrot.

"Where did you get those clothes?" she asked brusquely.

"I brought them over," Lexi answered, then drained her glass of juice. She rose from the table. "I figured I'd have to bring some over for Lance, and Hunter looks about the same size."

Hunter's eyebrows rose. She thought he was the same size as that hulk in the spare bedroom? He turned his arms, looking at his biceps. Maybe he'd bulked up in his prison, but he didn't think so. The gray long-sleeved T-shirt was loose, but comfortable. "Thanks," he said, smiling.

Lexi winked as she rose from the table. "Hey, I've had to do the walk of shame enough to recognize one when I see it. No dramas."

Hunter chuckled softly as Melissa choked on her coffee, but Lexi didn't seem to notice as she dumped the dishes in the sink and left the kitchen. He waited until Melissa stopped coughing and leaned back in her chair. He met her gaze as he raised the cup to his lips.

"You didn't tell her I was your prisoner." It wasn't a question. Lexi had treated him like a friend-by-association, easygoing and open. She'd brought him clothes and bacon—even some toiletries so he could shave, and for that, she had a new friend for life.

"Neither did you," she pointed out, folding her arms. That top looked so soft, and it showed off her breasts. His mouth dried. She wasn't wearing a bra.

Good God. He could feel himself swell in his hand-me-down jeans. He raised the coffee to his lips, trying to distract himself, but all he could think about was how those breasts had felt against his chest last night, and how he wanted to kiss her again, and this time not stop.

"Why didn't you?" he asked her. Talking felt like he

was trying to push his voice over rocks, so tight and dry was his throat.

She arched an eyebrow, and she went from gloriously tousled cutie to seductive vixen. His lips quirked. If she knew where his thoughts were going, she'd probably do some of her witchy-woo voodoo on him, make him a eunuch.

"Because Lexi is already worried enough. She doesn't need to know the man healing her brother tried to incinerate me in a fireball. Where did you sleep last night?"

"On your sofa." He put the cup down on the table. Her couch may have been a piece of furniture about a foot too short and not quite wide enough for his frame, but after sleeping on stone for the last five months it was almost bliss.

Almost.

It also faced a hearth. Would have been nice to have known that last night, too. They'd lit up Melissa's spare bedroom like a fairy wonderland, when he'd had a perfectly good fireplace in the living room down the hall. Had she been trying to limit his access to light? Still, he got the recharge he needed when he'd kissed Melissa, and he didn't regret that, not one bit.

Knowing that a soft and sleepy Melissa was just down the hall had been torture. He'd wanted to go to her. He'd had to keep telling himself it was because he'd been in captivity, months without a woman, and Melissa was right *there*. He almost believed himself, too, but as he didn't share the same hunger for Lexi as he did for Melissa, it wasn't quite convincing.

She was silent for a moment, then she flicked her hair back over her shoulder. "How is Lance?" she asked, her gaze on the table. He pursed his lips. She really did care for this friend.

"He's resting. I checked on him when I woke up. He's still battling the poison, but he's breathing easier." He eyed the kitchen for a moment, and a photo frame on top of the fridge caught his eye. He rose from the table. "Who's this?" He gestured to the frame. He'd seen other photos around the living room, some featuring the same guy. In this one, Melissa was sitting at a table, leaning against the guy whose arm was slung around her shoulders. She looked...younger. Not agewise. He guessed it was a recent photo, within the last couple of years, judging by her age. No, it was the easygoing smile, the carefree twinkle in her eye, the absence of...anguish. He blinked when he recognized it. Melissa carried a darkness within her now, something that she hadn't possessed at the time this photo was taken. The photographer had caught the couple in midlaugh. They looked relaxed, and very comfortable in each other's space.

She rose from the table and grabbed the frame. "None of your business." She held the frame behind her back, and lifted her chin to eye him squarely. "What do we need to do about Lance?"

His lips pursed for a moment. Whoever the guy was, he was important to her. As important as the guy lying unconscious in her spare room? How many men did this woman have dangling around her? Just the thought she was a player made him fold his arms and match her brusqueness.

"I'll work on clearing out the rest of the toxin, but I might have to halt after that. With the extent of his injuries, he's going to need a slow rehab." He made a split decision. "This could take a while." It wasn't quite a lie. He could justify it. He could speed up the process, but right then, he decided to take his time, take a little extra care.

She frowned. "A while? How long is a while?"

He shrugged. "A couple of days."

"Days?" Her expression was a combination of surprise, horror and frustration.

He smiled. "Yep. Guess we're going to be spending some quality time together." This was an opportunity to discover more about the woman who had held him captive. He should move on, but he convinced himself this was a strategic move—and nothing to do with a developing fascination for the woman. He'd initially sought her out to destroy any evidence that could convict his brother of murder. Now his desire to stay had nothing to do with Ryder, and everything to do with the complicated woman standing before him. She treated him as though he should behave better—as though she believed he was capable of being better. Everyone else took him at face value. He frowned. No, he mentally corrected himself. He was staying because he needed leverage against someone who could match him. The witch had managed to capture a light warrior and hold him prisoner. She knew his vulnerabilities. He needed to find hers to level the playing field—because he sure wasn't going to go through that hell again.

Her lips pursed, and his gaze dropped to her sexy little pout. She could be so sexy in a snit. "Just—just heal him, Hunter. As fast as you can."

He bowed his head. "But of course. A deal's a deal. I'm a man of honor."

She rolled her eyes and snorted as she turned to leave the room. "Please, we both know that's not true," she muttered as she walked down the hallway to her room.

He brooded as he watched her go. She was right. He took what he wanted, when he wanted, and it had served him well in the past. He'd almost killed her trying to hide what he thought was evidence against his brother.

When an Alpha Prime had died in his brother's dental surgery, he knew it was just a matter of time before his brother was punished—either through the Reform court, or through the Alpha Prime's werewolf pack. He'd seen the autopsy results, knew that the highly concentrated dose of wolfsbane that had killed the lycan leader could have only come from Irondell's premier apothecary. Even during their disconnection, he'd wanted to protect his little brother, had felt the need to look out for Ryder. Maybe it was a throwback to a time that was no more, when the boys had behaved like brothers, and there had been love and camaraderie between them. Or maybe it was a deep-rooted sense of duty as protector after his mother died. Either way, he'd done it because he'd believed it to be the right thing to do. A bad act for good reasons. He frowned. Sometimes, he did bad things. Sometimes he regretted it. Sometimes he didn't. It wasn't a question of honor; it was a matter of expediency. Sometimes those virtues couldn't coexist, and he'd never lost any sleep over it.

He eyed the closed door between him and Melissa. For the first time last night, though, he'd had trouble sleeping.

Melissa entered the spare bedroom carrying two glasses of water and halted. Her apartment was toasty. Like, the warmest she could remember. Candles were lit everywhere, and the fireplace in her living room was in full flame. She figured he'd find it sooner or later. While she might not know much about light warriors, she knew they needed light or flame, and with that they could create their own light and flame. She wanted Hunter to have the strength to heal her friend. She didn't want him to have the strength to level a city block.

Hunter now stood over Lance's still-unconscious body, but he looked different. He'd shaved, the dark beard gone to reveal a chiseled jaw. His hair had been trimmed, too. Gone were the dark, loose waves, and instead his hair was shorter. It was still long enough to curl, still gave him that rough edge, but the shaggy style made him look casual and presentable. She turned an inquiring gaze to Lexi, who nodded proudly, gesturing to the scissors that lay in the first aid basket.

Lexi had cut his hair. Melissa set the glass down on the bedside table. He didn't look like the man who'd been kept in a cell for five months. He no longer looked like her prisoner. Didn't look rough and dangerous, but instead looked much more civilized. Like a guy she'd pass in the street and probably turn to look at twice. Who was she kidding? She'd been thinking of him most of the day. Ever since that kiss, she couldn't get him out of her mind. She'd look more than twice if she passed him in the street. Honestly, she'd probably do more than just look, after that kiss. And that frustrated the hell out of her.

She stepped back. She didn't like the false air of civility he wore—and she knew it was false. He may have his hair trimmed neatly, be cleanly shaven and wear presentable clothes that clung to those broad shoulders before draping down to hide the washboard stomach she knew existed beneath. But that was the problem. She knew exactly what strength and lethal power were now hidden behind the facade of propriety—and she didn't trust him. Not. At. All.

She'd pushed her nightstand against the door last night, and since waking she'd installed spelled wards around her home and shop. He wouldn't be able to leave the premises—he couldn't get past her apartment's front door, but she'd taken extra precautions with her access points in the store below. He wasn't going anywhere, no matter how hard he tried. He wasn't in a cell any longer, but he was not free. He wouldn't be until Lance was healed. She was still in control.

Although, she hadn't been in control last night... Oh, there it was again, that mental image of him kissing her against the wall. No, damn it, he was her prisoner, not the hunk of her dreams. She refused to start thinking of him like that, kisses be damned.

She handed the second glass to Lexi, her gaze remaining on what Hunter was doing. She could see those light tendrils snaking around her friend's body. She'd had to go downstairs and open her store, and this was her first opportunity to return to check up on her friend. She wouldn't have left him alone in Hunter's care, but Lexi had taken up temporary residence watching over her brother—and playing hairdresser, apparently. That left Melissa able to tend her business.

Although all morning she'd been distracted, wondering how things were going in the apartment above the store. She told herself it had nothing to do with this good-looking angel of death, but everything to do with her friend.

"How is he?" she whispered to Lexi.

Lexi sighed. "He's improving, but Hunter is taking it slow so as not to hurt him more." The woman shook her head, her straight blond hair shifting with the movement. "I have to tell you, Mel, I've never seen anything like this. I don't know what he's doing, or how he's doing it, but Lance is improving." She raised the glass to her lips.

Melissa leaned against the wall. "He's a light warrior," she told her. Lexi coughed on the water, her eyes wide. She wiped her chin, and glanced between Melissa and Hunter, who seemed oblivious to their conversation, so focused was he on his patient.

"Are you serious? I thought they were extinct."

Melissa shook her head. That was the common belief and, until recently, it had been hers, as well. "Apparently, the reports of their demise are greatly exaggerated."

Her brother's friend, Vassiliki Verity—a half-blood vampire, and an annoying one at that—was defending a shadow breed dentist on a murder charge, and had tracked him down to the home of his brother—Hunter. The man who'd destroyed her apothecary. Hunter Galen and his brother were having an argument when she and Dave had arrived, and they'd hidden, managing to overhear snatches of the conversation. She and her brother had been astounded when Arthur Armstrong, a Prime of the human faction, had arrived. Armstrong was as wealthy as he was powerful, an active participant in the intrigues of the Reform elite—and father to Hunter and Ryder. Just as his light warrior ancestors before him, Armstrong had kept the light warriors' existence secret. Everyone assumed that Arthur Armstrong and his sons were highly skilled healers among the shadow breeds. Nobody had guessed it was their light warrior powers that helped them be so.

Armstrong had been manipulating various members of the shadow breeds for years, during their treatment appointments. Melissa stared at the man standing over her friend. Who knew what he'd done with his patients. Was he as sick and twisted as his father?

She folded her arms. Of course he was. He'd tried to kill her, hadn't he? Then he'd used her dreams against her, and finally he'd used her to recharge his inner battery by kissing her. Everything this man had done to her had been one form of deceit and betrayal after another.

"Don't leave Lance alone, okay?" Melissa told her friend quietly.

Lexi frowned, concern darkening her gaze as she stared at the man standing over her brother. "Why? What would he do?"

Melissa pursed her lips. "I have no idea, and that's what scares me."

Hunter lowered his arms, extinguishing his light, and turned to face them. He really was too damn good-looking. "I think that will do for today. Any more and I might overload him." His gaze was friendly, and mildly tired. He hadn't heard their whispers in the corner.

He saw the glass of water on the bedside table and his brows rose in surprise. "Thanks, Melissa." He reached for it and drank, swallowing the contents in two gulps. He smiled, holding up the empty glass. "Thirsty work. Appreciate it."

She nodded. "I have to go back to work. Let me know if you need anything," she told Lexi meaningfully, and left the room.

"Oh, wait," Lexi called, and stepped out into the hall behind her.

Melissa turned to face her, her hand already on the doorknob to leave the apartment. "What's up, Lex?"

Lexi grimaced. "I'll, uh, I'll need to head back home tonight."

Melissa's eyes narrowed, and her gaze dropped down to Lexi's hand. The green snakeskin jasper ring was still on her finger.

"I need to have a chat with my boyfriend," Lexi told her quietly. "I'd put it off, but after what's happened with Lance, I think there are some things I need to address."

Melissa nodded solemnly. "I understand. What time

do you need to leave? I'll make sure I'm back here by then."

"Five?"

Melissa hesitated, then nodded. "Sure. I'll get Jenna to close up. I'll be here."

"Thanks. I'll stay the night at Lance's place," Lexi told her, her hand gesturing toward the rest of Melissa's apartment. "It's pretty full here. Is that okay?"

While Melissa would love the buffer between her and Hunter, she realized Lexi's words were true. All available beds or furniture were taken with Lance and Hunter here. Besides, Lance was a dhampir, and his home was probably the best option for Lexi to stay at if she was leaving her vampire boyfriend.

"That's fine. Will you be all right?"

Lexi waved a hand casually. "I'll be fine."

Melissa frowned. She may have thought Lexi was annoying or frustrating, and perhaps a little insecure, but after witnessing the care and love the young woman held for her brother, Melissa was warming to her, a new respect dawning behind the exasperation. Trying not to, but she couldn't quite help it. Lance had asked her to look after Lexi, and she would, but now she'd do it possibly as much for Lexi as for Lance.

"You call me if you need me," she told the young woman, her tone serious.

"Oh, Mel—"

"Don't 'oh, Mel' me. If you're in danger, you call me. I don't care what time, okay?"

Lexi smiled. "Okay, but seriously, I'll be fine."

"Just call me when you get to Lance's place, okay? Promise?"

"Promise."

Melissa nodded, moderately satisfied, and left the apartment.

Hunter listened to the whispered exchange in the hallway. His hearing was acute, and he had no trouble hearing the conversation near the front door, nor the one that had occurred earlier in the room.

He frowned. Why would Lexi need help? Why was Melissa concerned? The fact that Melissa was so protective of Lexi was a surprise. Hell, he'd been surprised ever since Melissa had told him she had a friend, and one that she was prepared to surrender her own need for vengeance in order to assist. Now she was going all motherly protective over Lexi—admittedly in a fierce, kick-ass kind of way.

Lance stirred on the bed, his eyelids flickering, before his eyes finally opened.

Hunter was next to him immediately, and gave him a friendly smile. "Whoa, hey, you need to rest," he whispered, gently touching the dhampir's temple, and the man's green eyes glazed over, and he drifted off into unconsciousness. "Back to sleep, bud."

No, he wasn't ready for the dhampir to wake just yet. He still wanted to find out a few things about the witch, and Lance unconscious and still not quite healed was exactly the way things needed to be for now.

Chapter 9

Melissa hadn't needed to get Jenna to close up, after all. The weather had turned foul outside, with winds gusting and flurries of snow whirling down the street. Her store had emptied about an hour ago, so she'd sent Jenna home early. She was climbing the stairs when Lexi met her halfway.

"How is Lance?" Melissa asked without preamble.

Lexi smiled. "He's doing well. It looks like Hunter has been able to neutralize the poison, and he's working on the deep tissue cuts tomorrow. I think he's wiped out, though. He was passed out on your sofa when I left."

Melissa nodded as she turned to walk back down the stairs with Lexi. "Good. I'm not quite sure how it works, but I guess it can be exhausting, expending all that energy." They walked down the corridor to the door that opened out onto the street. Melissa had bespelled and warded this access point, too. She twisted the locks and hauled the heavy door open. It wasn't long after she'd set up her apothecary that she'd discovered some people viewed her store like a pharmacy, and she'd had a few break-ins, early on. Of course, when she'd tracked down the perpetrators and meted out her own form of punishment, word got out about what happened to those who tried to steal from a witch.

She didn't get burgled anymore.

Still, she'd learned personal and property security was important, and preferred to err on the side of extreme caution. She wasn't going to be vulnerable to attack. Never again.

She stepped aside to allow Lexi to leave. "Don't forget, call me if you need me."

Lexi nodded. "And you call me if anything changes with Lance. I'm not too far away."

Melissa waved, slamming the door shut and engaging all the locks.

She was almost at the base of the stairs when she heard the pounding on her door.

Hunter quickly settled himself on the floor next to the bed. Lance was breathing deep and even, a sign of the dhampir's rapid recovery. Lexi had just left the apartment, and Melissa would be up very shortly. He only had a brief opportunity to dreamwalk through Lance's subconscious, learn a little more about her, before her arrival.

He closed his eyes, allowing the rush of unconsciousness to sweep over him. In moments, he walked through Lance's memories. It was as though projector screens surrounded him, each playing different memories. He noted the darker one tinged with red—the one where he'd been hurt. He'd be interested to take a side trip into that, but later. Now he whispered a suggestion to act as a shortcut to the information he wanted to access.

Melissa.

Instantly, the screens flickered to life, and he selected the one furthest away. Their first meeting. Everything around him changed, and he realized he was in a back alley. It was late afternoon, the sky bathed in swathes of crimson and orange, but it was already getting dark in the alley. He glanced around, trying to get a read on the location, and noticed the Better Read Than Dead Bookstore lettering painted on one of the roller doors. The alley behind Melissa's bookshop.

Lance stood, leaning against a wall, his pose casual. He kept his gaze trained on the street, as though waiting for something—or someone.

Hunter heard the squeak as the door was rolled up, and he could dimly make out the figure of someone hauling down on the chains inside the dock as the door rose. Melissa.

She was younger, though. Early twenties, her red hair tied back into a ponytail. She wore a ratty T-shirt and jeans and scuffed sneakers, and already looked dusty.

Lance turned and frowned as Melissa emerged, glancing at her watch. "Go back inside," he called to her.

Melissa paused, noticing the man at the end of the alley for the first time. She folded her arms.

"I'm waiting for a delivery, bozo. You might want to move on, yourself."

"I said, get the hell back inside," Lance growled, his fists clenching, his shoulders slightly raised in a dominant pose.

Hunter's eyebrows rose. He looked threatening enough. He glanced to see what Melissa would do next.

She folded her arms, her eyes narrowing. "Get lost, before I call Reform Authority."

Hunter smiled. Ah, there was the shrew he knew so well.

Lance took a step forward. "It's dangerous out here. Go inside."

Melissa laughed, a sexy little tinkle as she stepped toward the edge of the loading dock. "I know this place far better than you, alley rat."

Something skittered at the mouth of the alley, and Hunter turned as shadows seemed to emerge from the encroaching darkness.

"Well, what do we have here, boys?" A masculine voice called out from the darkness, and a form stepped forward. He was tall, with blond hair and dark eyes. "Looks like the book witch has a new friend."

Hunter eyed the men stalking down the alley, and that's what they were doing, stalking. Their movements were smooth and predatory, and he watched cautiously as they fanned out in a strategic move that looked well practiced.

A vampire pack. Five in all, and very determined.

A second vampire stepped forward. He had dark hair, brown eyes and a coldness that seemed to emanate from his pores. "You were right, Ty. She is out tonight."

Hunter glanced back to the dock. Melissa eyed all of the vampires. He knew there would be no way for her to close the roller door in time, and the narrowing of Melissa's eyes suggested she'd arrived at the same conclusion.

Then she did something that surprised him. She laughed.

"Is that you, Dick? Did your little underling come crying to you? Is this your idea of some big, bad retribution against the witch?"

"I did try to warn you," Lance muttered as he shifted, subtly putting himself between Melissa and the vampires.

"Rick," the blond corrected through gritted teeth.

"Well, if the name fits…"

Rick laughed, showing his elongated fangs, as he nodded. "You're right. You might be a witch, but I'd prefer to call you dinner."

He opened his mouth in a snarl, and he and his pack moved as one, all springing toward the woman on the dock.

Melissa peered through the peep slot of her door, frowning. After a few minutes she turned to retreat up the hall, but then she heard a sound.

Sobbing. A painful, woeful, sorrowful sobbing, as though someone was mortally wounded, or their heart was cleaved in two. It was the kind of sound that reached deep into a person's conscience, and Melissa whirled back to the door. She craned her neck, twisting from side to side, peering into the darkness.

There.

Someone lay in the gutter, rocking, as the snow drifted around. Melissa frowned. It wasn't clear if it was a man or a woman—they were in shadow, their head covered with a knitted cap that even now showed the glitter of wet snow. She could see, though, that whoever it was wasn't wearing a coat.

Damn fool would freeze out there if they stayed much longer.

She opened the door, gasping as the bitterly cold air swept into the front hall. Then she stepped out and hurried to the person huddled in the gutter. She paused halfway across the sidewalk.

"Hey! You can't stay here," she called out. She flexed her mouth, then stepped forward again. "Hey, there, you in the gutter. You need to move on."

The person whimpered. Melissa frowned. It wasn't a normal whimper, she could tell; it sounded almost like a pup in pain.

"Excuse me? Are you okay?" She reached her hand out to touch the person's shoulder. The action seemed to make the person erupt out of the gutter.

Snow flicked in all directions, and the person's form twisted, a pained growl coming from them as they turned. It was a man, only it wasn't—not anymore, as his body morphed into lycan form.

Melissa turned to run back to her doorway, back to the haven that would protect her and prevent his entry, and halted.

Another werewolf had planted himself just in front of the doorway. Melissa raised her hands, summoning her powers as the lycans launched. She screamed as fangs tore into her shoulder.

Hunter watched as Lance and Melissa fought off the vampires. For a big guy, Lance could move like lightning, and if Hunter didn't already know Lance was a dhampir, he would have been impressed. Knowing he possessed similar attributes of strength and speed as a vampire made the brutal clash a little ho-hum, in his book. Still, it was interesting watching Melissa in action. She was like a virago, a whirlwind of red locks, flashing green eyes and hands that caused her opponents to scream in pain and clutch their heads at her softest touch.

Lance, on the other hand, was far more brutal, matching his strength against the vampires, his punches and kicks vicious. His expression was savage as his fangs elongated, and he bit into the necks of his victims.

He grimaced as Melissa touched one of the attackers, and he convulsed, screaming in pain as he fell. Lance ripped out the throat of another, and suddenly the numbers shifted from five to two dead, one who rocked, staring sightlessly at a crack in the pavement, one frothing at the mouth and unconscious, and the leader. Dick.

Oh, wait, Rick. Dick was Melissa's special name for him.

"Wait," she called, as Lance stepped toward the vampire.

He glared over his shoulder at her, eyes an eerie red, and blood smeared on his chin.

"He's lost his guardians. He's powerless now."

"He's a vampire," Lance stated roughly. "He should die."

Melissa strode up toward them. Damn, the woman didn't know the meaning of the word *retreat*. Hunter drifted closer to listen to the exchange.

Rick glared at them both. "This isn't over, witch. You think you can set up shop here and sell your poisons? Ain't gonna happen."

Melissa looked down the alley, then shrugged. "Looks like it just did." She put her hands on her hips, and gave the vampire a slow smile. "So you can go back to your little nest and tell Vivianne Marchetta that she doesn't own everything in Irondell. If she tries to mess with me or my store again, she's going to find out exactly how painful a curse can be."

Rick snorted. "We are going to rain hate down on you so bad—"

Lance reached out, his movements so fast they were almost a blur, and snapped the vampire's neck.

He watched in satisfaction as the body crumpled to the ground. "Sorry. I hate it when they go on, and on." He rolled his hand. "And on. Besides, all these bodies will tell Marchetta exactly what she needs to know."

Melissa assessed the man next to her for a moment. "You're not from around here, are you?"

Lance chuckled. "I was. Once. It's been a while."

"Oh? Where have you been?"

Lance took a handkerchief out of his back pocket and cleaned his face. "Prison." He said the word calmly, but didn't look at the witch.

Melissa digested that for a moment. "And yet you were in my back alley when these guys decided to pay me a visit. Why?"

Lance shrugged. "I've been trying to track this particular vamp, and heard he might show up."

"Dhampir?"

Lance nodded. "Yeah."

Melissa looked down at the bodies strewed around, and nodded. "Good job."

He glanced toward the entrance to the alley. "Hey, you don't happen to know if anyone's got some work going on around here, do you?"

Melissa shook her head. "Sorry, no." She turned, hesitated. Hunter watched her fleeting expressions with curiosity and amusement. First there was resistance, and she actually shook her head as though arguing with herself. Then there was guilt, followed by reluctant resignation.

"Wait." She turned around, and Lance halted. She sighed. "I'm looking for a store clerk. Minimum wage. Interested?"

Lance tilted his head, considering. "I tend to attract vampires."

She gestured to the bodies littering the alleyway. "So do I. I can live with it if you can."

Lance chuckled. "Then you have yourself a clerk."

The scream jerked Hunter awake. He lay on the floor, confused for a moment until he got his bearings. Melissa's spare bedroom.

Another scream, followed by a snarl.

Hunter rolled to his feet and made his way over to the window. He peered out to the dark street below.

Melissa was prone on the ground, one arm outstretched, as two werewolves circled her. Even from this distance, he could see the blood. It glistened down her arm, scarlet drops staining the white snow she lay in, and he could see the fine tremor in her hand as her lips moved. Whatever she was doing was holding them at bay, but they still prowled around her, snarling.

Even as he watched, one of the wolves launched at her.

"No!" Hunter roared as Melissa kicked at the wolf. He bolted through the bedroom, down the hallway, and yanked open the front door—and ran into an invisible barrier.

He growled with frustration, trying to bust his way through, but whatever ward Melissa had put on her home to keep him in was strong. He wouldn't be able to leave her home unless she allowed it.

He ran back to the bedroom, vaulting over Lance's body on the bed and landing at the window. He could open it, but encountered the same issue.

Melissa had trapped him inside her home.

Chapter 10

Melissa kept chanting the buffer spell. They'd caught her by surprise, damn it, and it was the first one that sprang to mind when the lycan's fangs had sunk into her shoulder. It created a small zone of protection, one that the lycans could pierce through, if they figured it out. She was on her butt, and using her good arm and legs to slowly shuffle back toward her front door. The snow was falling thicker, heavier, and the icy wind was numbing her. She was sluggish to move, sluggish to think.

If she could just get inside...the werewolves wouldn't be able to follow her.

She whimpered midchant, and one of the were-wolves pressed his advantage, barreling toward her. She started chanting faster, her arm outstretched as she focused her power on the wolves, and she cried out in pain as teeth snapped—and caught—her ankle. Even through the leather, she could feel those sharp fangs pierce her skin, heard the crack of bone, felt the snap deep inside.

She screamed, kicking out viciously with her other foot, the heel of her boot raking across the lycan's snout, and the werewolf recoiled.

She chanted faster, blinking furiously to try to stop the gray creeping in at the edges of her vision.

God, her arm was so heavy, stretched out like this, and she tried not to stare at the rivulets of blood that ran down her sleeve. So much blood. She could hear her heart pounding in her ears, see her fingers tremble as the painful heat of her shoulder started giving way to a cool numbness.

She shuffled back again, reciting the spell, thinking furiously. What else could she do? The shock of the attack was numbing her brain.

She heard a dull roaring from above, and thought for a moment she was going to pass out. A thump, followed by a crack, caused her to glance up.

Hunter was pounding on a window upstairs, his expression fierce. He was trapped. She kicked out again when one of the wolves came too close.

Her wards. If she died, her wards would still be in place. Hunter would be forever trapped—unless another witch managed to break the spells. She sucked in a breath, wincing as the gesture moved her shoulder.

If she broke the seal, he'd be free. Free to leave. He'd fulfilled his promise. If she didn't break the seal, he'd rot inside her home.

It was almost ironic that he'd tried to kill her, but in the end her death would be his undoing.

One of the lycans caught her eye, and she knew. It was going to push through her buffer. Funny how, even in their beast form, they could still telegraph their intentions.

A promise is a promise. Our word is our bond, and the only way a spell has any weight is because of the commitment we infuse in it.

The words sprang into her mind in the voice of her mother, and she bellowed, dismayed that the constant lecture from her mother had such a strong foothold.

The wolf sprang at her, and she raised her arms in a defensive motion as the furry bulk hit her in the chest. Teeth clamped around her right forearm and more teeth caught her on her left thigh.

She squeezed her eyes shut, whispering the words that would unlock freedom for her light warrior.

Hunter could sense when the wards dropped. There was high pressure that built in on him whenever he tried to ram his way through the door, or break through that open window. And then there wasn't…

He launched himself through the open window, sliding down the first-story roof, his hands outstretched as he summoned his light force.

He already had a fireball in each hand when his feet cleared the gutter, and suddenly he was free-falling down to the pavement.

He flung his fireballs at the lycans, and hit the ground in a roll to absorb the shock. He rose to his feet, smiling grimly as he heard the yelps and whimpers of the wolves as they felt the heat.

Melissa cried out, and he frowned. The werewolves didn't turn, didn't slow down. He summoned more energy and created two more fireballs. This time he threw them with force, and the lycans howled as their coats were consumed by the fire. He scooped up Melissa and strode to her doorway, not even bothering to look back.

His flames would finish the job for him. He kicked the door shut on the painful howls and whimpers outside, and jogged down the hallway to the stairs.

Melissa tried to lift her head, and she murmured something.

"Shh," he whispered as he climbed the stairs two at a time. "I've got you."

"A promise is a promise," she whispered, her head lolling against his shoulder. "You kept yours." She gasped in pain as he leaned forward, twisted the doorknob in his hand and shouldered his way into her apartment.

"Take it easy, Mel," he told her. She'd lost a lot of blood; she needed to conserve her energy. He trotted down the hallway to her bedroom, placing her with care on her bed.

"I kept my promise," she told him, her eyes flickering as though she was battling unconsciousness. "You're free."

He frowned. He had no idea what she was talking about. Delirium was setting in. "Shh, I'll look after you."

Her eyelids rose slowly, as though their weight was almost too much for her, and he found himself staring into the most mesmerizing green eyes. Her lips pulled down. "Is it going to hurt?" she whispered. There was just the faintest flicker of fear, and her bottom lip trembled, until she caught it between her teeth.

He stroked her red hair back, such a contrast to her pale, almost gray complexion. He smiled at her gently, wanting to reassure her. "Trust me," he whispered. "I'm a doctor."

He caressed her brow, and watched as her eyelids slid

shut. She went under so fast, it alarmed him. She was so hurt, so damn weak. His lips firmed.

He would look after her. And it wasn't because she was annoying and feisty and had managed to entertain him and challenge him with every breath she took. It wasn't because she was so damn vibrant and lively and luscious. She thought she was dying, and she'd set him free.

Damn it, how could he hate a woman when she put his needs before hers? He frowned. It was just like her to entangle him with guilt, with duty and loyalty. Damn witch.

He got to work.

The dark seemed to waver, lift, waver, lift…it took a hell of an effort, but Melissa finally managed to open her eyes. She stared up at the pressed ceiling. Her bedroom ceiling. She flexed her feet beneath the covers, grimacing at the pull on muscle. Must have slept in a funny position. She was warm. So warm and toasty. She stretched, wincing at the ache in her shoulder and arm. The brush of cotton sheets against her naked skin was oddly liberating, and she sighed softly. Thirsty. She was thirsty.

Her bedroom curtains were open, and sunlight was streaming in. Candles, half-spent, were on every available surface, and Hunter sat in a chair next to her bed, in a pool of light from the window, his arms folded on the bed, his head down.

Hunter. In her bedroom.

Melissa shrieked, hauling her sheet up to her chest as she sat up in bed.

Hunter flinched, his head whipping up, and his chair

tipped back, upending him on the floor. He glanced around wildly for a moment, his hair tousled.

"What are you doing in here?" she screeched at him, her voice hoarse.

He held up his hands, wincing as he moved gently on the floor. He blinked rapidly, as though to get rid of the sleepy cobwebs in his brain.

"Hey, take it easy," he soothed, rising to his feet, grimacing.

"Take it easy? Get out of my room!" She flung her arm up to point to the door.

"Settle down," he snapped, arms out toward her. "You're still going to be tender, and I don't want you to rip open any of my work."

She frowned. "What?"

Even as she said it, she realized her shoulder had begun to throb from the startled movement, and her ankle ached beneath the sheet. She glanced down to her arm and gasped. Pink slashes marked her skin—on her shoulder, her arm… She cautiously slid her ankle out from beneath the sheet. It was mottled with purple-and-blue bruises, with marks that looked a lot like puncture wounds, only they were already healing.

Melissa sat up in bed, dragging the sheet up with her. She frowned, touching her forehead. Last night…

"What do you remember?" Hunter asked as he righted the chair, but set it a cautious distance from the bed. He approached the bed, eyeing her warily, and slowly reached for the glass of water on the nightstand, offering it to her.

She took it from him, gulping it down.

"Easy," he told her. "Just—take it slow."

She eyed him over the glass, wanting to drain it all in one gulp, just because she didn't want to do as *he* said. Reluctantly, though, her stomach was already telling her to be gentle, its roiling and small wave of nausea a warning of what could happen if she didn't. She sipped the water, then held the glass to her chest as she stared at him.

Foggy visions, of him banging on a window and glaring at her. She frowned. "It's a little hazy," she admitted, worry creasing her brow. She normally had near perfect recall.

"That's probably due to the loss of blood," he murmured, subsiding in the seat.

She took a deep breath, focusing on the end of her bed. "I remember saying goodbye to Lexi… I remember your thumping on a window." She glanced at her bedroom window. Despite the sun, snow still clung to the sill, and icicles hung from the roofline.

White snow. Bitter cold. Crimson blood. Lycans. Fangs.

Her gaze flicked to Hunter. "I was attacked, wasn't I?" she said hoarsely. The memories were starting to stir in her mind, of being stalked, of being bitten. Two werewolves. It had been a while since the last attempt on her life. She'd grown complacent. The fuzzy visions were coming into focus, at first jumbled, then slowly becoming a part of a logical timeline. Supplying spells and potions to arm humans against shadow breeds meant attacks were a hazard of the job. She should have been more alert though, especially after what had happened with Lance—although his being a dhampir meant he was even more prone to attacks than she was.

Hunter nodded, and for the first time she noticed the dark circles under his eyes, the lines bracketing his mouth. He looked tired. She turned her arm over again.

The memory of the werewolf sinking its teeth into her flesh warred with the vision of healthy, pink skin.

"You…?"

He nodded.

He'd rescued her. She tightened her grip on the sheet at her chest, not quite sure what to do next.

He'd saved her. She didn't know quite what to say, how to react. Gratitude felt so weird after all this time hating him, being so angry with him. After everything he'd done to her, and after all those things she'd done to him…

He rose from the chair, his hands sliding into the back pockets of his jeans. He looked about as comfortable as she felt, lying in a bed with only a sheet as protection. Sure, it provided adequate cover, but she still felt so damn exposed.

Vulnerable. That was it. She felt vulnerable. She didn't like feeling vulnerable. Not at all. Blast it.

He gestured awkwardly to the door as he stepped around her bed. "I'll, uh, go check on Lance. You need to rest. You lost a lot of blood."

She nodded, then her eyes widened. "Oh, God, my store—" Panic set in as she realized the sun was high in the sky.

"It's Sunday," Hunter reminded her gently, and she subsided against her pillows. Her store was closed on Sundays.

Silence stretched between them for a moment, then Hunter scratched his head.

"I, uh, I need to sit in front of the fireplace. Recharge," he said, backing away.

She remembered another way he could recharge, and her cheeks warmed. His lips against hers. His chest against hers. Their bodies, naked and entwined. She was nude under the sheet, after all. The warmth of her cheeks bloomed to a scorching heat. The thought should have horrified her, but she noticed her natural resistance to getting anywhere close to this guy had drained out of her. The idea that she would willingly be a source of energy for the man, a source of *that* kind of energy... She suddenly knew what those vamp slaves must experience, the eagerness to sacrifice personal safety for extreme pleasure, even if it did come at a high cost... Hunter's eyes flared, as though following her train of thought, and he bumped back into her bedroom door. "So, uh, I'll go. Now."

He opened the door, his heated gaze resting on her lips, her bare shoulders...the sheet she clutched to her chest.

"Why?" she whispered, battling her confusion. His eyes met hers. She wasn't asking him why he was leaving, and he knew it.

His gaze flickered away for a moment, and shadows darkened his eyes. He shrugged.

"You needed me." He shut the door, effectively ending further conversation.

She stared, nonplussed, at the white timber.

Hunter tilted his head back against the door.

You needed me.

Ugh. It sounded so corny, so...banal. He'd rescued her because she'd needed him. His brother would be laughing until he cried if he'd heard that one.

Hunter tried to focus on the last five months, on huddling in a dark brick-and-stone cell, on being chained to a wall by cuffs that singed his skin with every movement. On dirty, ripped clothing. On being chilled and tired and uncomfortable. On never having a full belly or a truly restful sleep. On those spiders she'd poured in through the peephole. Not literally, of course, but he hadn't realized it was an illusion spell. It had felt damn real at the time.

Oh, and the snakes. Let's not forget the snakes.

She'd held him in the dark, intentionally withholding light from him.

And in her last conscious moments, she'd delivered on her promise to him. He dragged a hand over his face.

He was a sad and sorry sap, that one promise could affect him so damn much. He'd tended to her wounds, stripping her, cleaning her, healing her... He'd even ignored her attributes, so to speak, in his focus to heal her. She'd been naked, and he'd been completely professional.

Mostly.

Because she needed him.

He levered himself away from the door and made his way to his other patient. He would check Lance's wounds, ensure he would still remain under the blanket of unconsciousness for the foreseeable future, and then he intended to open all the curtains in Melissa's living room, start the fire and sit there for the rest of the day. He would try not to think about the bravery Melissa had shown in her first meeting with Lance, her kindness—reluctant though it was—in offering an ex-con a job, and her loyalty to the vow she'd made to him, or the fact that she was down the hall, naked.

No, he would not think of that. He would sit in front of the fire, nurse that bottle of bourbon and get pleasantly drunk.

Melissa padded down the hallway, her blush pink silk nightgown flowing behind her. She flicked her hair back over her shoulder. Wow, whatever shampoo she was using was working. Her red locks were artfully curled and all glossy and shiny, cascading over her shoulders. She couldn't quite understand why her hair was perfectly styled so early in the morning, but didn't question it. She entered the kitchen and halted, her eyes rounding.

Hunter stood at the stove, frying bacon. He looked over at her and his lips curled in a sexy grin.

"Hey, beautiful," he murmured.

She swallowed.

He was wearing an apron. *Just* an apron.

The muscles of his arms, shoulders and chest bulged, and she could see the dusky disks of his nipples peeking out on either side of her *I kiss better than I cook* apron—which looked like it was made for a kid when he wore it, revealing more than it concealed.

His broad shoulders tapered down behind the fabric—which ended mid–muscled thigh. His legs were toned, just like the rest of him. She didn't know why she was surprised.

"What—what are you doing?" she breathed. She should be stunned, should be shocked. Instead, she was…interested. Bacon sizzled, and the smell was so damn good, mingling with her favorite scent of well-made coffee.

"Making breakfast," Hunter responded with a wink, then turned back to flip the eggs in the frying pan. "Got to keep your strength up."

Her eyes widened as she saw his muscled back and perfectly shaped butt. Oh, dear heaven. That butt. It was—she lifted her chin, trying to tear her gaze away from his butt—it was gorgeous. Sexy…and her eyes were still glued to his butt.

The kind of butt that made you want to reach out and squeeze it.

"Oh, wait, I have something for you," he said, lifting the pan off the burner and flicking the gas off. Her mind immediately suggested all sorts of wicked somethings he could offer. He reached across the counter and poured—oh, sweet mercy—percolated coffee into a mug for her, and spun with an athletic grace to present it to her, his movements graceful and strong, his lips tilted in a half smile that was all knowing and wicked.

"For me?" she breathed, accepting the mug, the enticing smell of coffee and bacon entwining with his own personal scent of amber and musk. It was heady, and she took a sip, her eyes never leaving his.

"Uh-huh." Hunter's brown eyes flared with the beginnings of those mesmerizing amber flares, and his expression relaxed into a sensual invitation as he watched her drink.

"I'd like to taste some of that," he murmured, and his gaze dropped to her lips as she lowered the mug to the counter next to her.

"Yeah?"

"Yeah."

"Well, what's stopping you?" she whispered, her lips lifting in a smile meant to dare. She couldn't believe she was being so flirty, so relaxed and encouraging.

"Nothing," he breathed as he lowered his head.

Chapter 11

His lips took hers in a searing kiss, his hand delving into her curls, grasping her head and angling it to his liking. His other arm curled around her back and pulled her closer.

Melissa moaned as her body came into contact with his. Over and over, his tongue slid against hers, and her hands slid up those glorious biceps to twine around his neck.

He leaned forward, his hands lowering to clasp her buttocks, and she moaned into his mouth as he pulled her up against him, his groin against hers. She wrapped her legs around his waist, twisting her head to meet his lips, over and over, as he turned and walked them over to the kitchen table.

He swept his arm across the surface, sending plates and cutlery crashing to the floor, then sat her on the edge of the table.

Melissa gasped as his lips left hers to trail a hot, wet caress down her neck. She clasped his head, her fingers delving into his short hair, and he growled softly at the sensual head massage. He tugged her forward, her hips against his, and kissed his way down her neck to her chest as he bore her back down to the table.

She trembled as he flexed his hips against hers. Liquid heat pooled between her thighs, and her heart thudded as he licked and nipped his way across her collarbone. Her breasts swelled and heat bloomed. Everywhere.

She gulped. Who knew that was such a sensitive zone? Her eyelids fluttered open, and she stared sightlessly up at the ceiling as he dragged the spaghetti strap of her nightie off her shoulder and down her arm.

She wriggled her arm, arching her back as he slid the silken fabric down her body, revealing her breasts.

He levered back for a moment, eyeing the bounty he'd just revealed, and those amber flecks in his eyes turned to molten gold.

"Damn, you're beautiful," he whispered, an expression of hot appreciation and something softer, bordering on sincere. She raised her arms to caress his shoulders.

"So are you," she told him, her fingers lightly trailing down to his pectoral muscles, where she gently flicked his nipples. He shuddered, dipping down to take her lips again in an intense kiss before shifting to kiss her chest, brushing his lips over the tops of her breasts as his hands cupped them, lifting them. He swept his thumbs over the peaks of her nipples, and she caught her lower lip between her teeth as her nipples tightened.

He rubbed himself against her, his hips moving with the grace and rhythm of a dancer. But a built dancer, like a stripper, not the ballet kind, she found herself thinking, and then her thoughts scattered. He lowered his lips to one nipple, and she closed her eyes on a breathy moan as he drew it into his mouth, lashing it with his tongue. His erection rubbed against her, finding that place that needed his attention.

She flexed her hips against his, her head tilting back as he suckled at her breast. She clasped his head to her, not wanting him to move, it felt so good. But move he did, and darn if he didn't make it feel even better.

He released her nipple with a soft pop, switching his attention to her other breast, his hands sliding down her body to pull up the hem of her nightie.

Her nails scoring down his back in a slow glide, she pulled him closer, hands covering that beautiful butt.

He groaned. "I have to be inside you," he whispered.

She nodded. "Yes. Now." She couldn't agree more. She dragged up the apron, and he positioned himself. She could feel him, ready at that spot that wept for him, needed him, and she gazed up at him as he—

Pounding on the door jerked Melissa awake, and she rolled onto her back, scooting up to the headboard, the sheet wrapped around her.

Eyes wide, her chest rising and falling with her agitated pants, she glanced wildly around the room.

"Melissa," Hunter roared from the other side of her bedroom door. "Wake the hell up."

The bedroom door was finally flung open, and an angry Melissa emerged, shrugging a plaid shirt over a white T-shirt. She wore jeans and was still jamming one foot into its sneaker, and her expression promised punishment.

His body hummed with desire, a painful arousal and a rage born from shock. "What the hell do you think you're—?"

"You bastard," she hissed, her eyes spitting green fire. "I told you to stay the hell out of my head."

Hunter's eyes narrowed. "I did," he exclaimed hotly.

"I bet you're all recharged now, aren't you?" she said, her tone accusing.

"Thanks to you," he gritted. She was right. He was. And he was so damn hyped up he could throw a barbecue for the damn city.

Her fingers curled, and she raised them in a way he knew from experience meant pain would follow. He held up his own hands, and flames flickered from the tips of his fingers. "Don't even think about it," he warned, frowning fiercely. He was so damn angry with her, although why the hell she was acting as though *he* was the bad guy, he had no idea.

"I told you to stay out of my head," she hissed at him, fingers curled like claws. He could feel the pain starting in his head, as though her nails were slowly sliding into his brain. "Do you think this is a game? Do you think you can come in and twist my mind to your own devices?" Her voice was climbing in volume.

He blinked, confused on so many levels, and trying to think past the mental burn. "You think *I* did this?" He flicked his finger and a little flame zinged off and around behind her. She squealed, flinching at the hot sting that bit at her butt. It was only brief, and only a warning, but it was enough to distract her, and to eject those talons of pain out of his head. "You think that was me?" He didn't bother to hide his disbelief. "You were in *my* head, Melissa. I don't know how the hell you did it, but I don't like it and it stops now."

Her eyes narrowed and she glared at him, ready to inflict more pain, but his words halted her. "What?" she asked, angling her head, her fingers still poised, eyes full of suspicion and confusion.

She didn't know. Good God, she didn't know. The anger still coursed through him, the shock and frustration, but she was so eager to accuse him, to deliver pain as punishment for something she thought he'd done. She had no idea.

He extinguished his fire, his hands dropping to his sides as he stared at her, incredulous. "I was sleeping," he told her, his voice low and rough. "And *you* walked into *my* head."

Now it was Melissa's turn to be confused. *"What?"*

Her fingers relaxed, but he wasn't sure if it was intentional, or if she was thoroughly distracted. He knew he was sure as hell distracted.

"What are you talking about?" she asked, and he could see she was struggling with the concept. Join the club. He was totally stumped. "I was sleeping, and all of a sudden you were prancing through my dream."

He held up a finger. "One—I do not prance." He raised another finger. "Two—that wasn't your dream, that was mine."

She stared at him for a moment, blinking, and then she lowered her hands. "Wait, so…you were dreaming about…me?"

He frowned. "Yes, damn it." He looked away. Talk about damned awkward.

She rubbed her chin. "I don't understand how this works," she admitted, a little embarrassed. Of course, her little embarrassment paled in comparison to his abject mortification. He took a deep breath. Now that he could see she truly hadn't intended to dreamwalk in his mind, he'd gone from wanting to strangle her straight back to wanting her. Period.

He wanted the bitchy witch. He dragged his hands over his face. "Oh, this is so wrong."

"I don't get it," she said, arms out in a helpless gesture.

His eyes narrowed. "How can you not get it? You just did it." She was more skilled than he'd first thought—and he didn't like underestimating his enemy, damn it.

To his knowledge, only some light warriors had this particular gift. He'd inherited his from his father. He knew vampires could compel others. He knew witches could cast spells and unlock secrets of the mind with incantations and touch, and they could see visions, etc. He'd never heard of another breed being able to do as he could.

It scared the hell out of him. The crapstorm he had going on up there, he didn't want anyone to see. He didn't like the exposure, the lack of control.

"You dreamwalked," he told her. He put his hands on his hips. "Tell me how."

She shrugged. "I have no idea." She tried to step around him, but he blocked her way. He was determined to figure this out—and prevent it from happening again.

"Try again," he growled.

She tilted her chin to meet his gaze, and he couldn't help but recognize the challenge inherent in the movement. "What bugs you more? The fact that I 'dreamwalked,'" she said, wiggling her fingers to parenthesize the word, "or that I busted you dreaming about me?"

He fixed his gaze on the door behind her, clenching his jaw, and she swept past him.

"I don't know how your party trick works," she said over her shoulder, and then she held up her hand. "Although, if I can do it in my sleep, well that kind of implies it's not so tricky."

She laughed, a sound that came out part husky tinkle, part unladylike snort. He thumped his fist against the doorjamb. Damn it.

She'd tiptoed through his dreams. Actually, no, she'd swept through it in a lustful haze, leaving him horny, frustrated and shaken. She wasn't supposed to be able to do that. The only other person he knew capable of dreamwalking was locked up in a Reform cell. Although his father hadn't been able to intrude in Hunter's dreams; his own shields were too strong for that.

But apparently not strong enough to withstand a bitchy witch.

He ducked his head. Fine. This had been fun, but it was time to wrap things up. He didn't quite understand her, or why she was so hell-bent on annihilating shadow breeds in general. Lance was a dhampir, and she considered him a friend—and would go to considerable trouble for him. His lips pursed. That was nice. Sure, he could admit that. What she'd done for Lance, that was nice. Of course, he had to reconcile that with being chained up and locked away in a cell for five months. Not so nice.

He straightened and turned in the hallway. He had that knack for pulling the not-so-nice out of people. His mother had left him—well, okay, she'd died, but his brother had walked away from him, and this witch had imprisoned him. Even Debbie had chosen Ryder over him. There was something wrong with him. He was not-so-nice.

And she was tiptoeing through his dreams. The woman who had made his life a living hell now had access to his hidden secrets. Definitely time to leave. He shouldn't be messing around with the witch, anyway. He should be getting back to work. At least there he was—different. There, there was a little glimmer of light to rail against his darkness. He needed his light. It was the only thing he had going for him. He sauntered down the hallway. Time to wake up his patient.

Melissa sat in the chair in the corner as Hunter did his work. He'd told her that he thought Lance could wake up, and then hadn't spoken a word since. He stood at the foot of the bed, hands clasping Lance's ankles, and Melissa could see the tendrils of light worming their way through Lance's body. She never got tired of watching; it was beautiful.

She glanced briefly at Hunter's back. Who would have thought a man so capable of violence could also be capable of such beauty? He'd taken such care with Lance, so cautious with his treatment. So gentle. It was hard to reconcile this man with the healing light with the warrior who had turned her apothecary into a Roman candle.

Her gaze dropped, and it took her a moment to realize she was staring at his butt. This time it was covered in denim, though.

She blinked and looked away. He did have a great butt, though. She peered at him briefly. At his butt. She still couldn't believe she'd walked through his dream. *That* dream. She puffed her cheeks out on an exhalation of breath. That had been one hell of a dream.

But she hadn't tried to fight him off. Hadn't tried to blast him, sear him, or otherwise make it painful for him. What was up with that? She hadn't been with anyone since Theo… She realized she hadn't even thought of her fiancé during or since that dream. That guilt weighed heavily on her. It felt like such a betrayal. She still didn't quite understand what had happened, though. Did they do the horizontal tango because he wanted it, or she wanted it, or they both wanted it? No, damn it. She didn't want *it*. Not with him. After everything that had happened between them, that would make her pathetic.

Damn, this was giving her a headache. She straightened in her chair. Maybe the dream wasn't supposed to be literal. Some dreams meant something vastly different than the experience they actually portrayed. She sighed. The problem was, she was a witch, and she had a better idea than some when it came to dream interpretation. If a client had come in with that story, her analysis would be…that one or both of them were as horny as a…well, something really horny.

Hunter stood back and rolled his shoulders. He slowly turned to her.

"He's going to be fine. We'll just let him wake up naturally, and then he'll be good to go." He folded his arms. "Which means I'll be good to go."

"When Lance is awake," she clarified. She didn't want Hunter skipping out until she was certain Lance was well and truly fine.

"When Lance is awake," Hunter repeated, nodding.

Melissa looked away. When her friend woke, Hunter's part of the deal would be delivered. Then it would be her turn. A promise was a promise. Hunter would be free to go.

And she would be alone.

She rose from the chair. "I, uh, have to catch up on some paperwork."

Hunter nodded. "I'll wait here."

She left the room and strolled down the hall to her living room. Hunter would be leaving. She frowned. Good grief, she wasn't getting morose about it, was she? She should be happy he was going, and good riddance to him. She may not feel like she'd truly delivered vengeance against the man who'd destroyed her business, her craft, and had tried to kill her in the process—but at least something positive had come out of it. Lance survived what would otherwise have been a fatal attack. She should focus on the positives.

She wouldn't have to make Hunter any more peanut butter and jelly sandwiches, or take down a dinner that even the rats preferred to leave alone. No more being on alert every time she ventured down to the basement. No more having to watch her back, or second-guessing what her prisoner would do.

No more bacon and coffee for breakfast. The thought came out of nowhere, surprising her. No more Hunter and his light. No more fires. No more breath-stealing, resistance-draining, knee-weakening kisses...

She took a deep breath. She wasn't going there. No. If she was distracted or tempted, she'd just have to remember what Hunter had done to her on their first meeting. If that didn't work, she'd think about Theo.

As usual, the guilt flared up, and she almost cried in relief at the familiar emotion. The guilt and the sadness were still there. She couldn't entertain any thoughts about Hunter—about any man. Theo had been her love, and he'd forever hold her heart. This craze with Hunter was just that—a craze. A temporary period of insanity. And then things would finally return to normal when Hunter was gone, back wielding whatever dark power he liked to use in his family's medical clinic.

It was so quiet. She rubbed her arms. So quiet and so cold. She crossed to the hearth and started a fire, then grabbed her shoe box full of receipts, dockets, invoices—a tissue?—and started to sort her paperwork. This was one part of owning a store she did not like. She grabbed the remote and turned the television on, just to have some background noise.

That was one thing she couldn't quite get used to. Her store was generally busy, but ever since Theo had gone, her apartment felt like a crypt when there was only her in it. She couldn't hear Hunter or Lance down the hall. She could have been all by herself. She turned the volume to low. Just having those voices in the background gave the illusion that she wasn't alone in the world.

She'd been working for over an hour when she realized she wasn't alone anymore. Hunter was leaning against the doorjamb, watching her.

"Oh, I didn't see you there."

He shrugged. "I didn't want to intrude. How are you feeling?"

He levered away from the door frame and sauntered close.

She frowned. "Fine."

He lifted his chin toward her shoulder. "How is your arm?"

"It doesn't hurt," she answered honestly. She didn't know how he did it, but it worked.

"Do you need me to—" Hunter hesitated, then tried again. "Will you be safe when I leave?"

She frowned, surprised by the question. "Yes, Hunter, I'll be fine. I can look after myself." She'd been doing it for some time, now.

"Those werewolves…" he began, and she waved a hand casually.

"Oh, that's nothing."

Hunter arched his eyebrow, and she made a face. "Okay, maybe they came close this time, but I'll be more careful next time. It wasn't my first wolf attack, and won't be my last, I'm sure."

Hunter dropped onto the sofa facing the fire, and frowned. "Do these attacks happen a lot?"

She turned back to her paperwork. "I'm a witch, Hunter. It comes with the territory. I give humans some measure of defense against the shadow breeds. My job is to try to even out the balance of power, or possibly tip it in our favor." She shrugged. "That means occasionally the shadow breeds try to take me out. Vampires, werewolves…you."

She lifted her gaze to his briefly, and noticed a flare of something…regret? Remorse? Just as quickly he schooled his features, and she couldn't be sure she'd seen anything.

"Those lycans, Melissa… I hit them first with a flare. It didn't stop them. Didn't even give them pause."

She shrugged again. "Maybe you're losing your touch?"

Touch. She remembered the dream, the way he'd touched her breasts, her thighs… Warmth flared in her cheeks. Okay. Stop thinking about *that*.

"Or maybe there was something else driving them," Hunter suggested. "I know I hurt them, but they kept at it. Almost like they were compelled."

Melissa lowered the dockets she held to the shoe box. "Lycans are supernatural. They can be compelled, but it would take a strong being to get past their natural defenses. I think you're reading too much into it."

It was Hunter's turn to shrug. "Maybe. All I know is I had to kill them to stop them. Just…bear that in mind."

She kept her gaze on the beaten shoe box on the coffee table. "I will."

The fact that she still lived due to Hunter's interference didn't escape her. She opened her mouth, then hesitated. She'd lowered the ward that trapped him. He could have escaped, could have left her to the wolves, but he hadn't. She didn't understand why he'd stayed, or why he'd acted to save her life. She wanted to understand, but was afraid where that conversation might lead, especially in light of their shared dream. Asking Hunter why he'd stayed, when he had every reason to leave, would only lead to an uncomfortable discussion.

For the first time, Melissa backed down from a conversation, and shut her mouth. Leave it alone. As soon as Lance woke up, Hunter would leave, and they could both go on with their separate lives, ignoring each other's presence and pretending this had been but a minor episode in their lives. It didn't have to be more than that.

The buzzer rang, and Melissa looked up in surprise.

"Are you expecting anyone?" Hunter inquired as he rose.

"No."

Hunter nodded, and she didn't know what was more disturbing, that on her one day off she didn't expect visitors, or that Hunter thought that was a normal state of affairs for her.

"I mean, my brother drops by occasionally, but I'm not expecting anyone," she clarified, just so she didn't seem like a complete loser.

Hunter strode to the living room window and peered down into the street. "It's Lexi."

Melissa smacked her palm to her forehead. "Of course. She broke up with that bloodsucking boyfriend of hers last night." She rose from her seat and hurried down the hallway to press the button that would unlock the main door briefly to allow Lexi up.

She couldn't believe she'd forgotten all about Lexi, and the fact she was leaving her manipulative boyfriend. She lifted her finger off the buzzer and opened the apartment door for Lexi. She started toward the kitchen. "I'm going to put the coffee on," she called out to Hunter. "Want one?"

"Sure."

Hunter glanced over at the TV as Melissa puttered in the kitchen. He reached for the remote, turning the volume up slowly. It looked like the price of iron was up, he noted, due to some arrangement between Marchetta Enterprises and the Alpine Pack. Hunter arched an eyebrow. Vamps and werewolves in business together? What the hell had happened while he'd been chained to a wall?

He continued to watch the news report as he heard the footsteps in the hall behind him. Some prisoner killed a security guard and had escaped a Reform maximum security prison. He glanced over his shoulder. "Hey, Lexi."

Lexi halted briefly, scanning the room. "Where is Melissa?"

Hunter's eyebrows rose at her brusque tone, lack of greeting and the determined set of her jaw. "She's getting her domestic vibe on in the kitchen." Thankfully she was only making coffee. He didn't think he could stomach one of Melissa's attempts at a meal.

Lexi left the doorway, and Hunter frowned. He'd come to think of Lexi as something approaching a friend, but this morning she'd barely acknowledged him. Had something bad happened with the boyfriend?

Lexi had always treated him with respect, and despite Melissa's warning, she'd been friendly and trusting. That had been rare for him, and he appreciated it more than she or Melissa would ever know. He rose from his seat. If Lexi needed help, he'd be happy to fry a vamp for her.

"Hey, Lexi, how did it go?"

Melissa's voice was soft, caring, and he halted for a moment, intrigued by the tone. He'd never heard her speak like that before. It was like a warm embrace, something that curled around, attentive and supportive.

"Melissa."

"Lexi? Are you okay?"

So Melissa had noticed their friend's mood. He started to walk toward the kitchen.

"I'm sorry, Melissa."

"Lexi? What's going—where is your ring?" Melissa's voice sharpened, and Hunter frowned.

"Put the knife down, Lexi," Melissa warned, and then Hunter heard a clatter of dishes, the sound of glass breaking and then a shriek. Hunter ran.

"Stop it, Lexi," Melissa yelled, and there was another crash.

He skidded to a stop at the kitchen door. Melissa had raised a chair, both as a shield and as a weapon, its legs pointed toward Lexi.

Lexi stood close, a knife from Melissa's butcher block clasped in one hand. The coffeepot lay in jagged pieces on the floor, and brown liquid dripped from Lexi's arm, leaving a blooming scald mark behind.

"Lexi," Hunter called softly, his arm out, but Lexi ignored him, her attention on Melissa. The woman shook her head, tears flowing down her cheeks.

"I'm sorry, Melissa," she repeated. She pushed the chair legs aside with considerable force and her arm flashed out, the wicked blade slicing through the air.

Melissa dropped the chair and dodged, but Hunter heard her hiss, saw the red mark bloom on her sleeve. She hadn't avoided the blade entirely.

"Stop, Lexi," Melissa cried, her expression a combination of shock, fear and anger.

Hunter stepped in, and Lexi whirled. He jumped back to avoid being slashed across his middle.

"Stay back!" Lexi yelled, her features harsh as she glared at him briefly. His eyes widened.

"Lexi, it's me, Hunter." He'd never done anything to hurt this woman, yet here she stood in the kitchen, trying to kill them both. The woman before him stared at him with wild eyes. There was recognition, but it was like a wall was erected between them.

"Put the knife down," Melissa told her, trying to back away, but Lexi was slowly advancing on her. Hunter watched in horror as the woman he'd decided was a friend went after the witch who had freed him. Torn didn't begin to describe his emotions. Saving one would mean betraying the other. He couldn't get close enough to touch Lexi, to render her unconscious, but if he didn't do something, she was going to hurt Melissa, possibly kill her.

Lexi darted forward, and Melissa jerked out of the way, sending more dishes from the counter spilling to the ground, breaking and scattering across the floor. She managed to deflect the knife, catching and clutching Lexi's wrist.

"Hold her," Hunter called, and stepped forward, his arms raised. He summoned his light force. Large arms wrapped around him from behind, forcing his arms down and lifting him off his feet.

Hunter's eyes rounded as the arms clasped around him tightened, squeezing so hard his lungs couldn't expand fully.

"Do not even think about hurting my sister," a deep voice rumbled against his ear. Hunter didn't have time to let his disbelief take control. He kicked, trying to land against the cupboard door to give him some resistance, some way of shoving against the man mountain that embraced him, but his patient—back to full strength, apparently—shifted, and Hunter's feet kicked at the air.

"Lance," Melissa screeched as Lexi continued to struggle. "Help."

Lexi raised her hand, the blade gleaming in the sun-light streaming into the cheery kitchen, the whites of her eyes visible, and she swung.

Hunter curled his fingers, summoning a small flame in his hands and pushing it at Lexi. The giant hold-ing him roared, flinging him out into the hallway, and his flame caught at the kitchen table instead. Hunter bounced with considerable force against the plastered wall of the hallway and crashed to the floor. He gri-maced at the pain, and coughed as his lungs filled with air.

Lance, wearing a pair of jeans and no shirt or shoes, advanced toward him, a dark murderous glint in his eye.

Chapter 12

Melissa ducked under Lexi's arm and brought her elbow up to smash into the woman's back. Lexi screamed in pain and rage as she fell forward against the sink. Melissa grabbed the frying pan that hung from a hook on a frame above the stove and whirled, using it as a shield. Her eyes widened when she heard the scrape of metal on metal, felt the force as Lexi's blade hit the back of the pan that she held in front of her face.

She heard a bellow from the hallway, followed by a crash, and then Hunter skidded into the room again, his face bruised, his arm raised and fury in his gaze. She saw the fireball flare in his hand, and her stomach lurched as she recognized his intent.

"No," she yelled in protest. She held one hand up in defense, then used the pan like a tennis racket and swung it at Lexi's head. She flinched at the clunk it made when it caught the woman on the upper jaw, and Lexi's head whipped around, smacking into the fridge door. She fell, unconscious, to the floor, collapsing among the broken shards of crockery and strewed cutlery. Melissa hurriedly used a tea towel to put the small fire on the top of the kitchen table out, smoke and scorched wood permeating the air.

Hunter frowned fiercely at her. "Why did you—"

A large body crashed against his, and suddenly the doorway was empty as Lance tackled him. They crashed toward the living room.

"No," Melissa yelled, skirting around the inert Lexi, kicking the blade away under the table and hurtling out of the kitchen. She winced as Lance punched Hunter in the stomach with a force that had the light warrior doubling over in pain.

Hunter glared at the dhampir, anger flaring, and Melissa saw the fireball leave Hunter's hands and launch toward her friend. She flung her arm out, muttering a dampening spell that turned the fireball into a puff of smoke.

"Don't," she cried as Lance strode toward Hunter. She sprang in between the two men, arms out. To their credit, both men halted immediately.

"He was going to attack Lexi," Lance gritted.

"He saved your life," she snapped, and Lance halted, frowning.

"She was going to kill you," Hunter grated, gesturing toward the kitchen.

"I'm going to kill you," snarled Lance, stepping closer.

"Oh, bring it on, bigfoot," Hunter challenged, beckoning him with one hand. Lance took another step, and Melissa found herself wedged between two very big, powerful and angry men.

Lance's eyes widened. "Is that—is that my *shirt*?"

Hunter's shirt was ripped open, revealing his toned chest and washboard abs. Not that now was the time to notice his toned chest and washboard abs.

"Stop it, both of you," Melissa said through gritted teeth. She pointed a finger at Lance. "You need to bring it down a notch." She used her other hand to point at Hunter. "And you need to stop trying to set everyone on fire."

She swallowed, then nodded, finally acknowledging Hunter's point, her heart still racing at the threat. "She's under a compulsion," she told him. "Lance is protecting his sister, Hunter." She turned to Lance.

"Hunter was just—" She blinked, still trying to process it. "He was looking out for me." She turned her gaze to Hunter, and he glared at her with an intensity that revealed something she wasn't sure she could identify properly, as her instinct didn't make sense. But she wasn't going to query it. She dropped her gaze but gave a little nod. He'd saved her life yet again.

"Someone better tell me what the hell is going on. Now," Lance demanded.

"Why don't we secure psycho sis first," Hunter suggested. "Then we can catch you up over tea and scones."

Lance narrowed his eyes, and Melissa turned to him, bracing her hands against Lance's chest. "He's got a point. For some reason, Lexi feels compelled to kill me. When she comes to, she'll start again, and none of us want to see her hurt. At least, not more than she is already."

"Let me at her," Hunter said, and she felt his sigh against the back of her neck. His anger had cooled.

Lance shook his head. "That's not going to happen," he muttered.

"No, wait," Melissa said, then turned to face Hunter, curious. "What are you suggesting?"

He was standing so close she could feel his breath against her collarbone. His brown eyes were dark with turmoil, and she couldn't quite get a read on his emotions.

"While she's unconscious I might be able to do a scan, maybe even break the compulsion."

Melissa gaped for a moment. "You can do that?" she breathed. To her knowledge, a compulsion could only be broken by the one who set it, or by their death. To learn that there was possibly another option was like finding an undiscovered loophole in the laws of nature. Exciting and frightening at the same time.

Hunter shrugged. "It's possible," he admitted. "It depends on how deep the compulsion goes."

"I'm not letting this fire-freak anywhere near my sister," Lance stated, folding his arms, and Melissa placed her hand on his arm.

"He's not just a fire-freak." She ignored the exasperated sigh of the man behind her as she gazed up at her friend. "This man saved your life, as a favor to me, and to your sister. If he thinks he can help Lexi, I'd suggest you let him try," she told him softly. "I don't want to hurt Lexi, Lance, but if she comes at me again, I'll be forced to defend myself."

"Trust me," Hunter said, "I'm a doctor." Melissa could hear the sarcasm in his tone, just as she knew Lance could.

The muscle in Lance's jaw flexed, and his gaze shifted between her and Hunter. Her friend's green eyes narrowed. "Are you vouching for him, Mel?" The question was loaded with meaning, and it took Melissa a moment to digest it. Did she trust Hunter? That's what

Lance was asking. Did she trust the light warrior enough to place another friend's life in his hands?

Finally, she nodded. "Yes, I'm vouching for him."

Lance stared at her for a long moment, before dipping his head. "Fine. Do it." Hunter stepped toward the kitchen, and Lance reached to grab his arm. "But if you hurt her…" His expression turned hard and threatening. Hunter flashed him a tight smile.

"I saved you, didn't I?" He shook his arm free and stalked into the kitchen. He scooped up Lexi's unconscious form and carried her out to the living room, placing her gently on the sofa. Melissa and Lance followed closely.

"Why don't you tell me exactly what the hell has been going on here?" Lance asked Melissa in a low voice. "Who the hell is this guy?"

Hunter ignored Lance and Melissa's conversation, although he didn't completely push them from his mind. Largely because he didn't trust the Paul Bunyan wannabe. The guy was massive, and Hunter's ribs still ached from their encounter—he'd felt one crack, but he was healing fast.

He knelt at Lexi's head and gently rested his fingers against her temples. He still struggled with the homicidal vision of her in the kitchen. She'd borne very little resemblance to the woman who'd brought him bacon and eggs, and who had teased him as he'd prepared breakfast in the room she'd just turned into a battleground.

She'd threatened Melissa.

He closed his eyes, summoning his light force to enter her mind. He winced as he noticed her concussion, and he siphoned some energy off to heal her, reducing the swelling as he also delved into her mind.

He didn't dreamwalk—didn't trust Lance enough to slide into unconsciousness anywhere near the dhampir, but instead checked for previous assaults on Lexi's mind. He found plenty, and his lips tightened as he realized how vulnerable the young woman had been. He saw clumsy strokes of coercion with the unmistakable taint of a vampire, but they were aged, and though not completely severed, there was a definite weakening… He angled his head, feeling something warm and protective there. He didn't know why, but Melissa immediately sprang to mind. Had she tried to protect Lexi?

Normally he didn't worry himself too much with this kind of attack on a patient. He dulled trauma, if need be, but it was mainly the physicality of a body that he concerned himself with, believing that if a person exposed themselves willingly or not to psychic attack, then they should deal with the consequences. He had no issue with implanting suggestions. He did it with patients trying to kick addictions or lose weight all the time. Okay, so he may have dabbled once or twice with nonmedical stuff, but that was purely for amusement's sake to see people do things they wouldn't normally do.

Having seen the consequences of downright forceful manipulation firsthand, though, in a woman who had done nothing to deserve the removal of her free will… For the first time, Hunter was annoyed. He severed the coercions easily enough. It was a darker lock on her mind that concerned him. He skirted around the edges, impressed despite himself at the finesse of the block. Someone had implanted a series of suggestions in Lexi's mind with great skill. Every time he tried to unlock it, another barrier revealed itself. His brows pulled together. He hadn't seen this level of artistry since… He stilled.

No. He denied it immediately. It couldn't be. And yet,

there was only one person's persuasion that had ever really fooled him, only one person's prowess that he was unable to break.

He opened his eyes, withdrawing his touch from Lexi's temples.

"Well?" Melissa asked softly. He looked up. Melissa and Lance stood behind the sofa, leaning on the backrest with arms folded, looking down at him expectantly.

"I've gotten rid of the lame attempts from some vampire to control her, but there is something in there…it's so deeply buried that if I try to destroy it, I'll hurt Lexi. Badly." He reached for the remote control on the coffee table and turned up the volume, then flicked through the channels.

"I hardly think this is the time for watching TV," Melissa commented, frowning, but he shook his head, stopping when he found a twenty-four-hour news station.

"I can only think of one person capable of this kind of compulsion," he said absently, reading the newsfeed scrolling across the bottom of the screen. There had been something about…

He sucked in his breath when he saw the headline. "Son of a bitch."

In moments the news anchor announced the story. "In further news, authorities have identified the escaped inmate from the Oodvark maximum security prison as Arthur Armstrong, currently awaiting trial for conspiracy to murder Alpha Prime Jared Gray. Armstrong killed a female security guard during his escape, and is considered armed and dangerous. Authorities are warning the public not to approach this man if sighted, and to call Reform Authority."

"You've got to be kidding me," Melissa breathed. Hunter rose from the floor and crossed to the window.

He placed a finger against the curtain and slowly, gently, pulled back the fabric to peer out.

It was late afternoon, and already the gloom was setting in. The snow was turning to gray slush on the ground. A movement across the street caught his eye. Someone stood in a doorway, flicking ash from a cigarette. Hunter angled his head. A guy who looked like he'd slept in the clothes he wore for a good few months leaned against a shop window farther down, and a couple of men lurked up toward the other end of the street. Even as he watched, he could see a group of men approaching from about three blocks away.

"We have company," he muttered.

Lance went up to the other living room window and peeked out. "Werewolves."

Hunter nodded. "I don't see any vamps."

"It's still daylight," Lance murmured. "Besides, they're not going to come out with this many lycans about. One bite and they'd be dead."

"What's going on?" Melissa asked, coming up behind Hunter.

He turned to eye her. "Either you've pissed off a great many lycans, and—" He held up a hand, saying, "I'll give credit where it's due, I think you're totally capable of doing it, or someone is compelling an awful lot of folks to marshal an attack."

Melissa frowned. This close, he could smell her, feel her warmth, her body so close to but not touching his. He frowned when he noticed the bloodstain on her shirt. She'd been cut. He reached out, clasping her arm gently, and sent a warm tendril of light from beneath his palm to gently heal the wound. Melissa gasped, glancing down at her arm, then up at him. He winked, then turned to stare out the window again.

After a moment, Melissa stepped closer to peer over his shoulder, then shrugged. "They can marshal all they want, but my place is a fang-free zone, current company excepted," she said, indicating Lance. Hunter's gaze flicked over to the hulking giant. What was so damn special about this guy that he got a special hall pass from a witch with a fang phobia? Was there something more than just friendship between them? He wasn't sure. They didn't seem amorously inclined, but she had been able to stay the big guy, just with a frown and wagging finger.

"What about tomorrow?" Hunter asked quietly. "Will you open your shop?"

Melissa lifted her chin in that challenging, stubborn, try-me gesture he was beginning to recognize. "They're not going to run me out of business. They've tried many times, and they'll try more, but they won't succeed. We're not even sure who *they* are."

Hunter rolled his eyes. "Save the pep talk for someone who will swallow that crud," he told her. "Have you ever been under siege? What about your customers?" He pointed to Lexi. "She doesn't have fangs, and she damn near made a pincushion out of you." He folded his arms. "And I think you and I both know who is behind this."

Melissa mimicked his stance, folding her arms. He decided this was his favorite position for her, when her arms pushed her breasts up like an offering. A movement caught his eye, and he dragged his gaze up from Melissa's chest to Lance, who glared at him with narrowed eyes. Lance shook his head ever so slightly, as though in warning.

Hunter smiled. He rarely did as he was told.

"What would your father have against me?" Melissa asked, oblivious to the exchange.

Hunter looked back at her, his brow dipping. "Seriously? Maybe the fact that you and some other witch used your powers to help my brother and me battle our father, which ultimately led to his arrest and incarceration? Or maybe the fact that you kept his son chained to a wall?" He shrugged. "Or maybe he has a thing against gingers, who knows? My father isn't exactly on an even keel, if you get my drift."

"Like father, like son," Melissa muttered.

Hunter wheezed a chuckle. "Like your family is perfect. Pot, meet kettle." He'd seen enough in her dreams of the interaction between her and her mother to know she could also boast of a dysfunctional pedigree.

Lance sighed brusquely. "Well, this is all very entertaining, but what do we do?"

Hunter glanced over at Lexi. She was still unconscious, but her color was good, and she'd probably come to, minus the concussion, within the next half hour or so. "I can't get rid of that compulsion, which means she'll come after Melissa again when she wakes. You need to get her out of here."

Lance shook his head. "I'm not leaving Melissa defenseless against a pack of wolves."

"She won't be defenseless—I'll be here. The wolves can't breach Melissa's barriers. At the moment, they're just waiting for her to come out. If she stays inside, she's safe."

"Not until tomorrow, when any compelled human can come after her," Lance pointed out.

Hunter nodded. "True. So I will call my brother, and he'll come down and help me get rid of them."

Melissa frowned. "I thought your brother was just a dentist?"

"He is, but I don't know anyone who has teeth who isn't afraid of a dentist."

Lance put his fists on his hips. "How are the two of you going to get rid of a pack of wolves?"

"Let's just say my brother and I have a special set of skills," Hunter stated calmly, and brought forth two small fireballs dancing on his palms. He rolled his palm, and the fireball rolled with it, until he gave a flick of his fingers and the fireball disappeared.

Lance frowned. "What the hell are you?"

"Hot stuff," Hunter answered, grinning. Melissa rolled her eyes, then turned to Lance.

"Don't worry, I'm not defenseless, either. We'll be fine, but they're here for me, not you or Lexi. You need to get her out of here before she wakes up and becomes part of the problem."

Lance glanced between his sister and his friend, and Hunter felt a little sympathy for him. Not much, but a little. He could relate—as much as anyone could relate to a giant, blond dhampir who sucked on vamps yet was afraid of what would happen when his kid sister woke up.

Melissa rested her hand on Lance's arm, and Hunter eyed the movement closely. Neither had an issue with personal space, he noticed. "I'll be fine, Lance. You know me. You know I can take care of myself."

Lance sighed, then nodded. "Fine."

Melissa smiled. "Good. I'd suggest going up to the roof. There's a ladder up there we use to stretch across the ally for roof parties with the neighbors." She started to walk toward the hallway. Lance turned to face Hunter, his expression harsh.

"If she gets hurt or killed," he began, his voice soft with menace.

Hunter held up a hand. "Let me guess. If Melissa gets hurt or dies, you're going to kill me." He sighed. "You and Melissa need a new playbook."

Lance leaned forward. "What about this one? Mess with Melissa, and you mess with me."

Hunter rolled his eyes. "I get it." He almost told Lance he was renowned for his messes, but didn't think the big guy shared his sense of humor.

Lance strode over and picked up his sister, hoisting her unconscious body up over his shoulder in an effortless fireman's lift. Hunter shook his head. "You guys are related? Unbelievable." Lexi was tiny in comparison to her brother. But then, most people would be, next to this big lug.

He followed Melissa and Lance, carrying Lexi, up to the roof. The sky was bathed in pink and orange, with indigo and purple creeping in, and already the night shadows stretched across the streets. Hunter helped Melissa place the ladder over the facade edging to bridge the gap between Melissa's building and the next. He frowned at the ladder, then glanced over the edge. It was a long way down to the alley.

"You walk across this a lot?" he asked, eyeing the distance between the buildings. It looked like a whisker away from suicide.

Melissa nodded. "Uh-huh. I generally do Halloween, and Hal over there does Christmas."

"Why don't you just use the door?" Hunter asked as Lance stepped up on the ridge of the facade.

"Where's the fun in that? Besides, I'd have to walk all the way down, then all the way up, and Hal would have to do the reverse. This is much easier."

Hunter shook his head as Lance carefully stepped across the divide. The witch was a daredevil, or just a touch crazy. He held the ladder to make Lance's trek across as stable and secure as possible, and then helped Melissa drag the ladder back, stowing it against the roof's capping. Lance jogged across the roof to the door that led to the interior of the neighbor's building.

"Oh, wai—" Melissa held up a hand, but Lance either didn't hear, or chose to ignore her. He tried the handle, then stepped back and kicked it open. Hunter's eyebrows rose. It had taken the guy just one blast with his foot to break open a security door. It was just as well they were on the same side. He eyed Melissa. Sort of.

He shoved his hands in his pockets and strolled to the front of the building and looked down. The street below was in dark shadows, the sun sliding behind Irondell's northern skyscrapers. The numbers below had increased. Hunter frowned.

So many werewolves—wait. Now there were vampires, too, their pale complexions visible in the encroaching darkness. Hunter's frown deepened. But—but vampires and werewolves didn't work together. They hated each other. A lycan's bite was lethal to a vampire. He shook his head at the weirdness of the sight. He estimated there were a good twenty people gathering in the street. A small group turned a corner, striding down toward the bookstore. *More.*

"Uh, Melissa, we should go in." He didn't like the looks of this, not at all.

"Why, what's up?" Melissa asked, crossing over to him. He watched as a couple of vampires bent their knees, looking up at the roof.

"Inside. Now," he stated, grabbing her hand and pulling her back toward the door that led to the upper level of her building. He heard the soft thud of feet on the roof behind them, and dragged her faster.

Chapter 13

"Oh, my God," Melissa gasped behind him, as she saw the three vampires land on the roof, and then suddenly she overtook him, dragging *him* into the building. She slammed the door closed behind them, muttering a protection spell as she slid the lock home. Thuds and cracks echoed on the other side of the door, and Melissa flinched as the door shook.

"How long will that hold?" Hunter asked. She turned to him. He wasn't even panting, not like she was.

"A little while," she said, and turned to clamber down the stairs toward her apartment. "Those spells are durable against a shadow breed." She shook her head. "They were vampires. I don't understand. Since when are the vamps and mutts in cahoots? They hate each other."

"Well, let's see," Hunter said as he trotted down the stairs behind her. "How likely is it that you would piss off both the lycans and the vamps so much, at the same time, that they would band together against you?"

Melissa drew to a stop outside her apartment door, and bit her lip. Uh-oh. "Well, um…"

Hunter shot her a resigned look. "What did you do?"

"I may have substituted silver for steel cutlery at the Reform ball this year." Silver was toxic for both vampires and shifters, and touching silver was about the same as caressing acid for them. Silver cutlery wasn't enough to kill the shadow breeds, by any means, but it had made everyone who came into contact with it damned uncomfortable. Her mother had been furious, and had banned her from the winter solstice celebrations as punishment.

It had been totally worth it.

Hunter gaped. "Silver? At the Reform ball?" He closed his mouth and gave her an assessing look. "You can be so devious," he murmured, and she blushed at the amused appreciation she saw in his eyes.

She ducked her head. "So you see, it might not be some twisted plan of your father's," she admitted. The cutlery switch wasn't intended as a fatal attack on the shadow breeds, but it had provided enough of a disruption that some of the more secret conversations couldn't be conducted, with everyone eyeing anything that looked remotely metallic with suspicion.

She pulled the keys out of her jeans pocket and slid one into the lock.

Hunter braced his hand against the wall beside the door, and her awareness narrowed down to the bunched biceps so close to her head. "You know, you really are a—"

The loud crashing from one floor below startled them both, and Melissa clutched her chest as Hunter took a few steps down the lower stairwell and peered around the corner.

"It's okay, that door is warded, too."

Hunter looked back at her, his expression grim. "Something tells me that's not going to stop them this time."

She frowned and removed her keys, jogging down the steps to check it out. Her wards were impenetrable. She'd used a lot of magic, and she'd even had her brother, Dave, assist her in creating a blood lock.

"No fangs, remem—" Her throat closed over when she saw the peephole forced off its runner, and a muscular arm slid through to wave around. Yells and jeers could be heard from out in the street.

"Human," Hunter stated. Melissa paled, and she took a step back. Hunter reached for her, his warm hand grasping her arm.

"If we go back up there, we'll be trapped between a human mob and the vampires on the roof."

"I haven't pissed off any humans," Melissa whispered. She frowned. "At least, I don't think so." She glanced up the stairwell. She could still hear the muted thuds from the door on the roof. The vampires were still trying their best to get past the door. She swallowed.

"There's a fire escape in the alley," she said, and her stomach coiled. If there were humans on the ground, there could be humans making their way up to the roof. Hunter was right. They would be trapped.

She whirled and ran down the stairs two at a time. "The store," she muttered. "We can call for help."

She flinched when she heard something launch at the door that led from the corridor into the street. They were going to break it down.

"Hurry," Hunter urged as she fumbled with the lock.

"I'm trying," she rasped. Hunter slid his hand over hers, steadying it, and together they slid the key into the lock. The door at the street buckled under the force of whatever was hitting it.

Melissa twisted the key and turned the knob, and Hunter pulled the door open as the front door at the end of the hall burst open. Hunter shoved Melissa in front of him and followed closely, dragging the door shut and flipping the internal locks as footsteps ran down the hall toward them.

Melissa backed away from the door, shaking.

"Where's the phone?" Hunter asked, and she pointed to the front of the shop.

"Behind the counter."

They ran up the aisle, and when Hunter halted suddenly, Melissa plowed into his back.

"What—"

Hunter pushed her behind him, and started to retreat. "Tell me there is another way out," he said, his voice calm but grim.

Melissa peered over his shoulder, and her eyes widened. A group of men stood at the front door, hands pressed up against the glass as they peered into the store. Neither werewolf nor vampire, they were definitely human.

"Loading dock," gasped Melissa, tugging on Hunter's arm. She started to run to the back of the store, but halted when she heard the thumping from the rear.

"No," she whined, "seriously?"

There was a yell from the front of the store, and then the sound of fists thumping against glass.

"Melissa," Hunter's low voice prodded at her. He pointed to the doorway that led down. She grimaced.

She didn't want to go down. There was a way out, but they'd possibly be facing something far worse.

Glass shattered at the front of the store, and the intrusion forced her decision. She muttered quickly, gesturing with her hands and the door clicked as the locks disengaged.

"Come on," she muttered, grabbing his hand. Maybe they could hide down in the basement until help came.

"Wait," Hunter said, his voice rough, and he turned to face the men now climbing through her broken shopfront, scattering and trampling over the display books. Hunter lifted his hands, palms up, and Melissa grabbed his shirt so forcefully it ripped.

"No!" she cried at him. "They're compelled, Hunter. It's not their fault."

Hunter glared at her briefly, then sighed harshly. "Fine. I'm going to apologize now, though."

"Apologize for what?" She asked warily, then huffed as he pushed her into the stairwell.

"Just remember, I'm doing this for you," he muttered, then raised his arms, hurling the fireballs at the shelves of books.

She gasped in horror as fire tore through her bookstore, and the men screamed, retreating from the flames. Hunter slammed the door shut, cutting off her view of the firestorm. "Lock it," he said fiercely as he stepped past her.

Her eyes burning with unshed tears, she murmured her barrier spell, then shook off Hunter's hand as he grasped her arm. He shot her an exasperated look, then stepped aside, gesturing for her to precede him.

"After you."

She could hear the crackle of flames beyond the door, already feel the heat. He'd effectively cut them off. There was only one way, and it was down. She stomped down the stairs and flung open the door that led to her apothecary.

Hunter watched as she spelled the door, heard the locks engage with a viciousness that made him flinch.

"You can't be pissed at me," he exclaimed as she turned to face him. Her lips were tight, her cheeks flushed, and her green eyes glared at him with fury.

So, maybe she could be pissed at him. Hunter shot her a look of surprised innocence. "What?"

Her eyebrows rose in disbelief. "What?" she repeated softly.

Hunter's eyes narrowed. He'd learned that Melissa was a passionate, vibrant and lively woman, but when she went all quiet, it was like the silence found in the eye of a tornado, with destruction sure to follow.

"You set fire to my store," she said, and took a step toward him.

He didn't budge. He thought about budging, but then realized it would make him look weak—and any hint of vulnerability with this one was like a mouse pausing within reach of a cat's claw. Dangerous.

"Because you wouldn't let me set fire to them," he protested.

She slapped her forehead with her palm. "You can't set everything on fire," she exclaimed.

"Not everything," he argued. "Those men upstairs are fine. They're not dead. Most of them aren't even singed."

She blinked, her mouth open as she tried to find her words—unsuccessfully.

"Hey, you have to admit, that was close," he said, gesturing to the door. "They would have had us if I hadn't done that."

"You set fire to my store," she exclaimed.

"And you can thank me, anytime," he hinted. What the hell was her problem? She was alive, wasn't she?

She made some garbled noise in frustration, closed her eyes and did an intriguing little stomp-dance with her hands fisted by her sides.

"Why are you so angry?" he asked, confounded. "We were surrounded by guys who apparently want you dead, and they would have had their wish granted if I hadn't put them on pause with that fire barricade." He shrugged. "Be angry all you want, but just know the reason you *can* be angry is because I saved your life. *Again.*" He emphasized the last word as her fingers curled, just to make it clear she owed him, and to keep her painful talons out of his brain—or delusions of snakes or spiders or whatever other nightmare she could conjure up.

"Maybe we could have reasoned with them," she said through gritted teeth. "But we'll never know because, yet again, *you torched my shop.*" She yelled the last words at him.

Hunter folded his arms. "There was no talking them down, and we both know it. That was a homicidal mob with one intention. To kill you." He'd seen their eyes. He'd seen the murderous glint, the compulsion. They intended to do Melissa harm. "You can hate me all you like, Red, but you can't deny that I'm efficient. You might not like my methods, but I'll get the job done, and today that job was saving your life." Damn ungrateful witch.

Melissa rubbed at her temples, as though trying to soothe a migraine. Or else she was trying to summon more magic to smite him with.

"That fire won't hold them for long," he warned her,

just in case it was the latter. "It's burning hot and fierce at the moment, but—"

An explosion above them interrupted him, and they both ducked instinctively. Dust filtered through partition boards in the ceiling.

Hunter eyed the door warily.

"What was that?" Melissa whispered. "A gas tank, maybe?" Her hand rose to her mouth. "Oh, my God. All those men…"

Hunter shook his head. "I don't think so." It had been over too quick—a short, violent burst. He knew fire, and that was not a gas explosion. He crossed over to the door and placed his hand on the surface. It was cool. He hadn't expected it to be hot to the touch, but he'd expected some warmth from above. He put his nose to the crack between door and frame. He could smell smoke, but the acrid scent was only mild. He twisted to place his ear against the crack instead, listening intently. He could hear talking upstairs, then the sound of wood sliding across the floor. A male voice, one he recognized, had him backing away.

"Get your sneaky little door open, quick," he ordered Melissa, his muscles tensing.

She didn't hesitate, but turned and did some sort of graceful hand gesture, her lips moving soundlessly. The door that was neatly hidden in the painted mural swung open.

He grabbed her wrist and pulled her toward the dark space.

"What's going on?" Melissa asked as she trotted alongside him. For once, she wasn't pulling back, wasn't trying to fight him. He guided her gently down the steep stairs, grabbing the torch and handing it to her as he turned to grab the door.

"I think I just heard—"

Another explosion rent the air, and the door on the far side of the empty apothecary blew in. The force of the explosion hurled Hunter and Melissa into the darkness, and slammed the mural door shut.

Melissa hissed as she rolled over. Every damn bone in her body ached. Her muscles felt like jelly, and she covered her mouth, trying not to puke.

For a moment, all she focused on was the pain, the discomfort. Her elbows were grazed, her wrist and hip throbbed where she'd fallen heavily at the bottom of the stairs and sharp pain seared through her ankle each time she tried to move it.

Hunter lay across her thighs, and he groaned as he stirred.

He levered himself off her, rolling across her legs in a move that had her biting her lip to stop from screaming. She used her good foot to shove him off her before he did any more damage.

"Ow," he moaned as her foot found his shoulder.

She swore as she tried to roll to her feet. Her ankle gave way when she tried to put her weight on it. She flung her hands up, unbalanced in the darkness, and caught herself against the brick wall. She hopped in a small circle, so that she could lean her back against the surface.

It was pitch-black inside the corridor. Heaven only knew where the torch had landed.

She was totally in the dark. She listened as thumps and thuds and male voices filtered down to them. A lot of male voices. Then she heard the sound of metal scraping, clanging and crashing. They were pulling the shelving apart.

They were wrecking her apothecary. Tears welled in her eyes as she listened to the destruction above. She pursed her lips so tight and held herself so rigidly that she didn't even breathe until she had to suck some air in. Her bookstore was gone, and so too was her clandestine little clinic. She dragged in her breath, a whispered sob in the darkness.

Damn it. She'd worked so hard on that damned space. She'd scrimped and saved, she'd worked on the reconstruction herself, after work and on the weekend, painting, hammering...she, Lance and her brother had worked tirelessly. It was a clichéd statement, but she really had shed blood, sweat and tears in that work.

All for nothing. She flinched as something big and heavy was thrown against the door above their heads.

Her fists clenched, and she could hear Hunter shifting in the darkness.

That bookstore had been her livelihood. There were so many dreams and hopes wrapped up in that business. She had started it, but then Theo had joined her, and together they'd made plans, grand plans, special plans.

And in the space of one evening, her income, her vocation—her future—everything had been reduced to ashes.

It started to unfurl in her gut, a burning rage that turned ice-cold, spreading through her. She raised her arms, readying to pour all her fury into her own destructive spell.

Hunter's hands clasped hers in the darkness. "Don't," he whispered, stepping closer to her until she could feel his body, so close to hers.

"Don't even think about stopping me," she said, her voice so low, but she knew he heard in the darkness. She tried to free her hands, and he pulled them above her head, bracing them against the wall. This time his body did lean into hers, all heat and muscle and strength. His scent drifted to her. She could feel the delineation of his chest muscles against her breasts, and despite herself she reacted, her nipples tightening against the wall of his chest.

"Don't," he told her, his voice husky but clear in its warning. "You can't win. My father is up there, and he's stronger than I am. You try to tickle him with your spells, and he will turn you into ash without a moment's regret."

"Your father?" For a moment, cool reason intruded in on her anger. She'd seen Arthur Armstrong in action. It had taken both Hunter and his brother, Ryder, and Melissa and her own brother, to subdue him, and that was because she and Dave had had the element of surprise on their side.

She wanted to scream in frustration. The man destroyed lives without any conscience. When she most wanted to, needed to, she couldn't just go up and bewitch her way out of a problem. Again. Memories of the only other time that had happened to her, and the way that situation had ended, still haunted her. For only the second time in her life, there was someone more powerful than she, and she had to stay her hand.

And listen to him destroy everything she lived for in the process.

"If it's your father, why don't you just go to him? If this is some attempt for him to save you, he can have you. I'm not holding you back."

Hunter stilled next to her. "He can have me?" he repeated. His tone was mild, but she sensed the tightening of his chest muscles, the rigid set to his shoulders.

"Nobody else needs to be hurt, Hunter. If he's doing

this to get to you, maybe we should just open the door to him and let you go to him." And maybe stop him from transforming her apothecary into rubble.

"I'm not sure how your family works, Red, but blowing up a building is not our usual greeting. My father might be pissed at you, but he would be incensed by what I did to him. No pun intended." Hunter angled his head, his nose brushing her hair aside. "If I go to him, he will kill me. Is that what you want?"

Melissa frowned at the loaded question. Did she want Hunter dead? Five months ago, she would have said yes. Without hesitation. Five minutes ago, she may have said yes, after the stunt he pulled in her bookstore. But with everything he'd done for Lance, for Lexi—even for her... she didn't try to sugarcoat it. He'd saved her life. On the one hand, she was very tempted to let the light warriors duke it out.

But then Hunter might lose. He might...die.

With her own mother being so politically minded, with every move, every word part of a hidden agenda, and having experienced firsthand the hurt and betrayal from a parent, she didn't wish that on anyone—although she didn't think her mother would actually attack her.

"Wow, you really—"

"No," she admitted in a whisper, interrupting him. "That's not what I want," she grumbled. There was silence for a moment, then Hunter chuckled, his breath gusting against her neck. "Careful, I might think you actually care."

She lifted her chin. She didn't want him thinking *that*. "Hardly. My mother would not be happy if anything bad happened to the light warrior within my care—even if it was at the hands of his own family."

"You sentimental thing, you."

The sounds of destruction got louder, as though they were systematically making their way around the room.

"This isn't fair," she whispered, all the frustration, the desolation and the fury poured into those three little words.

"What can you do about that door?" Hunter asked, his lips next to her ear. Her eyes narrowed in the darkness, despite the fine tremble his breath caused in her. Did he not understand the true import of what was happening above them? Did he have no sympathy, not even buried deep in some forgotten place? "My father and his mob will find that door eventually, and they'll come down here. We'll both be finished. Do you have anything in that pretty little head of yours that will help us?"

If she tried to attack the Warrior Prime above them, his retaliation would see them both dead. She could at least do something about the door, though. Her lips lifted. Actually, that would be fun.

She nodded, and for a moment Hunter remained where he was, his chest against hers, his strong hands gently gripping her wrists. He stepped back so slowly it was like an incremental distancing of their bodies.

She clasped her hands together, calling on her magic. There were no elements down here save for the stone bricks beneath her feet, but even that was not natural. She focused inward, feeling the stirring of her essence. She leaned forward, just a little, until her hand brushed the steel supports of the stairs. Using an old spell her brother had once taught her, she could feel the stairs become thin, wavery, insubstantial within her grip. She sent the magic up the railing, mentally wrapping it around the treads as well, until she sensed the door. Keeping in touch with the railing, she spread the magic over the door, letting it embed within its surface. Then she muttered the final verse of the spell.

Beneath her fingertips, the railing disappeared. She added a new line to the spell, adding an extra punch line to it, then she drew back.

"Well?" Hunter asked beside her.

"I've cloaked the door, given it some substance so that even if they do a tap test, it's going to look, sound and feel like wall from the other side. It's not completely impenetrable, but they'll have to be very lucky to find it."

"Which means we'd be very unlucky if they do," muttered Hunter. "Is there another way out of here?"

Melissa considered the tunnels, and grimaced. "Not really." She didn't like it as an option.

"Not really isn't a no. What gives?"

"If we follow that corridor to the end and climb down one level, we can access the tunnels of Old Irondell. We could possibly make our way through the ruins to my brother's shop." Dave's tattoo parlor sat above one of the old caverns, with access to the tunnels, but where she cringed at the underbelly of Irondell's new Reform society, her brother seemed to revel in it.

"Great."

"No, not great. You don't know what's down there."

Hunter leaned forward. "As my father's son, I can tell you it can't be as bad as what is waiting for us above."

"Maybe we should wait. I mean, someone will notice my flaming beacon of a bookstore and come to help." Maybe her brother, for instance. Or maybe Lance, once he'd safely contained Lexi.

"Or, considering all the enemies you've made over the years, perhaps they'll bring marshmallows and sing songs around the bonfire," suggested Hunter.

Melissa pursed her lips, but didn't argue. Sadly,

each option had an equal chance of fruition. Despite the shields she'd put in place, they could still clearly hear the men above. She didn't know how long they could wait it out, how long it would take before her mother decided to pay her daughter a visit and negotiate a truce—because Eleanor Carter wouldn't actually defend her daughter until she'd wrung every ounce of advantage she could out of the situation. And then Melissa would have to listen to her mother's lecture about it being her own fault.

"I wonder what thoughts are whirling through your head," Hunter murmured.

Melissa sighed. It was the thought of her own mother, more so than Hunter's father that made her decision for her. She refused to be beholden to that woman, for anything. If the White Oak Elder Prime had to bring any influence to bear on a situation of her daughter's creation, then her mother would ensure there was a debt for Melissa to pay.

"Fine, let's go."

She took a step forward in the corridor and crumpled, hissing in pain. Her ankle was throbbing, but any weight on it was unbearable.

Hunter was by her side immediately. "What is it?" he asked, his hands moving gently and efficiently over her body. She halted. Did his hands linger on her breasts?

"My ankle. I think it's broken."

His hands still hesitated at the side of her breasts.

"That's not my ankle," she muttered.

"I know," he whispered back, and she saw a flash of white in the dark, and then shuddered when his hands slid around to her front, almost but not quite cupping the mounds. The jerk was laughing. He moved his hands on before she could slap them away, touring down the indent of her waist, the swell of her hips—even there, he paused briefly—and then on to caress her legs through the denim. She heard him sigh.

"Yeah, it's broken, but I can't do anything about it here. My father will sense the light, and then he'll find that door." He pulled her arm behind his neck and helped her up. His arm slid around her waist. "Let's get into Old Irondell first, then I can do something."

Chapter 14

Hunter slid the heavy metal grate across the hole, letting it drop as quietly as possible into place. He snapped his fingers, and a small flame hovered above his hand. He glanced around. They were in a tunnel. A big one. The walls were made of different kinds of brick, and the surface they stood upon was dark and hard. It took Hunter a moment to realize they were in a narrow street, and the wall of bricks was simply different buildings.

His eyebrows rose. Hot damn. Those old stories were true. Present-day Irondell had been built on the skeletal remains of the old city. He frowned. He wondered if all of the stories had an element of truth in them. Like the Darkken.

No. Their luck couldn't be that bad.

He eyed the gaps between the buildings. It was so dark down here. He turned to face Melissa, infusing the flame with a little more light to see her more clearly.

Her face was pale and drawn, the lines bracketing her lips deep with strain. He had to remind himself she was still recovering from her wolf attack the night before. He was surprised by a need to take care of her, make her comfortable. It went beyond his usual attention to patients in need. He frowned. It made him feel soft. He didn't like it.

"Come on, let's find some shelter and get you sorted." Ah, now that had been brusque. Firm. Much better.

She levered herself away from the wall, her eyes wide and anxious as she glanced around. This was the first time he'd ever seen her skittish. "Relax, Red, there is no bogeyman."

"It's not the bogeyman I'm worried about," she whispered. He pulled her arm around his shoulders and tugged her close, trying to bear as much of her weight as she'd allow. She hobbled along beside him until they reached the corner, and he pulled her gently across to the wall, using it as cover as he peered around.

His light force shed a little beam, and he gauged the area. He could hear the drip, drip, drip of water leeching through the bricks from above, could smell the faint scent of rot and decay, and it was blessedly cool—not cold. No breeze stirred the underground. He spied a door in the wall. It was a good ten feet away, but poor Melissa was hurting. He could see the sheen of perspiration dotting her brow, her lip.

Screw it. He lifted her into his arms, hushing her to quiet her protests, and hurried down the alley. The door was locked. No surprise, he guessed. Nobody had officially lived in this part of the city for a good century or two. He turned until his back was to the door and gave a short, sharp back kick. The door bounced open, and he cringed at the noise. This place was creepy quiet. Too quiet.

He stepped into the darker interior, flaring his light force to make sure there were no surprises inside. The place was empty. He glanced around. It looked like the place had once been a diner of some sort. The leather booths were torn, the laminate on the tables cracked, dust and grime coating every surface, but it still looked relatively untouched. A veritable time capsule.

He lay Melissa down on a booth cushion that didn't look as worn, ripped or filthy as the others, then gingerly cradled her foot. She rubbed her lips together, as though trying to stop any noise from the pain. He met her gaze. After her little temper dance and attempt to blast his father away with her magic, she hadn't complained. Hadn't blamed him. Hadn't bitched, moaned or tried to kill him.

She must be in considerable pain.

"It's okay, I can fix this," he whispered, and rolled the pant leg of her jeans halfway up her shin. He slid his hand down her leg. For a moment he was distracted by the sensation of her silky smooth skin, the toned muscle, the warmth…and then he felt the heat, the swelling just above her shoe. Even in the dim light, he could see the dark shadow of substantial bruising blooming above the sock line.

He grasped her ankle gently, and even though he took great care, he still felt her flinch. If they were going to get anywhere close to Melissa's brother, she needed to walk. If necessary, she needed to run.

Closing his eyes, he poured his light force into her. This was going to hurt. He couldn't afford to knock her unconscious—she needed to be alert, but he couldn't expend that much energy, not without a backup source to recharge with. He filtered energy through her, creating a warmth, a lethargy in her that relaxed her tense muscles enough to aid his healing.

He focused on the bruised tissue, delving deeper until he found the bone, and started to knit the calcic fibers back together. It took a great deal of concentration, pulling strands together and fusing them, strengthening them so her bone would be as good as new, if not better.

It took some time, and he could sense her sliding in and out of a daze. Eventually he sagged against the back of the bench seat. Done. He raised his eyelids slowly, battling weariness. Bone reconstruction always took it out of him. First there were the bones, then the damaged blood vessels and tendons…

He withdrew his warmth from her, and Melissa sat up, blinking. She stared down at her ankle, then flexed it cautiously. Her eyes widened at the movement, and then she rolled the ankle, shaking her head.

"Those are some mad skills you have there, Doc." She tilted her head, as though mulling something over, and her brows dipped, just a little. "You healed my broken bone in what, twenty minutes?"

He shrugged. He'd lost track of the time. He'd been focused on her, not the ticktock of a clock.

She swung her legs down to make more room for him on the seat, and he shuffled across gratefully. He'd been perched on the corner, and now he could lean properly against the backrest of the booth. He tilted his head back and closed his eyes. He needed to rest. Just a little.

"Twenty, schmenty."

He could feel her moving, shifting a little in the seat to face him.

"So why did it take you—what, two days?—to heal Lance?" He opened his eyes and stared at the opposite wall of glass that looked out onto a darkened corner. Uh…damn, he must be tired, he couldn't come up with a convincing lie fast enough.

"Uh…" He tilted his head, just a little, to peer at her out of the corner of his eye. She looked genuinely curious.

"I mean, sure, he had more injuries, but they seemed kind of superficial. Except for the bullet wound," she added.

She was too curious for her own good, damn it.

"Poison," he muttered, mentally scrambling. He didn't know how she'd react if she discovered he'd intentionally delayed her friend's recuperation so that he could find out more about the woman he'd once considered his enemy. He drew his brows together. When had he stopped thinking of her as the enemy? "The poison did some damage. Took a while to metabolize it."

She eyed him for a moment, before finally nodding, accepting his words at face value. Relief relaxed his shoulders for a moment, but something niggled at him. It took him a moment before he identified it.

Guilt.

Good grief. Out of all the lies he'd told in his life—and he'd told a few—why did lying to this woman bother him? He had to get over himself.

She twisted to face the same direction as him, gazing at the dirty window that looked out on the darkened street. He dimmed his light force, conserving his energy. Hiding behind the mantle of darkness.

They sat for a moment in silence. He could hear her breath, sense the rise and fall of her breasts, the slide of her hair over her shoulder as she tilted her head against the backrest. Her scent, that same sexy combination of cinnamon and smoke, teased at him.

"Why didn't you leave when you had the chance?" she whispered into the darkness, and his muscles tightened at the question. He could hear the hesitancy in her voice, the curiosity…the vulnerability.

It was a raw question, leading to exposure for her, and for him. He swallowed. He was tempted to lie again, make up something believable—he was good at that. For once, though, he didn't want to go to the energy of creating a lie, of deceiving another. Maybe it was seeing his father in action, the master manipulator… Or maybe he was just tired of trickery and deception.

"You had a chance to go…"

He sighed. "You…you kept your promise."

"Of course I did. You kept yours."

His lips lifted at her statement. As though it was a normal, everyday occurrence. "You were dying." And with her last burst of energy, she didn't try to save herself, she'd tried to save him.

He blinked in the darkness. More than keeping her word, it was that selfless act that had really hit home for him.

"But what about before?"

He frowned. "Before? When?"

"When I showed you Lance, and you—" Her words halted.

When he'd kissed her, and stolen some of her energy. When she'd gotten him so damn aroused it had been the hardest thing for him to pull back. When their passion had, ever so briefly, made him feel and act like a different man.

"When you put me to sleep," she finished in a low voice. "You made Lexi go home, Lance was unconscious and I was out of it. You had every opportunity to leave.

I couldn't have done anything to stop you. You didn't think about it?"

"Oh, I thought about it," he admitted, his lips twisting in a smile that held no humor. "Contrary to popular belief, I do actually keep my word. Every now and then," he clarified. "But don't worry. I figure there's a cure for that."

She chuckled softly, and he nearly jumped when her hand brushed his in the darkness. "Maybe, Hunter, some things don't need to be fixed."

He turned to her, wishing he could see her expression in the darkness. What exactly did she mean by that? Did she—did she mean that she thought he was…okay? That he wasn't a completely irredeemable bastard?

Her fingers tightened around his, and he sensed the tension radiating up her arm. "I just saw something move," she whispered.

He swung his head to the window, and caught a vague impression of a darker shadow, streaked with gray, moving at speed. Then the glass window broke, and a dark mass exploded into the diner, barreling toward them.

Melissa didn't have time to scream before Hunter shoved her down along the seat. He rolled over the top of the table, legs lashing out, and she heard a grunt—although whether that came from Hunter or whatever the hell was in the diner with them, she couldn't say.

By the time she peered up over the rim of the table, Hunter was grappling with a figure. It was about the same height as Hunter, but bulkier. That was about as much as she could make out. She saw the light blur as Hunter's fists struck out, his torso a paler shadow in the dimness.

She heard flesh strike flesh, and the figure stumbled

back against the table, before righting itself, squaring up against Hunter. Melissa didn't think. She climbed up on the seat and launched herself at the back of the creature.

She hit with enough force it shocked her as much as the creature she tackled, and they both crashed down to the floor.

"Melissa," Hunter yelled, and light flared.

Melissa blinked at the sudden brightness dispelling the dark, and the creature beneath her recoiled, covering its face. She could feel the muscles move beneath her, and she frowned. She looked up at Hunter. He had a small fireball in his hand and was raising his arm as though to hurl it.

"No, wait!" she cried, flinging up her hand.

Hunter's eyes widened midswing, and he had to jerk back, pulling his fireball with him.

"What the hell?"

"I think—I think it's human," Melissa said, levering herself off the figure beneath.

The figure curled up on its side, hiding its face from the light, but she could feel the frame beneath the heavy garb. Definitely human.

"*It* attacked us," Hunter rasped, his fireball churning and writhing in on itself, as though fueled by fury.

The figure on the floor shook visibly, and it emitted a garbled noise, somewhere between a keening wail and a harsh sob.

"Hey, shh," Melissa crooned, reaching out tentatively to touch his back. She could finally see enough of it, in the light cast by Hunter's fiery glow, to see that it was a man. Long, dark, oily hair, face and hands covered in grime, and a stench that could make your eyes water.

"My house," the man sobbed, curling into the fetal

position and rocking. "My house, my house." He kept crying it, holding his knees tight, his eyes squeezed shut.

Melissa sighed as she backed away. "He lives here," she whispered.

"He still tried to kill us," Hunter said, his eyes narrowed as the fireball flared in his hands.

"You're scaring him," she snapped as the man on the floor whimpered. She flicked her fingers, using her signature dampening spell to turn Hunter's fireball into smoke.

Hunter turned on her, his face angry. "You need to stop doing that."

"Doing what?" She hissed at him. "Stop you from setting everyone who threatens you on fire?"

"No, you need to stop thinking I will back down from a fight just because you want me to," he grated at her. "I'm not some torch for you to flick on or off at whim. I'm a light warrior, damn it. Fire, light, this is who I am."

She gestured to the vagrant on the floor who was still rocking, but his sobs had quieted down to hiccups. "This is who you are? Some big bully who uses his powers against those weaker than himself?" She didn't want to remember what he was like. She wanted to hold on to the guy who healed her ankle, who would talk quietly and hold her hand in the dark.

"If someone comes after me, or those I—" He halted for a moment, his fierce gaze wandering over her face before he swallowed, and continued, "or those I am with, I will fight back."

Her eyes narrowed. That wasn't what he'd been about to say. As though sensing her suspicion, her doubt, he stepped up to her, his expression ruthless. "I can heal, but don't mistake that for weakness, Red. I can also destroy. Yin and yang, baby. You don't get one without the other. You need to remember that."

"Why?" she whispered, her gaze trying to read his emotions behind the rigid mask he was now using.

"Because I am not my Goody Two-shoes brother, or some noble knight. Never was, never will be. So stop looking at me like that's what you want me to be, and neither of us will be disappointed."

He looked down at the man on the floor, then extinguished his fireball in an exasperated sigh. "Now you've ruined the buzz. Let's go, before any of his friends decide to defend their territory."

He strode toward the broken window, glass crunching underfoot as he stepped through the opening. He paused on the street, and turned in one direction, then the other. His torn shirt framed his torso, and for a moment that was all she could see—an indistinct pale blur framed in darkness.

"Which way to your brother's?" he called softly, but she could hear the impatience in his voice. She gazed down at the figure on the floor, and winced.

"Sorry," she whispered, then jogged over to the window, stooping a little to avoid any jagged pieces of glass still in the frame. She glanced around briefly, trying to get her bearings. Old Irondell didn't come with a map, and she was trying to figure out where her store was, and where they needed to head in order to get to her brother's tattoo parlor.

"This way," she said finally, indicating right, and Hunter nodded, striding briskly down the street.

She followed, but stopped short of catching up with him. Was he right? Had she started to think of him as a noble knight? The thought was laughable. Hysterical, even. Hunter Galen, her knight in shining armor.

He had saved her life, though. Twice. And he'd saved Lance's life—although that had been part of a bargain to earn his freedom. She watched him walk, his long legs eating up the distance in the darkness, the torn shirt swinging to reveal glimpses of pale skin in the darkness.

Did she really expect him to behave differently? Was she trying to hold him to a forced, false ideal?

An explosion shook the earth, and glass shattered in nearby windows. Hunter dived for her, tackling her to the ground and rolling her under him as bricks and crumbling mortar tumbled to the dark street around them, and Hunter covered her body with his, protecting her from any debris.

It took a while for the dust to settle, but Hunter finally lifted his head. He gazed around in the darkness, his body tense, his expression alert. "What the hell was that?" he whispered.

"It looks like your father found the door," Melissa said, shrugging, although she didn't try to hide the triumphant gleam in her eye.

Hunter's eyes narrowed. "What did you do, Red?" he inquired silkily.

"I added some extra zing to the cloaking spell," she admitted.

His lips quirked. "You're actually quite proud of yourself. What did you do, exactly?"

"I added an element of reflection, and then magnified it."

His head tilted. "And for those of us not criminally witchified, what does that mean?"

Melissa smiled. "It means that whatever your father threw at that door was reflected back at him, a hundredfold." The light warriors may have set fire to her bookstore and apothecary, but she'd just flattened the building. "I'm hoping your father burned right along with it."

Hunter shook his head. "Sorry, but a light warrior can't be killed by fire." He levered himself off her, and held out his hand, pulling her to his feet. He gazed around the street. Broken glass, timber and bricks littered the area. It looked like a war zone. He shook his head, whistling soundlessly. "I am so turned on by you right now," he admitted, eyeing the destruction.

She rolled her eyes and started walking, stepping over a partial wall that had collapsed. "Let's go."

She was trying not to think of the way he'd grabbed for her, covered her with his hard body to bear the brunt of any damage. He'd put his body between her and danger. Again.

It would be easy to believe he was exactly as he claimed—a man who could kill or cure with no conscience.

She realized her ankle didn't hurt. At all.

He'd healed her. He'd taken away her pain, and he'd protected her from a bomb of her own making. Was that good in him really just a front for his bad, or did that good go just a little bit deeper?

Chapter 15

Hunter plodded along, stopping every now and then to look at Melissa for guidance. She hung back, reluctant to walk beside him. He nodded to himself. This was for the better. Every time they encountered anyone, she expected him to behave like some damn hero.

He was no hero. He did bad things. Most of the time to people who deserved it. He pursed his lips. He'd tried to be good, once. It didn't work out. Even now, when he thought of Debbie he felt the instinctive shame, the guilt.

He had to tell himself it wasn't entirely his fault, what had happened to Debbie, but it was hard to break the cycle of self-hate. He had loved her. Well, he thought he'd loved her. It turned out he'd loved the false impression she'd made.

He didn't blame her, though. She'd been but a pawn in his father's machinations. For a while, he'd hated her, and that had just increased the guilt a hundredfold when he'd discovered the truth. No, that blame fell squarely on his father's shoulders. He clenched his jaw so hard it began to ache. His father had cost him so damn much.

He and his brother had met Debbie at one of the many parties his father had thrown in his endeavors to force the powerful Reform elite to accept them into the higher echelons of society, but without revealing their true identities. As the only light warriors in Irondell, and as the head of the Armstrong family, Arthur Armstrong was by rights the Warrior Prime of their clan. It was ironic, really. His father craved the power, the recognition of being a Prime, but could never claim it without exposing the existence of light warriors to Reform society, and potentially making them vulnerable to attack. In his bid to be the strongest, his father's secret in effect made him the weakest.

So his father decided manipulation, deceit and trickery would be their stock-standard weapons when dealing with others, and had drilled those lessons into his sons.

When Hunter had met Debbie, she'd been his kind of gal. He should have known there was no such thing, but, well, she'd convinced him otherwise. His brother had thought the same, though, and they'd fought bitterly over her. Debbie had eventually chosen Ryder.

Yeah, well, the less time spent on those memories, the better. He kicked at a pebble in the darkness, and it skittered across the road, disappearing into the darkness. They'd come to another fork in the road. Every now and then a manhole in the tunnel roof let in weak moonlight. He turned around. He didn't know how long they'd been walking for, but he was exhausted. He glanced up at the dark roof, spying the faint lightening of the gloom from what looked like a stormwater drain above him.

The only light he had access to was moonlight, and it was weak, at that.

"How far to your brother's?" he asked Melissa as she came up to stand beside him. She looked around, her eyes narrowed as she peered through the gloom.

"I'm not sure," she admitted. "Irondell and Old Irondell don't share the same road map. I think maybe another half hour or so. If we're going in the right direction."

His eyebrows rose. "If? What do you mean, *if*?"

"Look around, Hunter. We can't really ask anyone for directions."

Her tone was cool. She was still pissed about the homeless guy. He ducked his head. Not his finest moment, he must admit. Still, the guy had *attacked* them. He would not feel guilty for defending himself, or for defending Melissa. Maybe next time the guy would think about using his words first.

He took a deep breath, held it, then exhaled. "Which direction do you suggest we take, then?" he asked, keeping his tone mild.

He could sense her movements in the dark. She was twisting this way, then that.

Great. She had no clue.

"I think—"

A growl echoed down the street, and both of them froze. Now he could see the whites of her eyes in the darkness.

Another growl rolled through the darkness. This time it was closer.

Ah, crap.

Ever so slowly he turned, and he reached out to grasp Melissa's arm as she did the same. "Easy," he whispered.

They stared down the street, and Hunter edged them

slowly, silently over to the side, closer to the wall of a building. He was tempted to light up the street, but figured that would seem more like an invitation for whatever was out there. Something farther down the street shifted. He could see the movement, but not the detail.

He tried to push Melissa behind him, but she resisted, stepping up next to him. He frowned, but when he heard the pad of paws on the pavement he tugged on her, spinning around as something snarled and launched at his back. He fell to his knees, the scent of fur and something foul assailing him.

Hunter hissed as teeth sank into his shoulder. Melissa screamed, but it was more from anger than fear, and then the creature flinched behind him. He heard the enraged snarl, felt the werewolf turn, as though getting ready to attack Melissa.

"Come on," Melissa yelled, and out of the corner of his eye he saw movement, as though she was about to attack the lycan.

Hunter summoned his light force, and let it rain like cascading fire down his back. He heard the snarls turn into whimpers, and groaned as claws dug into his back momentarily as the lycan hunkered down, then jumped away from him.

Hunter rolled over, hissing at the burn of torn flesh in his shoulder and back, and squinted, watching the lycan skitter away.

Melissa curled her hands over, her teeth bared as she gritted out a spell in some archaic language, and the wolf recoiled. It stumbled back, panting, then flinched as Melissa raised one hand. She clenched her hand into a fist, then twisted it.

Hunter flinched when he heard the bones crack, saw the lycan's head twist, the neck snap at an unnatural angle, and then the lycan collapsed, its tongue lolling out, its eyes glazed and empty. Dead.

Melissa hurried over to him and slid her hand around his neck. "Why didn't you kill him?" she asked, her face pale and anxious as she smoothed his hair back from his brow.

For that moment, Hunter thought he was in heaven. It was either that or blood loss. Her clear worry, her tender touch... Then her words registered, and he frowned.

"Don't kill people, kill people," he said, wincing as he tried to sit up. "Make up your mind, woman."

"I thought you weren't my torch." She put her arm around his back, helping him get upright. "For the record, shadow breeds are fair game."

"I'm a shadow breed," he muttered as he rose to his feet. Damn, he hurt. His back felt like it was on fire.

"As you say, you're not perfect. Can you walk?"

He started to nod, but stopped when the world tilted. "Yeah," he lied.

Melissa pulled his arm over her shoulders, and he chuckled when she nearly fell under his weight.

"You're falling for me," he wheezed, then hissed as her arm moved around his back.

She gasped. "Hunter, you're bleeding, I can feel it."

He snorted as he concentrated on putting one foot in front of the other. "Funny, so can I."

"We need to find some shelter. I'm pretty sure that wasn't the only stray in Old Irondell, and we don't know what else might come out at the scent of blood."

Hunter grimaced. His vision was blurring, and his limbs were so heavy it was like he was wading through mud, but he could still recognize common sense when he heard it.

His toe dragged across pavement, then metal, and he halted. "Here." It was a drain in the gutter.

"You've got to be kidding. It'll be filthy. I need to get you someplace clean to patch you up. No, wait, you can heal yourself."

He shook his head, and then clung to Melissa like a drowning man to a life preserver. "I'm tapped out. I used a lot of energy in your bookstore, then on you, and all the friendly folk we've met in Old Irondell." He swallowed. His mouth was so dry. "We need to hide—I can't protect you at the moment."

Melissa gave an unladylike snort. "I think I've got this." She slid his arm off her shoulders and stepped toward the drain. Without her support, Hunter stumbled, then fell to the ground, groaning softly as first his knees, then his palms, hit the pavement. She glanced over her shoulder. "Oh. Sorry."

She bent over the drain, and he crawled over to help her lift it. He wasn't sure if he did actually help, he just knew his hand was on it, and the grate moved. With a little maneuvering and a lot of swearing, they both disappeared beneath the surface of the road.

Hunter must have blacked out for a moment, because he came to as Melissa was dragging his body down a dark tunnel. This one was narrower, with a lower roof. The original stormwater drainage system of Old Irondell.

Now, it was bone-dry, having not seen a storm for a couple of centuries. Hunter tried to look up, but his head lolled back, and he found himself staring into the glittering dark gaze of his witch.

"Leave me," he whispered, and he felt her stumble. Her grip under his arms tightened, and he grimaced as she pulled him farther along, panting.

"Shut up."

"Leave me," he said, his voice stronger. "Go find your brother. Then, if you want, you can come back for me."

Although why she would he had no idea. He hoped she would, but wouldn't blame her if she didn't.

She changed angle, and he vaguely noticed the anteroom she was pulling him into.

She pulled them well away from the doorway, then collapsed. He hissed as his back fell against the front of her body.

"Shh," she said, wrapping her arms around him gently. "You just need to rest."

His eyes fluttered open briefly. It was dark. So dark, and cool. The place smelled...old. Musty and dusty, but not foul. That surprised him.

He sagged against her. He was a light warrior. He was starving, and there was no light down here. No amount of rest was going to save him.

He lay there, half on top of Melissa, in the dark, the strong, regular beat of her heart thumping against his torn and bloodied back.

He was going to die. He sighed. He'd always wanted to go out in a blaze of glory, not bleed out in a puff of defeat. He blinked slowly. This wasn't the way he thought it would happen. He smiled in the darkness. Cradled in the arms of a beautiful woman. He couldn't think of a better way to go.

"Fix yourself," she whispered, her voice so close to his ear.

"I can't," he croaked. "No light."

Her chest paused beneath him, as though for a moment she'd stopped breathing. She realized, now. His lips turned down. He'd hoped she wouldn't figure it out until after he'd gone.

Her lungs expanded beneath him, and she leaned forward. Her cheek rubbed against his, and for a moment he felt the tiniest of sparks between them.

"There's another way," she whispered into the darkness.

This time it was his chest that stopped moving. He shook his head, taking a slow, painful breath.

"No. I'm not taking anything else from you, Melissa." He blinked, annoyed by an unfamiliar burn in his eyelids. "I've taken enough from you."

Her finger under his chin forced him to turn his face toward her in the dark.

"You're not taking," she whispered. "I'm offering."

And then her lips covered his.

Melissa moved her lips against his, so gently it was just a light brush of contact. Her heart thudded in her chest, and she startled when Hunter's hand grasped her fingers that were holding his chin.

"I don't want to use you," he whispered to her, his lips moving against hers. She could hear the need in his voice.

She smiled, enjoying the closeness, the shared breath, the contact of their mouths. "That's not what this is," she said honestly. She didn't view this as him taking advantage of her, of her losing her will and becoming just a food source.

He needed sustenance, and she could give it. Put simply, she didn't want Hunter to die. She wanted to do this. She'd had enough of dreams, enough tantalizing…she wanted more. She was doing this as much for Hunter as for herself.

She pressed her mouth against his, moving her lips gently, until his mouth opened beneath hers. She closed her eyes as she slid her tongue in, rubbing it against his.

For a while, that's all they did, lips and tongues moving against each other. He stirred something inside her, something hot and lazy. He let go of her fingers and slid his hand up to trace her jaw. That gentle touch, so delicate, set her to tremble.

It was as if that little telltale reaction, that sign that she was into this just as much as he was, acted as a release for Hunter. His fingers delved into her hair, his mouth widened and, suddenly, he was drinking in her passion.

Her breath caught as heat flooded her. Heart pounding, she cradled his head. He shifted in her arms, rolling to face her, and suddenly she was on her back and he loomed over her. Not once did their mouths break contact. He rose above her, his hips pressing against hers, and she drew her hand down his chiseled chest. He shuddered, and she liked it, so she did it again.

Over and over, he kissed her, lips and tongue tangling with hers. His hands swept over her body, and she moaned at his touch.

He raised himself on one hand, and used the other to cup her breast. His lips left hers, trailing down her neck. She arched her back, giving herself over to his caresses. Her pulse thudded in her ears.

Hot. It was so hot. She panted, trying to shrug out of her plaid shirt. Hunter helped her, pushing the garment off her shoulders. She wore a T-shirt under it, and Hunter's hand dropped to her waist, bunching the material in his fist as though trying to regain some control.

She writhed beneath him, eager to finally feel his flesh against hers. She'd dreamed it, she'd fantasized about it, now she was doing it, and it couldn't happen fast enough.

Hunter's hand slid up under the shirt, and her stomach quivered at his hot touch. Her breasts swelled within her bra, and she moaned with pleasure when Hunter's hand finally reached her there, cupping her through the lace-and-silk undergarment.

Hunter's lips skimmed down her throat, and she shuddered when she felt the hot lick of his tongue in the indent of her collarbone. At the same time his thumb swiped over her nipple, a delicious friction with the lace between them.

"Please," she moaned, not able to form any more coherent words.

"Yes," Hunter moaned back, levering up to drag at her T-shirt. Melissa sat up a little, helping him yank the fabric over her head, her hair falling down against her back.

"Oh, yes," Hunter groaned, as he looked down upon her, and Melissa realized she could see him. She had a brief impression of twinkling lights, like stars floating in the air around them, and then Hunter's lips lowered to hers again.

His hands skimmed over her body, molding her breasts before trailing down to tug at the button of her jeans. Her hips rose to meet his, and she dragged her nails over his chest as he unzipped her fly.

His fingers slid inside her jeans, beneath the lacy fabric of her panties, and her eyes widened as he toyed with her.

"Oh, wow," she gasped, then tilted her head back as he strummed her, the hot, slick slide of his fingers driving her to the edge.

"Yes," Hunter said, lifting his head to kiss her.

"Hmm-mmm," Melissa agreed as she kissed him back. Yes, yes, and hell, yeah. Heart thumping, thighs quivering, she climbed the peak of pleasure, and Hunter expertly pushed her over the edge.

Scorching bliss flooded her, and she floated in a cloud of intense satisfaction. It took several moments for her to catch her breath, and she realized they really were surrounded by light.

Hunter leaned over her. Gone was the pale, clammy complexion, his skin golden once more. His features were tight, his eyes shot with glowing amber flecks and he took a deep shuddering breath as he withdrew his hand from her jeans. She trembled, her body craving more of his touch, despite her recent orgasm.

"Thank you," he murmured.

Her chest rising and falling, she stared at him, astounded. That was—wow. That was pretty amazing.

She gulped. "You're welcome." Her gaze drifted down over his body. His hands were braced on either side of her body, and his chest rose and fell as he tried to catch his breath. The muscles across his shoulders were tight, his rippling abs taut with tension. Lower, his erection strained at his jeans. Hunter sank back on his heels, dragging a hand through his hair.

"Don't you want to…?" Melissa lifted her chin to his groin.

"Of course I want to," he said tightly. "But I shouldn't. I feel bad enough, taking so much from you." He exhaled roughly. Melissa felt disappointment, and her own edge of frustration creeping in, with perhaps a hint of embarrassment. She lay there in front of him, her breasts swollen and needy, her core damp and ready, and he was ready to stop.

He rose to his feet and turned away. His back was smooth once more, and there wasn't so much as a scar from the stray werewolf's attack.

"Oh, okay," Melissa whispered, reaching for her shirt.

Hunter looked at her over his shoulder for a moment,

his features harsh with arousal, and his eyes sharpened, the amber flecks brightening. "No, damn it, it's not okay." His gaze heated as he stared at her lace-covered breasts, then he turned to face her. "No. If I'm going to feel bad about this, at least let's make it worth it."

He strode over to her, dropping to his knees between her thighs, his hand sliding behind her neck to hold her for his kiss. She gasped as his tongue entered her mouth, lashing her with desire.

Just like that, her senses snapped to attention, eager to dive back into the passion. So quickly, Hunter had her panting, drawing her up to his chest, his hands sliding around her to expertly undo the back clasp of her bra. He slid the bra straps over her shoulders, trailing his fingernails softly against her skin, causing her to shudder. He pulled away slightly so he could remove the garment altogether, and he sighed as her nipples brushed his chest.

Liquid heat pooled between her thighs, and she moaned against his mouth as his hands cupped her breasts. She quivered as he gently pinched both nipples, and hot sensation zinged straight to her core.

Hunter's lips trailed down her neck, and he bore her back to the ground, kissing, licking and nibbling his way down to her breast. He drew a rosy nipple into his mouth, sucking on it and laving it with his tongue.

Melissa's eyes widened as sensations, hot and wicked, bombarded her. The lights in the little cavern flared and flickered, dancing above them. She trembled as Hunter released her nipple with a final tug, and switched his attention to the other breast. He was driving her crazy with need.

Well, two could play at that game.

She caressed his broad shoulders, her breath hitching as his hips moved against hers. She trailed her hands down to touch the chest that had drawn her gaze and had been the source of her fantasies for so long. His strength, his heat, was intoxicating.

She flicked his nipples, and smiled when he groaned. He rose up to kiss her on the mouth fiercely, then turned his attention to stripping her jeans and panties off, dragging her shoes off in the process.

She pressed against his chest, and he moved back. Melissa rose, her hands moving to his belt. In moments she had his fly open, and he lifted his hips as she stripped him. Her eyes widened when she revealed his cock, its rigid length drawing her touch. Hunter's head lolled back and he moaned.

She leaned down and pressed a kiss to his chest. His hand rose, fingers spearing over her scalp, and she kissed and licked her way down his washboard stomach. He groaned when her lips closed around him, and she used her tongue, lips and hands until his fingers clenched in her hair, pulling her off him. He drew her up, eyes boring into hers with an intensity that was all revealing, and all seeing. There was no escape from that gaze. That bold, hot gaze that showed her the depths of his desire, a hint of vulnerability and awe, and an awareness that left her nowhere to hide.

"I—" His lips moved, as though he wanted to say something, then he leaned forward and kissed her. Hard.

Something flared within her, something strange and new, a heat that crept over her with wicked intent. He dragged her closer, pulling her into his lap until she straddled him, his biceps bunching as he embraced her, his tongue sliding with the same rhythm as his hips rocking against hers. She could feel him, hot and hard, nudging against her.

She also felt herself, warm and wet, writhing against

him. Her eyes widened at the sensation. Hunter's hands slid down her back, cupping her butt and lifting her.

He slid inside her, and she felt *everything*. Heat built between them, but it was the sensations bombarding her, robbing her of clarity, of logic and reason until all she could do was feel. He slid inside her, stretching her. Her body surrounded him, welcomed him, and she could feel it all. She didn't understand how she could feel him, feel her, didn't have the presence of mind to question it, she just accepted it.

He gathered her close, and she sighed, feeling his strength embracing her, her softness against him, and their joining, exchanging heat, sharing friction. Writhing against each other, their hearts beating in syncopated rhythm, Melissa could sense her orgasm building. She could feel Hunter's pleasure, an exquisite torture as her senses overloaded, and then suddenly she was flying, and whatever connection they had between them kicked them onto a plateau of bliss that fed itself, creating, expanding, re-creating, until she collapsed against Hunter's broad muscled chest, a quivering molten mess.

Hunter dragged a deep, shuddering breath into his lungs. Holy smoke. He wrapped his arms around the trembling woman in his lap, her thighs clasped around his waist. He'd just glimpsed heaven.

He tilted his head, leaning his temple against the top of her head as they both tried to catch their breath.

Holy. Smoke.

He stared at the stone wall of the chamber they were in. He'd lit the place up as though it was Reformation Day, complete with little starbursts above their heads.

Okay, he needed to tone it down, but hot damn that was amazing.

He closed his eyes, drawing in his light force, dimming the room until there was just enough light to see each other. His lips lifted. So romantic.

She shifted, and his eyes rounded. Oh. God. He was inside her and could feel her surrounding him, but he could also feel himself inside her. As he had during the act.

"Oh, no," he breathed. No, no, no, no. no. *Hell, no.*

Melissa stiffened in his arms, and her head lifted, smacking him in the temple. He winced as she stared at him, her eyes narrowed.

"Oh...no?" she repeated.

She moved, and he helped by lifting her off his lap, his hands on her waist. For a moment, he gazed up at her, staring at her sexy body bathed in the golden glow of his light force. Quite simply, the most beautiful sight he'd ever seen, bar none.

And then he saw it. The cord that linked his heart to hers. Only rare, gifted light warriors could actually see a mating bond. Debbie had died before he'd even thought about a bond, but as it was, she wasn't truly his to bond with, anyway. He'd seen the one that existed between his brother, Ryder, and his mate, Vassiliki.

"No, no, no," he said, shaking his head in disbelief. It was a thing of beauty, an ethereal flow of energy, like cascading, dancing ribbons of color, all pinks and purples and—oh, God—white. "Oh, that's not good."

Crack.

His head whipped to the side as Melissa's palm connected briefly and oh-so-sharply with his cheek.

"Not *good*?" She glared at him, furious, but he saw the hurt, the humiliation in her eyes.

He held his hand up. "No, Red, that's not what I mean—"

"Screw you, jerk." She whirled around, her red hair flaring out like a vibrant curtain of fire, and she bent down to retrieve her clothes. Apparently she was completely oblivious to the strand of twisting colors between them. "And don't call me Red. God, what was I *thinking*?" She dragged her underwear on, the elastic of her lacy panties snapping audibly in the stone chamber. He rose to his feet, dragging on his briefs and jeans, hopping from one leg to the other as he dressed.

"No, this is all me," he tried to explain again, then flinched as she whirled to face him.

"Damn straight. I had a great time, and don't tell me you didn't, because we both know you did," she said, her teeth clenched. "You—I—" She gestured between them, her face a comical blend of horror and confusion. "What *was* that?"

"That was you being so unbelievably generous," he told her, trying to use a soothing tone, "and I really, really appreciated it."

Her eyes rounded. "You *appreciated* it?" This time her voice emerged almost as a screech, and Hunter winced. Ah, hell. He was making a colossal mess of this. Like usual.

He held up both hands, palms out. "Hey, it worked. I'm healed, I'm charged and ready to go—"

"You already went," she snapped, and Hunter's lips twitched. He certainly had. Then his humor left in the face of her fury—of her hurt. He'd done that, in his usual, stupid-ass way.

"And you are…okay?" He'd heard about the bond, the feedback of the link. Had never, never, *never* thought he'd ever experience it. But what if it was just talk? What if he still drained her of her energy? Of her life essence?

"Am I *okay*?" She dragged her T-shirt on over her

head and tucked it furiously into her jeans. "No, I'm not okay. I just—" she gestured to the ground where they'd just blown each other's minds, and then gestured to him, finishing "—with you."

She made it sound like she'd broken a law of nature. His lips tightened. "I meant, are you okay, physically? Are your energy levels sufficient to get you out the door, or have I—" he swallowed, finding it difficult to put into words "—have I drained you?"

He stared at her, concerned and just a little panicked. The pleasure, the energy that had been created between them, could have drained her almost to the point of expiration. If he'd taken that much pleasure from any other woman, he could have killed her.

She frowned, resting her hands on her hips. "I'm fine," she growled.

He raised a hand toward her, saw that it was trembling and clenched it into a fist. "I mean it, Mel. What we just did—I could have killed you. Are you okay?" He needed to hear it from her properly, not some glib assurance. God, how could he have let it go so far?

She must have seen his apprehension because she calmed, ever so slightly, and her brow relaxed. Slightly. "Yeah, I'm fine, Hunter. In fact, I'm good." Her eyebrows rose, as though surprised by the truth in the statement. Then she frowned at him again. "And you suck, you jerk."

She shouldered past him, and he turned to grab up the remains of his shirt. After a tussle with Lance, and a tackle from a werewolf, it was torn to shreds, so he dropped it and jogged after her. He cast a muted glow in front of them to light the way.

"Melissa, I'm so—" he began but she held up a hand, not bothering to turn.

"Save it. I don't want to hear it. We did what needed doing. You're all juiced up. Ace. Sorry it wasn't what you expected." She'd started off strong, but her last words were husky, and she cleared her throat, increasing her pace down the tunnel.

"Oh, it was a surprise, all right," he said quietly, eyeing the swirling ribbons of color between them. She turned on him, holding up both index fingers.

"Please. Stop. Talking."

He closed his eyes briefly. Maybe she was right. Every time he opened his mouth, he just made it worse. He nodded and opened his eyes as she continued walking, arms swinging as she set off at a cracking pace.

And the light warrior's mating bond stretched between them. He fell into step behind her. He couldn't be mated. He shouldn't be mated. There was something innately wrong with him. He'd dated women—hell, he wasn't a monk—but he'd only ever really fallen for one woman, and she'd rejected him. She knew what he was like, on the inside. She'd seen his darkness. And she'd died trying to get away from him.

He eyed the woman who was doing her best to put as much distance between them as possible. He should expect that. It hurt, but it wasn't really surprising. His own brother had thought him capable of murder, so Melissa, the one woman who had seen him at his worst, would definitely not want to be linked for life to him. For a moment he entertained the fantasy that perhaps she would, that perhaps this woman who frustrated him and challenged him and would not back down, that perhaps she would see the good just as she'd seen the bad. That she'd want to share more with him than just pity sex.

Her fists swung at her sides, and Hunter shook his head. Who was he kidding? Every woman he'd ever come close to loving either ran away or died. Or both. Mates were supposed to stay together, but out of all the women of his acquaintance, Melissa was most likely to run away. Or kill him. Or kill him and then run away. Their relationship so far hadn't really suggested long-term commitment to him.

Maybe he could fix this…?

He tried to grab on to the link, but it was more of an aura, and completely intangible. He swung his hand through it in something resembling a karate chop, and the ribbons just ebbed and flowed around him. He kicked at it, tried to pull it, then twisted, hoping it would wrap around him and sever.

It didn't. He tried to separate the strands, so intent on disconnecting the link that he almost tripped over Melissa. She stood in the middle of the tunnel, arms folded, a slight frown on her face.

"What the hell are you doing?"

He whipped his hands behind his back. "Nothing," he replied innocently.

Her eyes narrowed, and she looked at him as though he might be just a little crazy. He eyed the bond between them, and he wanted to laugh hysterically.

He wasn't crazy. He was royally screwed. He'd bonded with the bitchy witch.

She shook her head, then turned. She took four steps, and he watched the twisting band between them, and then something gray and fast tackled Melissa to the ground, a guttural snarl coming from its throat.

Hunter roared, shock and rage coursing through him as Melissa screamed, struggling on the ground with the figure. It had arms and legs and a head, and looked like a man—sort of. Hunter reached out, and a spark of light zinged from his fingers, catching the man off guard, propelling him back down the tunnel a good ten feet.

The man's head reared back, his eyes snapping red in the dark, and Hunter's light caught the gleam of his fangs. Hunter grimaced. It looked like a vamp, but not like any he'd ever seen. The gray vampire let out a howl, tipping his head back and letting the screech reverberate through the tunnel.

Then the vamp launched at them again, and this time Hunter didn't hold back. He let fly with a fireball that engulfed the man. Hunter grabbed Melissa's hand and took off running in the opposite direction, the agonized screams of the vamp following them, like a rolling wave of sound.

Only the sound didn't ebb, as it should have. Hunter glanced over his shoulder, and his eyes widened. More were running down the tunnel behind them. Gray-faced vamps with murder in their red eyes. Hunter swore, then tightened his grip on Melissa. He would not let them hurt her. They approached an intersection in the tunnel, and Hunter tugged her down the right fork. They rounded the corner, and Hunter skidded to a halt.

Before them stood a man. He stood with his feet shoulder-width apart, his hands at his sides. This one didn't have gray skin, though. He stood roughly the same height as Hunter, with broad shoulders, and strength that was evident from the tightly roped muscles in his arms and torso to his powerful legs. His complexion was pale, almost ghostly white, and his eyes glittered an eerie pale blue, although there was a glazed, unfocused look to them. Long white hair was tied back in a braid, and Hunter warily eyed the defined wall of muscle framed by the black leather vest he wore.

A white eyebrow arched, and the movement spurred

Hunter into action. They had a gray army bearing down behind them, or this single blind albino blocking their path. He knew which odds he preferred.

He flung a fireball at the albino, advancing forward to move around him, when the albino reacted, holding up his hands, and a dark shadow grew between them, capturing the fireball Hunter had thrown at him and dousing it effortlessly.

Hunter halted, shocked. "What the hell are you?" he snapped.

The albino smiled grimly, his vague stare victorious. "Your worst nightmare." The tall man turned his hands palm out to them, and a roaring cloud of darkness swept over him and Melissa, swallowing them into the pitch-black.

Chapter 16

Melissa cracked her eyelids open. Her vision whirled, and she wasn't sure if it was her head or the rest of the world that was spinning. She clung to stone, her fingers curled as she dug them into a crack to stop from flying away, and slowly her world settled. She was lying on the floor, her cheek resting on the blessedly cool surface.

"Well, hello, darlin'."

The deep voice rolled over her, and she blinked before she shifted her head. The albino sat on an intricately carved chair. A fire roared behind him in a hearth that could hold her whole kitchen. The hall they were in was massive, with walls inset with timber framing, and a large stone frieze above the hearth depicting a battle of some sort. What the hell was this place?

"Leave her alone." Hunter's voice was forceful, implacable, from somewhere beside her. She didn't have the energy yet to turn and look at him, but he sounded fine. Angry, but fine.

"What did you do to us?" she croaked at the albino.

He smiled, and there was something that caught her attention, something that seemed so familiar, yet she knew she'd never met this man before. Man. Vampire. Her muscles tensed. She was caught by a shadow breed. She didn't know what the hell he was, just that he wasn't an ordinary human. Goose bumps rose on her arms, and she had to swallow her fear. She wouldn't give in to the panic. This would not be like last time.

"I stopped you from hurting any more of my people," he told her softly, and she heard the menace in his tone. He tilted his head, his unfocused gaze curious as it flicked between her and something—or someone— beside her. Hunter, she presumed. She had no idea how much this man could see, perhaps it was just movement, but he seemed to be able to track both her and Hunter unerringly. "I must admit, it's not often we receive guests. What brings you into my territory?"

"Who the hell are you?" Hunter snapped from beside her, and finally Melissa raised herself into a sitting position. The grogginess was beginning to fade, leaving a faint headache behind. She glanced behind her. Hunter was on his knees, his arms twisted behind his back and held by two of the gray vamps. The hall extended beyond them, and flaming torches were set in intricate iron wall sconces that were placed at regular intervals. Enough to reveal the masses gathered behind them. Positively medieval.

Yet no guards held her. They probably thought she wasn't a threat, after Hunter taking fiery action—*again*. Yet another lifesaving debt she owed him.

Hunter met her gaze, and behind the fury she saw

his relief at her awakening. She gave him a small smile to reassure him that she was fine, then turned back to the albino.

The man rose from his seat and moved to stand beside it, his elbow resting on the carved backrest. "They call me the Dark Lord," he told them, smiling politely.

Hunter snorted. "Rather flashy, don't you think? Not to mention the contradiction…"

Melissa couldn't believe Hunter was calling out the albino for being…an albino.

The Dark Lord's pale eyes flared with something that was borderline humor, but mostly exasperation. "A little. But my clan seems to think it fits." He held out his arms. A cloud of darkness descended from the ceiling, and a coolness entered the room, the fire stuttering beneath the mantle of gloom.

It rolled over them with the weight of a heavy blanket, and Melissa blinked, trying to peer past it. She panicked when she realized she couldn't, and her hands rose to try to wave it away, like a fog.

There was the snap of fingers, and the dark cloud disappeared. A chill settled in the room. The fire had died in the hearth.

He swaggered down from the platform, his gaze on Melissa. "So, tell me, darlin', what brings you a-visiting?"

Melissa glanced around the hall and swallowed. A large crowd had gathered. All of the people had dark hair and varying shades of gray skin. Most had dark eyes, although she saw varying shades of eye color, as well. Good grief, the tales were true.

The Darkken. A race of savages living in Old Irondell, eking out a living from the land without light.

Although they didn't look terribly savage. A little girl

peered out from behind her mother's jeans. Her skin was pale gray, with a marbling effect of darker and lighter grays. It should have looked ugly and alien, but instead the blending of color was beautiful. The little girl popped her thumb in her mouth in a universal need for comfort.

No, the Darkken looked…almost normal, in a grayscale kind of way. Normal and alert.

Melissa frowned as she returned her gaze back to the Dark Lord. "We're just passing through," she told him. She didn't see any purpose in hiding their objective from the albino. She hoped he'd let them pass. She feared he wouldn't.

The Dark Lord frowned, and he stepped down toward her. "Well, see, here's the problem. You've killed one of my guardians."

"*I* killed one of your guardians," Hunter interrupted. "She hasn't done anything."

The Dark Lord tilted his head, switching his attention to Hunter. "Ah, yes. The fire starter." He rubbed his chin. "You killed Orion." His expression became harsh. "Orion was a good man, with a wife and a baby on the way."

"Orion was trying to kill *us*," Hunter pointed out. "It was self-defense."

"You were trespassing," the Dark Lord said, his tone mild. Melissa watched the exchange warily. Both men looked and sounded like they were having a casual debate, but there was nothing casual about being held captive by the Darkken.

The Dark Lord sighed as he folded his arms. "What am I to do with you?"

"You could apologize for attacking us and let us be on our way," Hunter suggested hopefully.

Their captor's eyes narrowed. "Or we could kill you now for your crimes," he suggested roughly.

"My crime," Hunter corrected again. "Let her go."

Melissa's eyes widened as she turned to gaze at Hunter. His shoulders were back, his chin lifted. For a moment, her vision blurred, and it was another man on his knees, his dark head tilted back as he begged for her life. She blinked rapidly, shaking her head. No. Hunter was not Theo. It didn't have to end the same way.

"But you're a couple," the albino said, glancing between them. "One in, all in, right?"

Melissa frowned. While she didn't agree with the Dark Lord's interpretation of their relationship, she wasn't about to abandon Hunter. Despite what had happened between them in the tunnel, Hunter had still fought for her, time and time again. He'd saved her life, and was now trying to negotiate her freedom at the risk of his own.

Just like Theo, damn it.

"I just want to go to my brother's place," she said, interrupting their exchange, calling the albino's attention back to herself. "That's all we want. We don't want any trouble…" Well, she didn't know about Hunter. He always seemed so ready for a fight. "We just want safe passage to my brother."

The Dark Lord's eyebrows rose. "Is he a resident of Old Irondell?" he inquired politely.

Melissa shook her head. "No, he's…above."

The Dark Lord frowned. "He's one of the Others…" He glanced down at his feet, his hand out as he gestured casually to her, palm up. "So, if you're from above—which I can clearly tell that you are, and he is above… why are you below?" He turned his wrist in an elegant roll to point at the floor.

Melissa looked at Hunter briefly. Hunter shook his head, just a little, but the Dark Lord caught the movement. He gave them each an assessing look, then leaned forward, his freaky pale blue eyes on direct level with Melissa's. "I have news of a light warrior who has ventured into Old Irondell, and is looking for a man and a woman. You wouldn't happen to know anything about that, now, would you?"

Melissa's eyes widened. "He's down here, too?"

The Dark Lord's eyes flared. "He's issued an alert. He seems very eager to find you."

Hunter lifted his chin. "We'd rather he didn't."

The Dark Lord smiled grimly. "I bet. But you see, he's sworn to kill a resident of Old Irondell for every hour it takes him to find you."

Melissa's eyes widened in horror as she thought of the vagrant they'd encountered. Old Irondell was home to the Darkken, and all manner of creatures, but also to humans who were homeless and vulnerable. She had no idea how many lived below, but from the numbers here, it could be substantial. Strays, the homeless…the Darkken. How could Arthur Armstrong be so angry with them that he was willing to kill so many?

"So you can see my dilemma," the albino said softly, and this time there was no mistaking the menace in his voice. "Not only have you killed one of my men, you're also responsible for the death of more people under my protection."

"Your protection doesn't seem to be worth much," Hunter commented sourly.

The albino didn't even turn. He lashed out, his fist catching Hunter square in the jaw. "I think I'll just kill the both of you and be done with it. Problem solved," he snarled.

Hunter's eyes narrowed. "Fine, kill me. I'm the one he really wants, but let her go."

"Hunter," Melissa gasped. Why was he on a kamikaze mission?

The albino stepped up to Melissa, and she tried to dodge his hand as he stroked her hair. "You're quite the catch, aren't you, little one?" he commented softly. "A light warrior prepared to kill for you, and another prepared to die for you..." He tilted his head, his pale blue eyes considering. "What makes you so special?"

She met his gaze solemnly. "Do you really want to find out?" She focused on the Dark Lord, calling to her magic.

"Melissa," Hunter warned in a low voice.

She ignored him. This—creature—hell, she wasn't sure what he was, exactly. He didn't have the blending of grays in his complexion like the rest of the Darkken, and his blue eyes were startling, mesmerizing. With his snowy white hair, he should have looked old, but his clear pale skin pulled tight over high cheekbones gave him an ageless appearance. She'd never seen anyone pull darkness forth like that, but she and Hunter needed to claw back some footing from this man, and from the Darkken. They were vampires, of a sort, that much she knew...but she also knew they were a breed apart. Living below as they did in Old Irondell, they were the very essence of a shadow breed, dwelling without direct access to light, other than what they could create.

And she didn't cower to the shadow breeds. She would never yield to the shadow breeds. Never. She focused her magic on the large man standing beside her.

The Dark Lord's eyelids flickered, and then he winced, raising his hand to his temple. She pictured her magic leeching into him, gently spreading like tendril roots from a plant, curling and sliding, delving into his mind. She did it gently, but she saw his eyes narrow, then his grimace as he held his hands to his head.

She expanded her reach, and the two men holding Hunter suddenly clutched at their heads.

"Stop it," the Dark Lord growled, peering at her with eyes that started to glow with silver flecks.

"Let us go," Melissa growled back at him. "We don't want any trouble. Let us go."

"I said, stop it," the Dark Lord argued, his voice rising with menace. Darkness started to curl up from the floor, and she could feel it pressing in on her knees, her thighs, as it slowly rose. Perspiration beaded on her lip as the darkness rose on a level with her chest, embracing her with a strength that was almost crushing. She panted, trying to catch her breath, but didn't release the grip of her magic.

"Leave her alone," Hunter exclaimed as he rose to his feet. He clasped both hands in front of him, and a swathe of light appeared, cutting through the fog of darkness that was even now trying to swallow Melissa. The surrounding Darkken gasped, some calling out in surprise and fear.

The Dark Lord turned to Hunter, and Melissa felt the darkness lift around her, just a little, as the albino warrior focused on the man who managed to split his gloom with the sharp length of light.

She could see the strain on the Dark Lord's face as he battled both Melissa's psychic attack and Hunter's physical one.

"Stop it, all of you," a woman's voice commanded from the side of the room. Footsteps echoed across the stone parquetry, and Melissa noticed boots with narrow heels stride into the corner of her vision, followed by two shapely legs covered in dark leather, and a coat that almost touched the floor.

"Mother," the Dark Lord growled, his expression fierce as he eyed Hunter, both of them battling to overpower the other with their talents. "This does not concern you."

"Of course it concerns me," the woman snapped, and Melissa tore her gaze away from the men to briefly eye the newcomer. Her dark hair hung like a curtain down her back, threaded with streaks of gray. She was an older woman, slim and still attractive. She eyed the two men with something that bordered on exasperation. "It concerns me when my son tries to kill his brother."

Both Hunter and the Dark Lord blinked, and Melissa's eyebrows rose as Hunter twisted to peer over his shoulder. The light in his hands flickered out, and his face paled in shock.

"Mother?"

Chapter 17

Hunter shook his head. No. It couldn't be.

The woman who approached smiled, her brown eyes sad. "Hello, Hunter."

He blinked, and his thoughts stuttered to a halt. She—What—? How—?

"No." He backed away from the hand she lifted toward him, and he saw the hurt that flickered briefly across those eyes, so similar to his own. "No, it can't be. You're dead." The face that stared at him was exactly as he remembered it; lines around the corners of her eyes and mouth that deepened with her smiles, the soft skin of her rounded cheeks that pinkened like a cherub with her laughter, the softness of her lips for when she'd kiss him and his brother good-night…

No. This could. Not. Be.

"My brother?" The Dark Lord extinguished his black cloud, and turned from Hunter to his mother, and back again. Hunter could see the incomprehension in the man's crystal blue eyes. At least the albino was just as surprised by this as he was.

"Griffin, this is your older half brother, Hunter," the woman said softly. She eyed both of the men for a moment. "Hunter. You have a new baby brother."

Hunter shook his head. "I don't want a baby brother," he exclaimed, and his mother gave him a tender smile tinged with humor.

"That's what you said when I brought Ryder home to you," she told him softly.

"Clear the hall," Griffin called, and one dark-haired vamp standing closer than the others nodded, then started guiding all of the gathered Darkken out of the hall.

Hunter stepped back as his mother reached for him, holding his hand up in warning.

"No. You *died*," he said fiercely. "I went to your funeral, damn it. I even wore a tie." It was such a trivial detail, but he'd always fought against the conservative, against anything expected of him—except for the day they'd entombed his mother. He would have done anything, worn anything, said anything, promised anything, to have his mother back.

She'd died, and he and his brother had mourned. He shook his head. This just didn't make sense. "Was this all a lie?" His shoulders sagged at the thought. She'd drowned when the car she'd been driving plummeted over a cliff and into a lake. The rescue crews were fast on the scene, but he was told she'd been dead when she'd been pulled from the water. "Whose coffin did I cry over?"

Amelie tilted her head, her brown eyes stared at him solemnly. "Oh, I died, Hunter. That you can believe."

The muscles in Hunter's jaw clenched, and he lifted his hand to point from her head to her booted toes. "And yet, here you are. Riddle me that, Mother Dear."

"My lover saved me," Amelie admitted, and for a moment he saw his mother's gaze flicker away. Then when she looked at him, her eyes glowed red, and her incisors lengthened. He heard Melissa's gasp behind him but all he could do was stare at the woman who had once tucked him into bed and sung lullabies to him. The woman who was now a vampire. He shook his head, trying to make sense of it all. Then her words registered.

"Your lover?" Oh. My. God. That was news. It was the first he'd heard of his mother's infidelity, and he wouldn't have believed it if the detail had come from anyone else. But here he was, staring at what should have been a ghost. He ran his hand through his hair and turned away, meeting Melissa's stunned gaze for a moment. She looked confused, confounded. Well, welcome to his hell. She stepped closer to him, and as he turned to face his mother again, he felt her hand slide into his. He almost pushed her away. He wasn't the type to lean on anyone, to depend on anyone. He didn't need anyone. His father had taught him that. Yet his fingers curled around Melissa's, and he drew her a little closer to him.

"Explain," he gritted. He lifted his chin. He was trying to hang on to his sanity, his calm, when all he wanted to do was release his light and screw the consequences.

"Yes, Mom, please do," the Dark Lord urged softly as he folded his arms. No, what had she called him? Griffin? He eyed his so-called brother briefly. His brother. Seriously? Admittedly, the guy looked about as comfortable with the connection as he felt.

Amelie walked over and rested her hand on the Dar—Griffin's shoulder. Hunter refused to call his brother by some fancy title. "I loved your father, Griff. Make no mistake." She turned to face Hunter, grasping her other son's hand. "I loved your father, too, Hunter, but I had no idea what he was really like until after the wedding."

She lifted her chin. "He was quite cruel," she stated calmly, and Hunter swallowed. He didn't want to hear this. He knew his father could be a dick. Present situation, case in point. Knew he was a difficult man to live with, to please...but hearing the intimate details of his parents' marriage was like sitting next to a banshee. Painful to the ears. Melissa's thumb caressed the top of his knuckles, and he realized he was squeezing her hand tightly. He tried to relax his grip.

"Arthur was lovely at first. The perfect gentleman." Amelie smiled dryly. "And then, on our wedding night, I discovered—"

"Mom, no, please." Hunter held up his hand. He did not want to hear about their bedroom antics.

"I discovered the real reason your father married me was for my money," Amelie finished in exasperation. "He made no secret how he viewed marrying the Galen girl and accessing her wealth was his biggest victory, so far." Amelie shrugged. "He had such grand plans for building up a medical empire that would have all the shadow breeds relying on him... He loved manipulating people, me included." She tilted her head, and Hunter watched the dark hair tumble over her shoulder, and the memory of her sitting at a dressing table, brushing the silken strands repeatedly, flared in his mind. He blinked and looked away. He wasn't going to get sucked into some nostalgic fog that blurred the reality of what he was now facing. His mother had left. *By choice.*

"Your father treated me like a piece of art, to be trotted out to impress when needed, and to be ignored for the rest of the time. If I was lucky," she added, her lips twisting. "And if I wasn't—well, let's just say your father had a unique way of using light."

Hunter shuddered. He could only imagine, and damn it, he didn't want to, because then he'd have to feel sympathy for his mother. He wouldn't be able to give in to the anger that fluttered inside him.

"You cheated on him." He said it as a statement. There was no accusation. His father was a jerk. He knew that. Accepted that. His mother and father were not a bonded pair.

Amelie smiled. "I fell in love," she corrected. "Besides, I was not the first to sleep outside the marriage bed."

Hunter grimaced. "Please. Don't." He did not want to hear or think about his parents' sex life—or lack thereof. He was already going to need significant therapy after all of this. He drew his shoulders back. "So you found love and left your sons." He nodded. That pretty much summed it up.

Her eyes narrowed. "I *died*, Hunter. The car I was driving went over a cliff, and I drowned. I did not leave you willingly."

Hunter smiled grimly. "And yet, you didn't come back. All this time, you've been living down here, and we've been living up there." He gestured to the ceiling. "And you never once thought to come for your boys." He glared at the albino. "But you stayed for him."

He wanted to feel hatred for the man who had stolen his mother, but more than anything, the anger he felt didn't even begin to compete with the hurt. "Was I so bad, Mother?" He whispered the words, and Amelie flinched in horror.

"No," she breathed, shaking her head as she stepped

toward him. Again, he retreated. He didn't want her touch, didn't want to crumble. His mother clasped her hands together, almost in a symbol of prayer. "Oh, Hunter, no." She swallowed. "The night I died, it—it wasn't an accident," she whispered.

Hunter's brow pulled into a deep V. "You did it on purpose?" Oh, hell, that was even worse.

"No!" Amelie's lips tightened in exasperation. "No, I was murdered. My car's brake lines were cut. I had no brakes as I went around that curve." Her clasped hands shook and her eyes darkened as though focusing on a chilling memory. She looked over at Griffin, and smiled. "I was pregnant, and your father found out, knew the baby wasn't his. If Griffin's father hadn't found us, both of us would have stayed dead." She turned and met Hunter's gaze evenly. "Just as your father planned."

Hunter shook his head in disbelief. His father was a bastard, and yes, a man capable of murder, but to kill the mother of his children…? He swallowed, then dipped his head. Well, yeah. He could see that happening, sadly. "My father seems to be capable of the worst acts," he commented, looking briefly at Melissa. Her green eyes were dark with shock.

"But when you—" He gestured to his mother, asking, "what, undied? Shifted?" He shook his head. That didn't sound right. He'd treated vampires for all sorts of ills, and didn't have any issues with them—or any of the other shadow breeds, really. He understood the mechanics of becoming a vampire. You needed to be fed a vampire's blood by the next full moon after your death, and then had to feed by the full moon after that to complete the process. He had no name for the procedure, though.

"Metamorphosed," his mother supplied.

He inclined his head. "Metamorphosed." Of course.

Like a caterpillar becoming a butterfly. "When you metamorphosed, why didn't you come back for us? You probably could have kicked the old man's ass…"

Amelie smiled, but this time there was no denying the sadness and guilt in her gaze. "I tried. By the time I felt strong enough to face him, everything was legalized. I was dead. My will was read, my inheritance disbursed. It would have been terribly inconvenient for your father if I'd approached Reform Court for a reclassification." She took a deep, shaky breath. "And he threatened to kill you and your brother if I came forward. I had two choices. I could try to claim you, try to rescue you, and you would die, or I could live below, with Griffin's father, and all of us could live in peace."

Hunter laughed, the sound harsh and tight in his throat as he remembered his childhood, about the continuous challenges his father had set for him and his younger brother, the constant attempts to gain his father's approval and never quite winning it, and the woman his father had brainwashed in a twisted attempt to have his sons compete against each other to prove each other's mettle.

"We didn't live in peace."

Amelie's lips rubbed inward, and she nodded. She would have known what she'd left behind, what she'd left her sons to face on their own. He wondered what life would have been like, living with his mother instead of his father. Well, it was no use wishing for what couldn't be—that ship had sailed long ago. He didn't want to think about it, didn't want to deal with it.

Didn't want to face the fact his mother hadn't died. She'd left.

Hunter faced the big, muscled albino. He already had a brother, damn it, and even that relationship was strained. This brother had powers like he'd never seen, but he suspected it was a result of the vampirism of the man's sire warping the light force of his mother. Fine, he was curious—purely from a medical line of inquiry, he told himself. He'd survived this long without his mother, without the brother he didn't know he had. He could plod along just fine without them.

"Now what?" he asked Griffin. Let him go, kill him for his crime—at this point in time, he really didn't care. He was done. "Are you going to let us go, or punish me for defending myself?"

Griffin shrugged. "Beats me. I've never had to kill a brother before." The albino folded his arms, his gaze assessing.

"And you're not going to kill one now," Amelie snapped. "You know the circumstances. Orion should have brought them to you, not tried to kill them on sight."

"He was defending the perimeter," Griffin growled. "And now we have a psychotic light warrior prepared to kill everyone he comes in contact with until he gets his son."

Amelie faced her white-haired son, and Hunter could see the fury in her gaze. "That psychotic light warrior killed your mother," she rasped. "What do you think he'll do to your brother?"

"Stop calling him that," Griffin snapped. "Just moments ago he was trying to kill me, him and his mate."

"You started it," Hunter called, and his younger brother rolled his eyes.

"You deserved it," Griffin retorted.

"Oh, bite me," Hunter returned.

"With pleasure," Griffin said, his pale blue eyes darkening to a fiery purple, his teeth lengthening.

"Enough!" Amelie held up both her hands, eyes flashing. "For heaven's sake, you're acting like children." She turned to Griffin. "Instead of focusing on your brother, focus on the real threat to your people, and you," she said as she turned to face Hunter. "You will both be our guests—"

"Mother," Griffin began, and Amelie shot him a dark look.

"Our guests," Amelie repeated strongly. "Show them to a guest room, Griffin, so that they can rest. From what I understand, they've been on the run for some time."

Hunter smirked as his brother rolled his eyes, the muscles in his jaw clenching as he beckoned over one of his men.

"Go to the light warrior," Griffin instructed him. "Tell him I'm prepared to parlay, but if he kills any of the Darkken, I'll hunt him down."

The Darkken nodded, then strode from the room. Griffin glanced over at Hunter, not bothering to conceal his irritation, then lifted his chin in a jerky motion, indicating they follow him.

Hunter pulled Melissa along behind him. There was no way he'd leave her side while they were "guests" of the Darkken. His brother may have them under some sort of control—something he didn't quite understand—but he didn't trust them. Nothing personal, he didn't trust anyone, really.

He glanced over his shoulder at the red-haired witch behind him. Except for one, maybe.

Melissa warily stepped past Griffin into the room he'd assigned them. She knew he had some vision limitations, but the man had an uncanny awareness, and a dark side that was more than just a thirst for blood. A shadow breed of a new dimension.

"What *is* this place?" Hunter asked, and Melissa looked away from the albino to take in the room. She gaped.

There was a large fireplace, with a roaring fire that provided the only illumination in the room. Still, the firelight was enough to see the four-poster bed butted up against one wall, with heavy golden drapes hanging from its canopy. A tapestry covered a large portion of one wall, and there was a leather settee and matching armchair facing the large fireplace, with a magnificent Persian rug covering most of the floor. A small lamp table sat between the chairs, and it bore a tray of bread, cheese and what looked like wine. A half-opened door revealed a private, marble bathroom. Melissa turned slowly.

It was— Wow.

Griffin smirked. "Apparently this belonged to some eccentric actor, back in the time before The Troubles. He built this mansion based on some castle in Old Scotland." He glanced up at the ceiling. "I hear there are mansions just as ostentatious above." A pale eyebrow rose as he looked over at Hunter for confirmation.

Hunter stepped over to the fireplace, holding his hands out. "Have you ever been? Above, I mean?"

Griffin's expression grew somber, and he nodded. "Once. Didn't like it."

Melissa looked at the albino with curiosity. He sounded so serious, almost sad. Griffin straightened. "Anyway. Rest. I'll have someone drop off some clothes for you to change into after you've slept. See you in the morning." He backed out of the room before they could say anything, slamming the door shut and sliding the lock home.

Melissa frowned. "So much for being a guest," she said dryly. She turned, and her eyebrows rose.

Hunter stood in front of the fire, and the flames seemed to arc and dance toward his fingertips, almost as though he was sucking in the energy through his pores.

He flexed his fingers, then turned to her. "Are you okay?" he asked her quietly. Her eyes widened, just a little. After everything that had happened in the hall, he was asking her if *she* was all right?

"I'm fine, Hunter," she told him. Admittedly, being surrounded and "hosted" by vampires was not on her bucket list, but she was living, she was breathing, and if she just kept reminding herself of that, she wouldn't lose it.

He frowned. "We're in the home of the Darkken, and I know how you feel about us shadow breeds."

She gave him a half smile. He had no idea how she felt about the shadow breeds. Not many did. She also noted how he classed himself as a shadow breed, yet she'd seemed to have forgotten that fact, or at least subconsciously decided to ignore it. She professed to hate the shadow breeds, but she feared them, too, and it was that fear that had almost frozen her when the Darkken guardian had attacked.

She was still trying to stop the memories from surfacing, but even now, she had to ruthlessly block out the echoes of her screams from her mind, of Theo's agonized cries…of what came next.

"I'm fine," she said, her voice stronger. She wasn't going to cave in to the panic. She wasn't going to surrender, not to any shadow breed. She eyed the dark-haired man as he turned to stare back down at the fire. She'd surrendered a lot to this particular shadow breed. More than he'd ever know.

He was the first man she'd lain with since Theo. She subsided into the armchair facing the fire, letting its warmth slowly chase off the chill of her anxiety, her fear. For the first time since she'd stormed off from him in the tunnel, she let herself face that fact. She'd made love with Hunter. The warmth blooming in her cheeks couldn't be fully attributed to the fire. Even now, those heated, whispery memories were swamping the other scenes that were trying to get airplay in her mind.

She'd made love with a light warrior. A shadow breed. The kind of guy she'd sworn to annihilate, not…love. She should feel guilty. She'd betrayed Theo's memory in the worst possible way. Not only had she lain with another, he was one of *them*.

And yet, the guilt was…missing. Maybe she was still in shock. Maybe, on some level, her mind was already running through survival scenarios. One thing it wasn't doing was wallowing in guilt, or shame. What she and Hunter had shared in that tunnel—well, it wasn't shameful. It had been beautiful. She was trying to grapple with the softer feelings that came along with that coupling.

And then the big jerk had reacted as though he was the one to experience regret. That gave Hunter a whole level of conscience she wasn't prepared to recognize. He'd tried to kill her, for crying out loud. And she'd made love to him? It was a habit she really needed to break. How could she forget a minor detail like attempted homicide?

And yet, the man who'd tried to kill her had saved her life more than once since. He'd had plenty of opportunity to leave, but instead he'd stayed. He'd sacrificed his own freedom for her survival. And he'd made love to her with a passion and care she'd never experienced before—and that she wanted to experience again. She swallowed. Now they were held hostage by the Darkken, and Hunter's father was going on a homicidal rampage to find them. She shouldn't be thinking about sex. No, not sex. Making love.

Oh, and Hunter had been reunited with his undead mother. She shouldn't forget that little gem. She lifted her gaze from the flames to Hunter. The firelight flickered, a play of light and shadow across his handsome features.

He still didn't wear a shirt. Not that she was complaining. Yet, right now, gazing at his profile, she could see the tightness around his lips, the tension in his jaw. She didn't quite understand how, but she could sense his shock, his…hurt. He didn't want to talk about it, though, she could tell.

Well, you didn't always get what you want, because otherwise they'd be trying out that massive bed.

"So, you have a mother, after all…" she commented. "I always thought you were the spawn of the devil, but it looks like you entered the world in the customary fashion."

Hunter blinked, his lips parted, and the look he gave her was a charming cross between grumpy and humorous. His lips curled in a wry smile. "Yes, it appears my dearly departed mother isn't so departed, after all." His smile dropped, and he returned his gaze to the fire.

Melissa stretched her arms toward the fire, letting the warmth curl around her fingers. She didn't play with the flames, though, not like Hunter did. This fire had to be recharging his batteries. Which meant they didn't need to make love again, not for that reason, anyway. Melissa frowned as she glanced down at her fingers.

She cleared her throat. "You know," she began softly, "even though she, uh, gave you guys some distance, it seems she loves you." She had seen the woman's pain, her sorrow and sadness, and her very real shame at leaving her family behind. It had been fascinating. Probably because she'd never seen anything like that from her own mother.

Hunter drew back from the fire to collapse on the settee. "She didn't 'give us distance,' Red. She left us."

"She died."

"And then she came back, but only for her white boy," Hunter pointed out.

"She loves you."

"She loves the white boy more."

"Stop calling him that, he's your brother."

"I don't want another brother. I have enough problems with the one I've got already."

Melissa sighed. "I've got a brother, and I'd be damned lucky if I had another sibling like him."

"Well, there's the difference. You and your sibling actually like each other."

"You don't like your brother?" Melissa leaned back into the depths of the armchair and raised an eyebrow at the handsome man lounging across from her. "You set fire to my apothecary for your brother. You tried to kill me for your brother. Don't try to tell me you don't have some feelings for your brother."

Hunter's mouth turned down at the corners. "It's complicated."

"Oh, seeing your family in action—a father who killed his wife, and tried to kill you and your brother, and who is now killing innocents in the underground until he can kill us, a mother who didn't stay dead, and a half brother you never knew existed and who seems to be an equal match for your powers—I'm beginning to think complicated comes with the territory when it comes to you."

He shot her an exasperated look. "It's not the kind of tale you tell by the fire," he said, casually gesturing to the fireplace, the rug and the room in general. The movement caused the muscles of his arm to flex, and his pectoral muscle bunched. She eyed his nipple for a moment, then lifted her gaze to meet his. She wanted to feel his body against hers again. She wanted to feel all those wonderful sensations he'd given her back in the tunnel, but more than that, she wanted to ease the pain she sensed in him, soothe all the anger, the hurt.

"Don't worry, I don't believe in fairy tales. Besides, what else are we going to do, trapped in this room until your brother figures out what to do with us?" She tilted her head to gaze at him in inquiry.

"Half brother," Hunter corrected.

She inclined her head, accepting his qualification. "Half brother."

Hunter sighed, then glanced around the room. She could think of something else to do than talk, and she knew the same thought had occurred to him when Hunter's gaze flicked from the bed, then back to her. His gaze darkened with arousal.

Then he blinked, composing his features as he sat up on the settee and leaned over to grab the bottle of wine and the two goblets.

"Well, if I'm going to tell this miserable tale, we're both going to need to get drunk."

Chapter 18

"So, your father compelled this woman to be the perfect woman for you, and the perfect woman for your brother, just to see who could win her over?" Melissa had curled up on the armchair, her legs tucked under her, her elbow on the armrest as she cupped her chin. He'd just poured her third glass of wine, and Hunter nodded as he emptied the bottle into his own goblet.

"Yep. Sick, huh? He said it was to give us purpose." Hunter shook his head. *Purpose.* He had been quite happy, working in the clinic. Sure, he may have planted subliminal suggestions in some patients that had ended up benefiting him, but he'd never done anything that had been detrimental to his patients, and that was a record he was proud of. Healing people may not have had all the glory and fanfare his father was hoping for, but it was a good vocation. "My work, healing people, that was purpose enough for me," he admitted quietly.

He'd never said it aloud, not to anyone. It made him sound like some sort of benevolent tool, and he knew he wasn't benevolent. This work was entirely selfish. It made him feel good.

Melissa traced the rim of her goblet. "I overheard your conversation with your brother," she admitted. "The one you had with your father."

Hunter's eyebrows rose. "So you saw our dysfunction firsthand." Wonderful. His mate had seen how sick and twisted he and his family truly were. He eyed the bond between them. It still flourished, still weaved and rose, like a beautiful collection of ribbons. His mother had left him, and everyone seemed to think the maternal bond was the strongest. If his own mother couldn't stick around, why would Melissa? He wasn't being maudlin, just realistic.

"How did she die?" Melissa asked quietly.

"My mother?"

"No, the woman you loved."

There was so much weight in that sentence. He had loved Debbie. He wasn't a monk, he'd had girlfriends, and he'd made sure he was careful with how much he consumed of them in their relationship, but Debbie... Debbie had been different. Special.

"My father threw her off an upstairs balcony."

Melissa coughed on the wine she was sipping. When she'd caught her breath, she stared at him with a deep sympathy that darkened her green eyes. "Oh, Hunter."

He shrugged. "I didn't know it, at the time. I thought, with this fierce contest between my brother and me, that Ryder had done it."

"Oh, that makes it much easier to process," Melissa muttered as she shifted in her seat.

His lips curled briefly, but his memories were depressing enough to rob him of his humor. "She chose him," he said quietly.

There was silence in the room, and he turned his head to gaze at the fireplace. The fire was dying. He rose, placing his cup on the tray, and crossed over to the pile of cut logs neatly stacked against the wall next to the fireplace. He picked a good, thick piece of wood and gently placed it on the embers. It came naturally, the little breath of light force that urged the flames to stir once again.

"She was compelled by your father. You have no idea what she really felt."

Hunter shrugged. "She came to me, the morning before she died. Told me she'd made the biggest mistake, and that she should have chosen me over Ryder." He sat down again. "I should have taken her away, then and there." He frowned. "Debbie might still be alive today, if I had."

Melissa set her goblet down on the tray with a distinct clink. "Did you say Debbie?" she asked, and Hunter's eyes narrowed at her oh-so-casual tone.

"I did."

Melissa nodded slowly. "I thought that's what you said."

She slid her legs down to the floor and rose to walk over toward the fire, her hands out as though trying to warm herself. Hunter noticed her hands were trembling, and then she quickly clasped them together.

Realization dawned, and Hunter sagged against the backrest of the settee. "My father mentioned Debbie visited a witch, one that blocked his ability to compel her. That was you, wasn't it?" Melissa was the most well-known witch in Irondell, with a solid reputation. The bookstore witch was rumored to be the best, if he was honest. If Debbie was going to visit a witch, it would have been her. What a cruel coincidence.Melissa turned to him, her expression haunted. "I had no idea, Hunter," she said, and her breath hitched. "I had a client, Debbie Philips. She came to me because she kept having blackouts, and found herself caught between two men, and not understanding how or why."

Hunter tilted his head back to gaze up at the ceiling. Talk about six degrees of separation. Melissa had been the witch to protect Debbie from further compulsion. How damned ironic.

His father had admitted he and Debbie had been arguing upstairs at the family home, and in the ensuing struggle his father had pushed Debbie over the railing. She'd died from her injuries moments later. Because he could no longer compel her.

"So, you knew where her heart really lay," Hunter commented.

Melissa caught her bottom lip between her teeth, and shook her head. "Don't. Hunter, please, don't."

"Which one of us did she truly love?" Hunter asked, ignoring her plea. "I don't know what was real and what wasn't anymore. Was she still under compulsion when she came to tell me she'd made a mistake picking my brother over me, or was that her real instinct?"

"Hunter—"

"Tell me, Melissa," he said as he rose from the settee. "Which of us did Debbie really love?"

Melissa gazed at him, her expression miserable, and she shook her head.

"Tell me," he insisted, his voice louder.

The woman standing before him looked like she wanted to crawl into the fire itself. She rubbed her lips together for a moment, then met his gaze.

"Neither," she told him in a whisper.

She may as well have shouted it at him. "Neither." He chuckled, the sound harsh to his ears. He really was fundamentally flawed. He swore softly.

Melissa strummed her fingers against her denim-clad thigh. "She, uh—she liked you both, thought you were good guys, but whatever your father did to her, those moments she was being the perfect woman to both of you, she was being someone she wasn't. The connections she had with you and your brother were built on a lie. She told me she had to do right by both of you, and end it."

Melissa grimaced. "I'm sorry, Hunter," she whispered.

He held up a hand and shook his head. "Don't be. First my mother, then Debbie. I'm beginning to see the pattern." The women he'd loved with all his heart didn't love him in return. Or at least, not nearly as much. For some reason, he couldn't make them want to stick around.

He glanced at the mating bond stretching between Melissa and himself. It was only a matter of time before Melissa left him, too. He pasted a fake smile on his face. "I'm fine. Trust me, I'm a doctor. I know how to get through stuff like this." Only, he couldn't dreamwalk through his own mind and switch off those painful memories.

For some reason, though, he suspected Melissa's leaving would hurt him far greater than his mother and Debbie combined. He cleared his throat. "Uh, I'm tired. Think I'll turn in." He indicated the settee he was sprawled over. "I'll take this, you take the bed."

Melissa's glance flitted to the bed that easily dominated the rest of the room. "There seems to be plenty of room for both of us," she suggested softly.

He met her gaze. There was empathy, there was

sadness, but there was also invitation. God, he was so tempted. So tempted to just once lie next to a woman, be held by a woman, be loved by a woman. *This* woman.

But that would just make the mating bond stronger, and more difficult to break. And break it would. He was a shadow breed, and despite her warm sympathy and listening ear, Melissa would never see him as anything more than that, and would never allow a mated commitment. He knew he was in for a fall, big-time, when she left. He just had to make sure it was something he could survive.

He shook his head. "We both know that if I get into that bed with you, neither of us will get much sleep." Even saying that, he couldn't stop his gaze from touring over her willowy body, those long legs that felt so right wrapped around his waist, the breasts that were made to fit his hands. He swallowed. God, he wanted her, and he wanted her to want him—for more than just pity sex. "It's better this way."

Melissa looked away and nodded, then made her way over to the bed. She tossed him a pillow and the extra blanket that was draped across the end of the bed.

"Good night, then," she whispered as she kicked off her shoes and slid beneath the covers. She'd taken his rejection so calmly, but he knew otherwise. Through their shared connection he could sense her hurt, her embarrassment. He stretched out fully on the settee, punching the pillow.

The connection was on a feedback loop. At the moment, Melissa was totally oblivious to it, and he wanted to keep it that way. He didn't want her to sense it, didn't want her to be aware of it—she'd probably kill him when she found out… But for now, she was in the dark. What she didn't know couldn't hurt her. He'd get her to her brother's place, make sure she was safe from harm, safe from his psycho father, and then they'd part ways. He sighed. A light warrior mated once in a lifetime. How fate had selected a fiery, sassy witch for him, he'd never understand. A fiery, sassy witch who hated all shadow breeds. Fate had a very twisted sense of humor.

Melissa sighed from the bed behind him, and he heard the linen rustle as she rolled over. She was lying there, mere feet away from him, all warm and relaxed and voluptuous, and he was sleeping on a settee that was about half a body-length too short, all because he was trying to be noble and not lock her into a bond she couldn't, wouldn't accept.

See, this was why he'd never tried to be noble before. Noble sucked.

Melissa woke in the darkness, the rocks beneath her digging into the bare skin of her shoulders above the back of her gown. She reached instinctively for Theo, and he grasped her hand.

"Stay calm," he whispered.

"Are they coming for us?" she whispered, trying to keep the terror out of her voice. The stiff fabric of her ball gown rustled as she sat up cautiously.

"I'm not sure," Theo said as he, too, sat up. "But don't worry, Mel. We'll get through this."

"I don't think I can go through it again," Melissa whispered, ashamed to admit her fear, her lack of courage. She swallowed. It had hurt so much...she hadn't been able to do anything to stop them, there had been too many of them.

Where was her mother? Or Dave? Surely they should have been rescued by now. She and Theo had been snatched as they'd left the Reform ball—what, nearly two nights ago? She shivered, and Theo took his jacket off and slung it around her bare shoulders.

"We're going to get through this," Theo whispered, staring straight into her eyes. She nodded. "You and me, Mel, we're strong together. We can han—"

"Oh, it's so sweet, listening to these two lovebirds," a feminine voice purred in a soft, Baltic accent, and the cellar door creaked as it opened.

"Yeah, so sweet, I think I might throw up," a masculine voice responded, the accent slightly stronger, harsher. Melissa flinched as the two vampires descended into the root cellar. She knew them. Had encountered them several times at the Reform balls and other Prime families' events. Natalia and George Petrovski. Melissa gazed past them. She'd counted seven vampires since their capture. Most were of the Saltwash colony, just like the Petrovskis, but two were from the Iron Peak colony, and she didn't know their names. Two colonies separated by hundreds of miles, yet united in their torture of her and Theo. She didn't know where they were being held. She'd just glimpsed a decrepit farmhouse in the darkness when she and Theo had been taken from the car and forced to enter the root cellar.

George Petrovski lifted a lantern, and beckoned to them. "Come, come closer."

Theo edged between her and the vamps. Melissa swallowed as the other five vamps climbed down the rough steps into the root cellar. No, not again. They'd fed on her and Theo until they'd both passed out, then had fed them vamp blood to heal their bite wounds so they could start all over again.

"Stay back," Theo warned, holding his hand up.

"Or what?" Natalia asked, then laughed, her eyes flashing red as she stepped closer. "You still have vamp

blood in your system. Your magic is useless until your enzymes break down the V-juice."

"And then we'll just feed you some more, and then some more, and then..." one of the Petrovski cousins interjected from behind, then chuckled. *"Well, you get my drift."*

Goose bumps rose on Melissa's arms as she stared at the advancing vampires. Two of them held lanterns that they hung up on hooks from the low ceiling. They were right. Both she and Theo were powerless against the vamps. She glanced wildly about the root cellar. The only way in or out of their prison was up the flight of rickety stairs to the double doors that hung open. They'd have to get past the vampires first, though.

Melissa slowly clutched hold of her skirts. The fabric was stiff from the dried blood—so much blood, but she was ready to run when Theo gave the signal.

"Why are you doing this?" Melissa asked, gazing at Natalia. She had no quarrel with this woman—at least, not until now. But these vamps had broken the sanctity of a Reform ball. *"My mother will—"*

"Your mother will negotiate for your release," George interrupted. *"Everybody knows Eleanor Carter will work a situation to her advantage."* He shrugged. *"Sure, we'll get a slap on the wrist, something that will make it look like we're not getting away with..."* He smiled, his incisors lengthening, as he finished, *"...what we're getting away with."*

Theo kicked the lantern out of George's hand, and Melissa sprang at Natalia, hands fisted as she punched the vampire in the jaw. She kept swinging until her arms were caught, and she screamed as fangs sank into her neck, and more fangs sank into her wrists. Her pulse pounded in her ears as she tried to struggle, tried to *thrash against the vampires holding her. With every beat of her heart, though, she could feel herself weaken, feel the chill creep into her limbs, feel the blood draining from her.*

"Enough," Natalia shouted. "We want her conscious."

Hands dug into her hair, and she winced as her head was roughly turned so she could see Theo.

She was held by Natalia and two of her cousins, while Theo was held down on the ground by the other four vamps. He cried out in agony as they ripped at his flesh with their teeth. Melissa screamed, trying to go to him, to help him, but the vamps held her back. He glanced at her, his complexion sickly white, his lips gray, his blood a dark crimson against his white dress shirt. George looked up, grinning when he saw he had Melissa's horrified attention.

"Hold," the vamp told the others feeding on her fiancé, and the other vamps reluctantly stopped, their eyes flashing red in the dimly lit room. They hauled Theo up to his knees, supporting him when he would have collapsed. Theo tried to talk, but only a garbled groan emerged. George smiled as he peered over Theo's bloodied shoulder.

"We don't think this witch is the right match for you," George said, grinning.

Melissa shook her head. "No, please don't." She could feel warm liquid streaming down her cheeks, her neck, confused between tears and blood. "Leave him alone."

"Should have thought of that before you accepted his ring," Natalia crooned in her ear. "We don't like the Sassafras Coven. Nobody likes the Sassafras Coven. Hawthorns are much better."

Melissa's jaw clenched. The Sassafras Coven was

good enough for Theo, it would be good enough for her when she married him and left White Oak. There was no way she'd go anywhere near the Hawthorns after this.

"Let her go," Theo croaked. "Please, take me, but let her go." *He looked so broken, yet he'd never seemed braver to her, there on his knees, his blood draining from him as he pleaded for her life.*

"Theo," *Melissa cried, again trying to reach him, again being held back. His blue eyes met hers, and she could see the glassy stare, the weakness creeping over him as his wounds continued to bleed.*

"But we're not cruel," *George whispered.* "We'll put him out of his misery." *He reached for Theo's head, and twisted his neck. Melissa flinched at the audible snap and screamed as the man she loved fell to the floor, dead. If it wasn't for the vampires holding her up, she would have collapsed.*

"Tut-tut," *Natalia tsked.* "Now look what you've done. You'll have to fix that."

George nodded, then bit at his own wrist, tearing at the skin. He knelt down to Theo's corpse, and placed his wound against Theo's lips.

Melissa's eyes widened, and she shook her head. "No. You can't."

George stood, the wound on his wrist healing so quickly he could pull his shirtsleeve back down without staining it with blood. "I just did."

"But—oh, God, what have you done?" *Melissa yelled.* "You monsters."

Theo's body flinched, his back arching as the vampire blood worked its way through his system.

"Have you heard of the old story, Romeo and Juliet?" *Natalia inquired politely.* "This is our version of it."

Theo's eyelids opened, and his blue eyes stared

blankly up at the ceiling for a moment, then he coughed, dragging in deep, ragged breaths.

Melissa shook her head in denial. Oh, please, no, no, no.

"Did you know, the metamorphosis kicks in quicker, the sooner after death you receive our blood?"

She could hear various cracks, and she shuddered when she realized Theo's vertebrae were slipping back into place. Theo sat up, rubbing his neck, and frowned.

"What the hell?"

"It takes a few minutes for the memory to kick in," George explained to Melissa in a conversational tone.

Theo glanced at George, then his eyes widened. "Why, you bastard!"

He launched himself at George, but the vamp tossed him off easily. "Easy, buck. You'll need a feed before you can fight a vamp."

"And fortunately, we have one here for you," Natalia said.

Theo stared at Melissa and shook his head in horror. "No." He rose to his feet, glancing around at the gathered vamps. Melissa trembled as she watched her fiancé's wounds slowly close, until not so much as a scar remained to tell the sordid story of his death.

"Yes," George said, grabbing on to Theo's shoulders and forcing him to face Melissa. The vamp tilted his head at his sister. "What say we make this interesting? Our new baby should learn to hunt, yes?"

Natalia chuckled. "You are so twisted, brother, I love it." She ran her finger along Melissa's neck, and Melissa tried to pull away, then watched in horror as the bitch vamp walked over to Theo.

"You need to feed," she told him, and Theo shook his head, gritting his teeth.

"*No.*"

"*You won't be able to help it,*" Natalia told him, drawing her finger along his bottom lip.

Theo's nostrils flared as he caught the scent of her blood, and Melissa's horror gave way to true fear as her fiancé's pupils darkened to crimson.

"*Let her go, boys. Let's give her a sporting start,*" George called, and the vamps who still clutched Melissa shoved her toward the stairs leading up from the root cellar.

"*Theo,*" she cried, hoping she could reach him, hoping she could stop this.

"*For God's sake, Melissa, run,*" Theo called to her, and she glanced over her shoulder to see that the vamps were trying to hold him back. From her. His eyes were bloodred, and he cried in pain as his incisors lengthened, his nostrils flaring as he stared up at her. He looked—blood-crazed.

Melissa gathered her skirts and ran up the stairs, sobbing, as she burst out into the night. One shoe fell off her foot, and she stumbled in the dark. She kicked the other shoe off, bundling her skirts in her fists, and pelted across the yard. She winced, gasping as sharp rocks in the dirt poked her feet, but she kept running.

She didn't see it in the darkness, didn't know the fence was there until she ran into it, bruising her chest. She wheezed in pain, her fingers reaching out to clasp the wooden railing. Oh, hell. She started to run alongside it, her fingers trailing along the wood. Her skirts were too full to squeeze through the slats. Hopefully she'd find a gate or something that would give her an avenue of escape.

"*Run, Melissa,*" Theo yelled behind her, and Melissa

picked up her skirts and ran. Moonlight gleamed on a metallic surface up ahead. A gate. An open gate.

Her breaths coming in harsh pants, she bolted along the fence line, hearing with every beat of her heart the pounding of her fiancé's footsteps behind her. She was almost at the gate when something hard and heavy thudded against her, and they crashed through the fence, timber snapping with the force of the hit.

Melissa hit the ground with a thud and wheezed, trying to catch her breath. Theo straddled her legs.

"Theo, fight this," she begged him. He gazed down at her, his expression tortured, his eyes red with bloodlust.

"I'm trying," he moaned as he dodged her fist.

"Try harder," she rasped, struggling beneath him.

"You're bleeding," he gasped, and he shuddered as he inhaled. Melissa stretched out her hands, looking for something, anything to slow him down. Her fingers found a piece of the fence, and then Theo's head whipped down to look at her. She trembled. His skin was drawn tight over his cheekbones, his eyes were red and glazed, and his mouth—the mouth she knew so well now belonged to a man no longer her fiancé.

He snarled, his teeth glistening in the moonlight as he dipped his head down to her neck. She screamed as fangs sank into the tender skin, and panic, anger and adrenaline flooded her as she pushed hard, trying to shove him away.

His body flinched, and he slowly raised his head, her blood dripping from his fangs, a stunned expression on his face. He rose above her, and she looked at him with confusion, until her eyes swept down and she saw the shard of wood she'd thrust into his chest. Her eyes widened in horror as she realized what she'd done.

Theo's hands shook as he clutched the stake in his

heart, his complexion graying as death crept over him, and he slumped over to the side. The bloodlust leeched out of his eyes, returning them to the blue she knew so well, until the eyes staring back at her were once more those of the man she loved, and not the crazed feral creature who'd attacked her.

"I'm sorry, I'm so sorry," she whispered over and over as she stroked his cheek and patted his chest so ineffectually. "I'm so, so sorry," she sobbed softly as her heart broke with remorse, and with guilt.

His lips curled as the gray crept up his neck. "Thank you," he breathed as the gray stole over him, stealing his dying breath.

Melissa squeezed her eyes shut, blocking out the sightless eyes as she felt the coolness creep into the body beside her. What have I done? *She sobbed quietly, trying to deny what she'd done, what had happened. It wasn't until she felt the ground dampening beneath her with her dead fiancé's blood that reality intruded, and she tilted her head back, letting out a heartrending wail of agony to the peaceful, moonlit sky above.*

"Red, Red, oh, God, Melissa, wake up, honey," a masculine voice intruded on her grief, and her eyes snapped open. She stared up at a familiar face, a face that didn't belong to the man she'd killed, but to the man she now loved.

Hunter.

Chapter 19

Hunter swept Melissa into his arms, rocking her as he pulled her out of the nightmare. His heart pounding in his chest, he swallowed as he held her tight, whispering nonsense into the hair that brushed his nose.

Hell. He squeezed her gently, rubbing his hand down her back in soothing circles. "It's okay, Red. You're okay." That dream had scared the crap out of him.

She trembled in his arms, and he heard her gulp. He rose from the bed and hurried into the bathroom, throwing a pale orb of light so he could find a glass and run her some water. He hurried back to the bed, holding the glass out to her, and she accepted it with trembling fingers. He watched closely as she drank the water, then took the glass from her when she was finished. He leaned over and placed it on the ornately carved bedside table, then gathered her in his arms again.

"I'm so sorry that happened to you," he commented

as he rubbed her arms. That had been one hell of a nightmare. He closed his eyes. He could still feel her terror, her sorrow…her guilt. He wished he'd been there for her, wished he could have helped her—and her fiancé. It was a horrific experience to endure, for the both of them. Even if the guy was his mate's love.

"You saw," she whispered, tucking her head against his chest.

"I saw," he admitted. "Not intentionally, though. We seem to be sharing dreams." He shifted, pulling her into the space between his thighs so she could lean against him, his heart thudding against her back. "I'm glad, though. That's one dream you shouldn't have to walk through alone."

She took a deep, shuddering breath. "I think being around the Darkken triggered it."

He nodded. He could see why being surrounded and held captive by vampires could remind her of a previous traumatic vampire experience.

"Lance went and tracked each one of them down," she said into the darkness. "They won't ever do that to another person."

Hunter had a new appreciation for the big lug.

"Theo helped me build the apothecary," she whispered, and he closed his eyes. "It was our vision. We were going to marry, and develop the apothecary so that folks could come and get the help they needed from the witches." She sniffed.

He gently bumped his head against the massive carved headboard. And he was responsible now for it going up in smoke not once, but twice.

He was silent for a while, then dipped his head to kiss her temple. "I get it now," he whispered.

"Get what?"

"Why you don't like us shadow breeds." She'd lost her lover twice. She'd lost her business. She'd lost the dream she'd worked so hard to achieve. The shadow breeds had taken pretty much everything from her.

"You keep saying that," she whispered into the dim room, and he frowned.

"What?"

"Us shadow breeds." She rubbed his arms, and he held her closer. "I—I haven't really thought of you as one of 'them' for a while now."

He arched an eyebrow. "How have you been thinking of me, then?" Naked, he hoped. Sweaty. He'd settle for naked and sweaty. In each other's arms would be better. He held his breath, waiting for her answer.

She shrugged, the lightest lift of her shoulders. "Just Hunter. I think of you as Hunter."

He stared at the tapestry on the opposite wall. Hunter. Just Hunter. Not pyro jerk, or any other name she'd called him since he'd woken up in her cell. Hunter. Not Light Warrior Hunter, not Shadow Breed Hunter, not Tried-To-Kill-Me Hunter. Just…Hunter.

He swallowed. Cleared his throat. "I owe you an apology," he murmured, and she turned to look at him. Her face was pale in the light cast by the fire, her eyes glittery green from her tears.

"What for?" she asked softly.

Well, he was building quite the list with her, but he needed to set something straight, needed to make right some of his wrongs, especially with this woman. He needed to say it, and she needed to hear it. Not some half-assed, lame attempt, either.

"I'm sorry for setting fire to your apothecary," he said, his gaze meeting hers. She moved, but he caught hold of her chin. This was about as genuine as he ever got with anyone, and he didn't want her to miss it. "I'm so sorry for nearly killing you," he continued softly. "What I did—" He cast about for the right words, but there weren't any. "It was wrong. I shouldn't have done it—I'm so sorry, and I'm so relieved you didn't die," he whispered. "Because—" He hesitated, swallowed. His gaze swept over her face. "Because I was so lost, and I didn't even know it until I found you."

Her eyes rounded, and she stared up at him, surprised. "I never thought I'd hear you say it," she admitted in a whisper. "Not for real."

And that was shameful. He dropped his gaze to her throat. "It shouldn't have taken five months," he conceded. "That was not—cool. Not cool."

Her lips twisted, as though she was trying not to smile. He frowned. "What?"

"I don't know if a fire starter could ever be cool," she murmured, her teeth catching her lower lip, but the smile still curved upward. "I think you're too hot for that." Her green eyes flared with something warm, something that was an undeniable invitation. An invitation he no longer had any intention of rejecting. Screw noble. Being disgraceful was so much better.

He arched an eyebrow. "Oh, you think I'm hot, huh?"

She twisted in his arms, her gaze never leaving his. "Uh-huh."

She leaned up to kiss him, her hand cupping his cheek. "I think you are so much more that you give yourself credit for," she whispered, and right then, he knew. He was gone. Totally, irrevocably lost to this woman. She raised her head to his, and he opened his mouth to her kiss.

She kissed him gently, she kissed him hotly, she kissed him until he was breathless and panting and

wanting so much more than just a kiss. The fire flickered, then roared, its flames creeping just a little higher,
spreading a golden glow throughout the room.

He cradled her head as she straddled and leaned over
him, his tongue sliding into her mouth as he dragged
her shirt aside from her neck. The fabric halted his ex-
ploration. He was tempted to tear it from her, but tried
to slow down, to regain some control. He pulled back
for a moment, whipping her T-shirt over her head, rising
slightly off the bed to take her lips again as he undid the
clasp of her bra and slid the straps down her shoulders.

Her hands slid down his chest. He moaned against
her lips, enjoying the sensation of her touch. Sliding, caressing, her fingers glided over his torso, teasing him,
pleasing him. She rolled her hips against him, flicking
her thumbs over his nipples, and his heart thudded in
his ears, heat building between them.

His arms slid up her back, her hair brushing his skin,
sensitizing him. He moaned as her lips drifted to his
jaw, nipping and licking down his neck. He could feel
the heat between them, their hips rolling and writhing as
though dancing to an unknown beat. She was so damn
generous, so giving, offering him such intense pleasure
so easily. He flinched when her teeth grazed his nipple.
He was so damn hard, so ready for her, but he wanted
this to be about her.

He rolled them over, and she gasped at the movement, then sighed as he took her lips in a hot kiss, their
tongues curling, caressing.

He skimmed his hand down her body, his hips resting
between her legs. He loved the soft feel of her breasts,
loved it when she trembled at his touch. He trailed his
lips down her neck, and she arched against him, as
though offering herself up to him. He dipped his head

to one rosy peak, laving it with his tongue, his hand cupping her other breast, and she moaned. He switched his attention to the other breast, satisfaction at her impassioned cries giving way to his own building desire.

He nipped and licked his way down over the gentle swell of her stomach, unbuttoning her jeans and sliding them and her panties down and off her legs as he went. He kept kissing her, and she gasped when he breathed against her warm, damp core. Her eyes widened, and she looked down at him.

"Wait," she gasped, and he smiled, a wicked need ensnaring him. Her cheeks were flushed, her red hair tumbled over her shoulders and her green gaze was dark with arousal. He clasped one of her hands in reassurance.

"Trust me," he said, and winked. "I'm a doctor." He lowered his lips to kiss her, his gaze on her as her head tilted back, the cords on her throat standing out as she cried in ecstasy. He made love to her, kissing her with a desire and reverence he'd never felt before. He loved this woman, and he was determined to show her. For once, he was determined that his bad was going to be very, very good.

Warmth rolled over him, and he realized he was surrendering to the mating bond again. He could smell her, taste her, touch her, yet he could feel his breath on her, feel the wicked sensations that flooded her from her core, and the awareness flooded his own groin with desire, their combined arousal building. He could sense her tightening, sense the climb, experienced the rush of her orgasm right along with her as it swept over her, and she screamed in pleasure, bucking against him.

He rose up over her, unable to hold off any longer. He thrust inside her. Felt the cradle of her core, the heat surrounding him, and felt her. Felt his length sliding inside her, sensitizing her anew. Light flared around him, little sparks that flickered and twinkled, creating a magical skyline inside their room. He plunged, again and again, and she met his thrust with abandon, twining her legs around his waist, clenching him. The tingle started at the base of his spine, and heat crawled over him, spreading outward in an explosion of exquisite pleasure that ricocheted between them. Her pleasure, his pleasure—he wasn't sure where one ended and the other began, it just rolled on, setting off minor explosions as they eventually subsided, panting, on the twisted sheets.

He slid to the side, rolling them over until Melissa covered his body like a sensual blanket. He could feel her heart pounding against his, and his lips lifted in a smile. For the first time ever, he knew true contentment.

He kicked at the sheet until he could grasp it with his hand and pull it up over her back, tucking her in on top of him. She lifted her head, her smoldering green eyes meeting his briefly before she yawned. Like a cat. She'd played hard, and now she was sleepy. He smiled again, cuddling her to him. She made a halfhearted effort to roll off him, but he stayed her, his hands on her hips.

"No, stay. I'm not letting you go anywhere."

Her head dropped to his chest, and she snuggled against him, her thigh sliding up against his waist. For a while, they lay like that, hearts beating against each other as their muscles relaxed. Hunter gazed up at the canopy of the bed, his arms enfolding the woman he loved. He couldn't let her go. Wouldn't let her go. If she tried to leave him, well, he'd just have to leave with her.

Melissa toweled her hair dry. The only reason she knew it was morning was because her watch read 7:32 a.m. They'd been woken up at six-thirty by a knock at the door and a delivery of clean clothes. Her cheeks pinkened. As soon as the door had closed, and the lock had slid home, Hunter had scooped her up and carried her to the bed to make love to her again.

Her teeth caught her bottom lip in a smile as she dropped the towel and scooped up the denim and underwear. Her body ached, but it was a glorious ache, one that told her how her body had been loved long and hard during the night. And in the morning. As well as the shower.

She'd dressed and was finger-combing her hair when she heard a sharp rap on the door. She peered out of the bathroom, and Hunter rose from the armchair by the fire. He wore fresh dark jeans and a white long-sleeved T-shirt that draped his body, emphasizing his broad shoulders and lean hips.

The door opened, and a Darkken vampire peered around the room until he saw Hunter. He beckoned him. "You need to come with me."

Hunter slid his hand into a back jeans pocket and leaned casually against one of the corner posts of the grand bed. "I don't need to do anything with you," he said dryly.

Melissa emerged from the room, plaiting her hair as she walked.

The Darkken frowned. "You need to come with me," he repeated.

"I'm not leaving her alone," Hunter said, inclining his head toward Melissa. She came up next to him, watching the Darkken warily.

"She stays here, you come with me," the vampire said, anger edging his tone.

"No."

"What's going on?" Melissa asked, eyeing the vampire with curiosity. The Darkken's lips tightened, then he sighed brusquely.

"The Lady Amelie wants to see her son. In private," he added.

Melissa glanced at Hunter, saw his hesitation, his curiosity, his wariness. "Go," she told him. "I'll be fine here until you come back."

Hunter turned to her, reaching for her hand. "I don't want to leave you alone," he murmured huskily. His need to protect her made her feel all warm and tender and, oh, damn it, fuzzy.

She met his gaze. "You need to do this," she urged. "You have a mother who wants to make things right with you." She glanced down at their clasped hands. "You don't know how precious that is, Hunter. Don't throw it away."

Whatever she said must have struck a chord with him, as Hunter nodded reluctantly. He dipped his head, ignoring the vampire in the room to kiss her lingeringly. "Be careful, Red," he murmured as he lifted his head, and didn't move until she nodded her promise.

"I will."

She watched as Hunter left the room, and she stood there for a moment after the door closed and the lock was engaged, her fingers keeping his kiss warm on her lips. She watched the ribbons of light that flowed from her chest to beyond the door. He still hadn't mentioned the bond, and she wasn't sure why. She'd felt the tug of it in the tunnel, had been surprised at each of Hunter's attempts to tame it, control it. Hadn't actually seen it, though, until last night. Which meant Hunter had seen it earlier, and hadn't mentioned it.

She sighed, twirled, then flopped back on the bed. She had a bond mate. A bond mate who didn't actually want to talk about their bond. She spread her arms out on the bed. She should be angry. Horrified. Running in the opposite direction… Instead she made a sheet angel, moving her arms and legs on the bed until she could feel the linen bunch beneath her. She was a witch. She'd heard of mating bonds, had even seen the glorious auras of some, and had envied those who shared one. She may not understand all of the laws of magic, but she knew only an idiot tried to ignore the laws of magic.

She giggled. She wasn't an idiot. She didn't think she could ever find love again, not after Theo. Didn't think she'd find a man worthy, and didn't think she'd get over the guilt. Sure, it hadn't been the best start to a relationship, but perhaps that was the universe's idea of a joke. Show the worst of the mate before slowly revealing the best.

She frowned. It had been a really slow reveal, though. She stared up at the canopy. Hunter hadn't said anything, hadn't indicated anything, had even tried to hide it from her. She should feel insulted, but she thought she understood him a little better now. First he'd discovered the woman he'd loved had been a lie, as was their love. Then he'd learned his mother hadn't actually died—well, she had, but that wasn't the reason she wasn't in his life. She'd left him. Unwillingly, but she could see he'd taken that news hard.

She lifted her chin. She'd just have to show him that not all women ran away from him.

Poor Hunter. He had no idea who he was up against.

Hunter frowned as he followed the Darkken vamp down a dark passageway, and then down some stairs. This wasn't the way back to the hall. He'd tried to memorize as much as he could, but they'd turned away from the hall about three corridors back.

"Where does my mother want to meet me?" he asked the vamp as they stepped down into another hallway, and rounded a corner.

"In hell, where you'll see her in good time," the Darkken commented.

Hunter halted, but something hard and heavy crashed into the back of his skull, and darkness snatched him away from consciousness.

Chapter 20

Melissa heard the bolt slide in the lock, and her eyes flickered open. She must have dozed off. Not surprising, considering her lack of sleep. She jackknifed off the bed, summoning her magic as the door swung inward, ready to annihilate any vamp that attacked her.

Lady Amelie's eyebrows rose in surprise, and she lifted her hands, palms facing her. "Good morning."

Melissa lowered her hands, but didn't completely relax. The woman was still a vampire. "Sorry," she said lamely. It wouldn't be the done thing to zap the mother of her bond mate.

Amelie glanced around the room. "I was hoping to talk with Hunter, if he was willing."

Melissa frowned. "He is. He was on his way to you."

Amelie glanced toward the door, a frown marring her brow. "What?"

"That vamp came to collect him—" Melissa glanced

at her watch. "Uh, nearly an hour ago. He said you wanted to talk to Hunter."

Amelie shook her head. "I sent no one for Hunter. I don't need anyone to act as an intermediary between my son and me. There are already too many misunderstandings and lost words between us."

Alarm grew in Melissa. "Well, someone came here and told him you wanted to see him, and he hasn't been back since."

Amelie reached for Melissa's hand, and Melissa stepped back. Amelie's surprised gaze slowly transitioned to understanding. She beckoned instead. "Come, we have to let Griffin know."

"How do we know Griffin didn't organize this?" Melissa asked as she followed Amelie into the corridor.

Amelie snorted as she strode along the hallway. "If Griffin wanted Hunter dead, he wouldn't be sneaky about it. He'd just kill him and be done with it."

"Oh," Melissa responded faintly. "Good to know."

Amelie shook her head. "An hour. A lot can happen in an hour." She broke into a trot, and Melissa increased her own pace to keep up with her. She followed the older woman through the labyrinth of corridors until they jogged into the great hall.

Griffin was on the dais, listening to a report from the vampire who'd urged everyone from the hall the night before.

"What do you mean, there's another witch?" Griffin exclaimed, his tone exasperated. "I feel like someone's declared Old Irondell as a top holiday destination. There are too many tourists traipsing around, damn it."

"He's searching for a woman," the Darkken supplied. "He identified himself to one of the perimeter guardians, and requested parlay."

"Parlay." Griffin shook his head, lips twisted. "Well, that's seems to be a loose term at the moment." He paused, then sighed roughly. "I'll still honor it, though. We're not allowed to kill him now. At least, not until he leaves Old Irondell." The Dark Lord waved his hand, a disgruntled expression on his face. "Fine, bring him in."

"Griffin," Amelie called.

Melissa gasped as she saw the crowd of Darkken part, and a familiar figure with shaggy dark blond hair, biker leathers and sunglasses stalked into the hall.

"Dave," she exclaimed, running toward her brother. Two Darkken vamps stepped between them to halt her, preventing her from reaching her brother.

"I'd suggest you get your hands off my sister before I remove them for you," Dave said calmly, but there was no mistaking his fierce expression.

"Let her through," Griffin called, then grumbled something to his Guardian Prime. The Darkken dropped their hold immediately, and Melissa launched herself at her brother, and he swept her up in a bear hug.

"Griffin," Amelie called, this time sharply.

Griffin rubbed his temple. "Yes, Mother?"

"Oh, it's so good to see you," Melissa breathed as she clutched at her brother.

"You don't call, you don't write," Dave responded, chuckling. "Don't you think leveling a city block to get my attention was a little overkill?"

Melissa paled. "Was anyone hurt?"

Dave grimaced. "Well, if you're talking about your business neighbors, seeing as it was a Sunday night, nobody else was around. But if you're talking about a whole bunch of vamps and lycans...yeah. There were a few fatalities."

"They were attacking me," she said defensively. Dave pulled back to gaze down at her.

"I figured that much, just by the sheer numbers. When they didn't pull your body out, though, I've been trying to figure out where you got to. Didn't think you had the guts to brave Old Irondell on your own, though, kid. Smart move."

"I wasn't alone," Melissa said, then turned toward the dais, pulling Dave along behind her.

Amelie was already talking with Griffin, who rubbed the bridge of his nose.

"What do you mean, he's gone?"

"He's been taken."

"Well, if he's silly enough to get himself nabbed…" Griffin halted when he saw his mother's expression, and he folded his arms as he faced off against her. "I got a delivery today. Do you want to know what it was? Gavin's head." His expression showed his pain, his anger. "I sent Gavin to your dear husband to invite him to parlay, and the psycho killed him. Do you want to know how many he's murdered since then? Six. Six people, Mom. All in the time it would have taken for Gavin to return. While. We. Slept." He said the last words through gritted teeth, then took a deep breath. "How many lives is your precious son worth?"

Amelie tilted her head to the side. "I would risk everything for all of my sons. We have to help him, Griff."

Griffin shook his head. "No."

"Yes." Amelie's eyes welled with tears. "I have already lost Hunter and his brother to this man once, Griff. I should have done something, all those years ago. I can't just sit by and let Arthur do this."

Griffin gazed at his mother, and his eyes shifted to stare blankly toward Melissa as she and her brother drew up close to the stairs of the dais. He was silent for a moment, thinking, assessing, before he finally leaned forward in his chair.

"I'm sorry, Mother, but I won't risk any more of our Old Irondell family than we've already lost."

Melissa blanched as Griffin rose from his seat. "I offer no protection to Hunter Galen. He has no claim to Old Irondell."

"Griffin! What you do…" Amelie shook her head in horror. Griffin stepped toward his mother and clasped her hands.

"Trust me to know exactly what I'm doing," he told her quietly. He turned to face Melissa and her brother, and Dave stepped forward, thrusting his hand out.

"Dave Carter—" He glanced at his sister and Melissa shrugged, as he had no formal title to add to the speech. Dave shrugged. "Tattoo Artist Extraordinaire, formally requests—"

"Save it. Parlay, I know." Griffin nodded. "You wanted to find your sister, she wanted to find you, you've both found each other, everyone's happy, you're free to leave," he said, and bowed. When he straightened, Melissa stepped forward.

"Are you seriously not going to look for your brother?" she asked.

Griffin nodded. "Seriously. And flippantly." He turned to go, but Melissa touched his arm.

The Darkken Guardian Prime stepped forward, but halted when Griffin held up his hand. "Yes, darlin'?"

"You know what this means, don't you?" she whispered.

The albino tilted his head, and his unblinking gaze met hers. His brows pulled into a slight V. "I'm curious. Tell me."

"It means that while Hunter was a guest in your home, one of your kind betrayed your hospitality, and your will."

Griffin didn't blink, but smiled tightly. "As I said, you're both free to go." He stepped back, arms out. "Hear this. The witches have free passage to leave. They will not be bothered."

He strode toward the exit, and Amelie stepped down off the dais. "Griff," she called in protest.

The Dark Lord held up a hand but didn't stop. "Can't talk now, Mother. You know how it is. Things to do, people to see. Old Irondell doesn't run itself." The albino strode from the hall, his Guardian Prime following behind.

Melissa covered her mouth. Hunter's brother wasn't going to lift a finger to help him. Dave glanced between Melissa and the doorway.

"Why do I feel like I'm missing something?" he inquired.

"Hunter's father is the one behind the attack on my store," Melissa informed her brother, and started striding down the hallway to the main exit. The Darkken crowd parted. True to their leader's word, neither she nor her brother was hassled as they left the hall of the Dark Lord. "He's come down into Old Irondell, looking for us." She halted, frowning. "But will he still be looking for me, now that he has Hunter?"

Dave looked back at her and shrugged. "Doesn't matter. After what he did to you and your store, I'm going to look for him. He's walking dead." Dave started to walk toward the main exit, but Melissa grabbed his arm.

"Wait, I can find him," she said, looking down at the coiling ethereal ribbons.

Dave arched an eyebrow. "You want to do a locator spell? Do you have something of his?"

"Kind of. I have his mate."

Dave waited for her to continue, then his jaw dropped as he finally realized what she was saying. Despite his sunglasses, she could still read the shock on his face. "You didn't," he breathed.

"Oh, I did," she said, nodding. "Quite a few times, actually."

Dave clapped his hands over his ears. "Lah-lah-lah—"

Melissa grabbed his arm and tugged him around the corner. "We go this way."

"You realize Mom is going to freak when she hears," Dave muttered as he allowed her to drag him along.

"She'll be ecstatic," Melissa corrected as she followed the bond link. "Which sucks. I really didn't want to make her happy at all. She thinks Hunter is a valuable asset, and will be overjoyed when she hears the news."

"You might get a shock when you get back above," Dave said as he trotted along beside her.

Melissa frowned as she halted at a door. She twisted the knob. It was locked, damn it. "Why?"

Dave drew her back, then placed his hands on the keyhole below the doorknob. He murmured something briefly, and an electric shock sizzled between his hand and the door. The lock clicked, and Dave twisted the knob, pushing the door open. He waggled his eyebrows. "Impressed?"

"Hardly. You're a witch. I'd be disappointed if a simple door lock foiled you."

"It foiled you," he pointed out.

Melissa shook her head. "No, I was winding up to blow it to smithereens."

Dave smiled. "Sometimes subtlety works better."

"I'll remind you of that if we ever have to save your mate," she responded brusquely as she stepped through the doorway and jogged down the stairs. "Why would I get a shock above?" she prodded her brother.

"Well, a lot of shadow breeds died outside your store, and some humans died inside," Dave said as he trotted along behind her. "They want justice for their dead."

Melissa didn't stop, but she frowned at her brother briefly, and he held up his hands. "I know," Dave said, "it wasn't your fault, but Mom is in damage control."

This time Melissa did halt. "No." Denial, disbelief, dismay—they all battled for supremacy.

He sighed. "Yep. She's negotiating."

White-hot anger coiled inside her, and she shook her head. "She's going to be very disappointed when she realizes it's all going to be undone."

"She's your Coven Elder, Mel."

"I'll withdraw from White Oak, if necessary."

"Melissa—"

Melissa shook her head and continued. "No. This is it. I'm done. You're not bound by the coven, so I won't be, either."

"You know it's not as simple as that. I'm different."

And didn't she know it. Melissa had grown up knowing her brother was "special," and not subject to their mother's rules. All duty and obligation had fallen to her, as the only child of the Coven Elder inside the coven. But if Dave could live outside the coven, so could she, damn it.

She lifted a finger, using it to punctuate her words. "She will get my loyalty, and she will get my respect, but only when she's worthy. I'm not going to worry about it now, though. I have a bond mate to locate."

* * *

Hunter opened his eyes, wincing at the jackhammering inside his head.

"Ah, finally. You do so like to laze about, don't you, Hunter?"

Hunter tried to lift his head, but hissed as an iron collar singed his neck. He frowned.

His arms were cuffed above his head, and if the burning at his wrists was any indication, he was bound by iron, chained to yet another wall. His shoulders felt like they were gradually tearing out of their sockets, bearing all of his weight as his feet dangled above the ground.

Cuffs were overrated.

He winced, trying to move his head without touching the collar to get an idea of his whereabouts. It looked like it was some sort of outdoor area of a tavern, covered over long ago. Tables with bench seats, flowerpots with nothing but dirt and what could have been a bar. There were at least a dozen men gathered, a motley crew of vagrants, vampires and a lycan or two.

Movement caught his eye, and he finally caught sight of his father. Arthur Armstrong stood before a brazier, flames flickering through the grate. His gray hair was smoothed back, his blue eyes brittle as he met his son's stare. He wore a suit, and was pulling on leather gloves. Hunter sniggered.

"You're a little overdressed for the occasion, don't you think?"

Arthur's lips tightened. "That's one thing I couldn't really instill in you, wasn't it? An appreciation for grooming."

Hunter shook his head, then grimaced at the hot kiss of iron on his skin. "You tried to groom me," he said, and smiled. "But you failed."

Arthur pulled a rod out of the brazier with a gloved hand, and Hunter's smile dropped when he saw the glowing tip. "Actually, you failed, son. I gave you the perfect opportunity. Ryder was going to go to prison—or die, whichever came first—and you would have been the sole Armstrong heir."

Hunter blinked, stunned at his father's words, at the deceit in them. "You do realize I was there, right? In the same room? You know, when you admitted to plotting to kill both Ryder and myself to get your hands on our trust funds?"

"One, that's my money, I earned it. Two, that's a charge I'm not guilty of," Arthur said as he stepped toward him.

"Only because you escaped from prison before your trial," Hunter pointed out.

"A prison you helped put me in," Arthur remarked conversationally, then drove the hot poker into Hunter's side.

Hunter growled, hissing in pain as the iron speared beneath his skin. Arthur withdrew the poker and tilted his head to the side as Hunter panted.

"I'm impressed. You're doing your own dirty work these days," Hunter gasped. Up until now his father had sat back like a master puppeteer, compelling and manipulating folks to do his evil deeds, so that he could keep his hands clean and claim innocence. Except for now. Hunter was almost flattered that he was the catalyst for his father getting directly involved, but the searing hot pain in his side removed any sense of levity.

"You should know by now," Arthur said as he turned away, handing the rod over to a vampire who walked back to put the iron poker back into the brazier's flames. Arthur turned to face him, his hands behind his back.

"We're light warriors. I am your Prime. You do not punish me—I punish you."

"Punish me for what?" Hunter shouted, incredulous. "What did *I* do? God, you are such a dick. You kill Debbie, you conspire to kill your sons—you killed your *wife*," Hunter spat. "You're not normal, Arthur."

Arthur's eyes narrowed. "Ah, I see you've found your mama. Did you also meet the white whelp? Did you know he's just removed you from his sphere of protection?" Arthur pointed to the vamp who'd lied to him to lure him out of his bedroom earlier that morning. "He's renounced any ties you have with his family, I've been informed." Arthur shrugged. "But I digress. Your mother abandoned us. She betrayed me, and she was going to birth another man's breed. Can you imagine the scandal?" Arthur shook his head. "No. I've worked too hard, for too long, to have our reputation or standing tarnished by a woman who couldn't keep her legs together."

"Please. It's not like you're some paragon of virtue." Hunter didn't hide the contempt in his tone, or his expression. Listening to his mother talk about her life, he may not have accepted her words immediately, but he knew, deep down, that living with Arthur Armstrong must have been hell for her.

Arthur smiled. "I'm the Warrior Prime of House Armstrong. It's my duty to spread my seed, to build a strong legacy. It was your mother's duty to be loyal."

Hunter's eyes narrowed. "Spread your seed? Hell, do you actually hear the rubbish that comes out of your mouth?" Then the words sank in, and he blinked. "Are you saying—do you have more kids out there?" Shock chilled his blood. He knew he was flawed, that he continually had to fight the darkness in him, but what if his father had had another child, one that didn't fight the darkness? One that was just as evil and arrogant as his sire?

Arthur nodded. "Of course. When I'm finished here, I will go introduce myself to my daughter. She's been brought up by her mother in the wild, sadly, completely unaware of her true family." Arthur shrugged. "It's such a pity you won't get to meet your half sister, Hunter. Just think, there is a light warrior out there, full of raw, untrained power. She's unconstrained, totally free to indulge in her nature." His father's hand rolled elegantly. "Of course, she'll need some guidance, some instruction, I daresay basic etiquette training will be a necessity, but I will make her my heir."

For a moment Hunter just stared at his father, unsure of how to process the wealth of information he'd just learned. He had a sister. A sister who apparently had no idea of her madman of a father, or her brothers. A sister who maybe had no other light warrior around to help her. And she would be his heir. Hunter accepted his father wanted to kill him, but there was still Ryder.

"You're still planning to kill Ryder," Hunter said. His hands fisted, and he ignored the hot bite of the iron. "You are a sick man, Arthur. You need help."

Arthur sighed. "I'm your father. Call me Dad." He turned and gestured to the gathered men, all filthy, grimy and waiting for his next instruction. "And I have all the help I need."

Hunter's eyes rounded. "I will call you a lot of names, you sick son of a bitch, but I will never again call you Father."

"Oh, you think you're such a good son?" Arthur exclaimed.

"Yes," Hunter responded. "As a matter of fact, I think I was a better son than you ever deserved. I tried so hard to please you, playing all those stupid mind games, working with you. Ryder left you. He struck out on his own, and I wouldn't go along with all those strategic plays you wanted to do with your patients in your clinic. But you couldn't handle that. You decided to kill your sons as soon as they started to show some independence. Do you know what that says about you, Arthur?"

Arthur nodded at the vampire at the brazier, who stirred the coals. The flames danced and dipped. "What, Hunter?" he asked, his tone bored.

"It tells me that you're a scared little man who can't allow his sons to separate from him because then it means he's no longer their number one. It means you're not as strong as you like to think you are, that if you can't control with an iron fist, then you've completely lost control—and that means you're weak."

Hell, how had he not seen this before? He thought his father was a cruel bastard. He'd never thought he'd be capable of all this death and destruction, though. How much of his father was in him?

"Shut up," Arthur roared, and gestured to the vampire. The vampire yanked the rod out of the brazier and strode toward him. "Shut up. You betrayed me, Hunter. You, of all people. You worked with me. You were by my side, nearly 24/7. I gave you a home, an education—a career, damn it, and this is how you repay me, by siding with your brother against me." He grasped the iron poker from the vampire, and drove it into the top of Hunter's left thigh. Hunter growled again, snarling at the man as he slowly withdrew the hot rod. His leg—the pain, the excruciating, burning agony, actually gave him a chill. Hunter realized his body was going into shock.

"You really have a selective memory, don't you?" Hunter breathed, beads of perspiration sliding down the side of his face and between his shoulder blades. He gritted his teeth, tried to ignore the pain, but damn it hurt like a bitch. He wasn't healing. The iron was constraining his light force, including his ability to regenerate. He blinked, glaring at the man who even now handed the iron rod to the vampire, and he watched the poker get shoved once again into the coals, stirring up the embers. He shook his head. His father's distortion of the facts was stunning. "You wanted to kill me, remember? Before my birthday?"

Hunter blinked. His birthday. He'd turned thirty while chained to the wall in Melissa's cell. Quite the nonevent, admittedly, but it had still happened. "My trust fund," Hunter breathed. He frowned. "Is this about revenge, or about the money? This attempt to kill Melissa, to track us down..." He didn't have a will. Had never really thought about it until the night his father's plots were revealed—and then he'd been taken prisoner by Melissa, and there hadn't been an opportunity to organize one. Not that it had been a priority for him over the last few months.

"Melissa?" Arthur frowned as he thought, then his brow smoothed. "Oh, the witch. No, I was doing that as a favor to you. Nobody locks my son up for months and gets away with it."

Hunter tilted his head back, grimacing as the collar shifted around his neck. "Great. The 'I want to kill you, but God help anyone who hurts you that isn't me' mind-set." He wheezed with weak laughter. "You know, there's a term for people like you," he said, gazing up at the ceiling. He had no idea where they were, but he didn't think he was anywhere near his brother or his mother—or Melissa. He swallowed. He was going to die. He didn't want to die. He wanted to let his mother know he forgave her. He totally understood why she'd fled his father. He wanted to tell Melissa he loved her, tell her about the bond, and live a long and happy life with her. He wanted to repair the relationship with his brother Ryder. Hell, he even wanted to get to know his ever-expanding number of new siblings. But instead, he would die from being used as an iron pincushion. Perhaps it was a fitting end for all the bad things he'd done. Melissa's face swam in his mind's eye. He wanted to spend the rest of his life doing right by her.

"What is it?"

Hunter blinked. Arthur was standing in front of him again, glowing poker in hand. Had he zoned out, just a little? He knew he'd lost a lot of blood.

"What?" He wrinkled his brow, trying to keep up with the conversation.

"You said there is a term for people like me. What is it?"

"Completely fu—" He broke off as the iron rod speared into his other side, and this time he bellowed with the pain before darkness swept over him, giving him some relief.

Chapter 21

Melissa halted at the low, long cry of pain, her blood chilling in her veins.

"Oh, my God, that's Hunter," she gasped, and started to run.

Her brother caught up with her, pulling her to a stop. "Be smart, Mel. We can't just burst in on a Light Warrior Prime. We have to find out what's going on first." His head twisted to the side, and he hesitated for a moment.

"We have to hurry, Dave," Melissa pleaded, trying to drag her brother along. "That is my mate, and he needs me, needs us."

Dave held a gloved finger to his lips, then rolled his hand. Melissa frowned. He wanted her to shush, but... keep talking? Dave backed up the tunnel, and made a beak with his hand, opening and closing it. Keep talking.

Melissa frowned in confusion, but did as her brother instructed. "I—" Her mind went blank. She normally didn't have a problem talking, but talking on cue took the spontaneity out of a conversation. Dave frowned, his beak-hand flapping open and closed faster.

"I love him," she stated abruptly. "I love Hunter, and I want to help him. I intend to spend the rest of my life with him. He's…not perfect, I'll admit—but then, neither am I."

Dave backed up against the wall just before a bend, and nodded. She continued. "I know he can be a little impulsive—but we can all be guilty of that sometimes, right?" She eyed her brother. "He's a good man. He's been hurt, and he's had to live with a cruel father, so I understand he's—adapted." That was probably the nicest way she could frame it. "But, Dave, he's strong, and—believe it or not—he's fiercely loyal, and very protective. He may sometimes get it wrong showing it," she admitted, "but I realize now, deep down, he's doing what he thinks is the best for those he loves." She hesitated. "And I would do the same," she admitted. "I would do the same crazy crap if it meant protecting—"

Dave whipped his hand out, grasping the arm of the person who had crept up to the corner of the tunnel, and slammed them back against the wall.

Amelie Galen gasped, her arms coming up to grasp the lapels of Dave's leather jacket.

Dave relaxed his grip immediately, but didn't let her go. "What are you doing?" he asked Hunter's mother calmly.

Amelie looked between the harsh expression of Dave, and over to Melissa, before swinging her gaze back to the big man who held her, gently but implacably, against a wall.

"I'm helping you," Amelie responded.

Dave arched an eyebrow. "By following us like a shadow, creeping along behind us?"

Amelie lifted her chin toward Melissa. "Griffin says she is my son's bond mate. I can't see the link, but I figure she's using it to track down Hunter. I want to help you save my son."

Dave pursed his lips for a moment, then grimaced. "And just how do you think your other son would view my taking his mother to a fight with a deranged light warrior, hmm?"

Amelie arched her eyebrow, and her eyes flashed red, ever so briefly. "I'm not defenseless. I ran away once, and left my sons in Arthur's hands, and that decision will haunt me forever. I will not do it again. I will not let that bastard kill any of my children."

"This is wasting time," Melissa interrupted. "She is responsible for her own decisions, Dave. Let her come, if she wants, but either way, let's go."

Dave let go of Amelie, stepping back with his gloved hands up. "Fine. But we do this my way. My rules. No innocents get harmed. Understand?" Amelie nodded, but Dave stepped closer. "That means you don't go off on some bloodlust craze," he said quietly. "Arthur had both lycans and vamps working together for him. The only way that happens is if they're compelled. They aren't in control of their actions."

Amelie nodded again. "Understood."

Dave nodded, satisfied, then strode toward Melissa. "Okay, sis, you're up. Show us where this mate of yours is." He shook his head as he fell into step alongside her.

"What?" Melissa asked.

"I can't believe you fell for the firebug. The guy tried to kill you."

Melissa nodded. "And I chained him to a wall for

five months. Neither of us is proud of what we did to each other."

"How the hell did you go from putting your little pyromaniac in chains to becoming bonded mates?"

"Long story," Melissa replied, as she broke into a jog, following the twisted ribbons of color through the darkness.

"I look forward to hearing it, when this is all over," Dave whispered, then pulled her against the wall as they came up to an intersection. Amelie followed suit. He crept up to the corner and peered around the brick wall. He quickly jerked back, then leaned over so that his lips were close to her ear. "I think we've found him."

He silently shuffled back so Melissa could take her place at the front, and she peered around.

Her mouth opened in a silent gasp of horror. It looked like the back alley of a row of what used to be restaurants. At the far end was a courtyard, braziers burning. A group of men were clustered about—vamps, vagrants, some Darkken…and a lycan? All either sat on the bench seats to watch the proceedings, or gathered for a closer view. An unconscious Hunter was chained up on a wall, his feet dangling three feet from the ground. Even from here, she could see the bloodstains on his white shirt, almost black in the dim light. She covered her mouth to stop from screaming, and watched as Arthur held out his arms, light arcing from his hands to the son chained to the wall.

Hunter's body flinched and jerked, his skin glowing, until finally his eyes opened, and he glared, gasping at his father.

The light flickered from Arthur's fingertips, extinguishing as the older man smiled triumphantly.

"Ah, much better. Now we can start all over again."

Melissa recoiled, darting back behind the brick wall. "We have to do something," she whispered to her brother.

Dave nodded. "If we make a move on Armstrong or Hunter, that little posse out there will take action. We'll have to take out Armstrong's men first."

"How? There's at least a mixed dozen out there. I can't touch them all at once." Melissa's favorite weapon was her sleep spell, but it usually required physical contact. "You're strong, but even you can't knock them all out at the same time with a spell."

Dave nodded. "So we'll have to go with shock and awe." He turned to Amelie. "When you metamorphosed, did you retain any of your light force?"

Amelie shook her head. "No, I fed it all to my son, to keep him alive during my death, and then the rest of the pregnancy. I'm just a vampire now."

Dave shook his head. "You're never 'just' something. Okay, here's what we'll do."

He quickly outlined a plan. Melissa's eyebrows rose. She knew her brother could be ballsy, but this was out there, even for him. They were outnumbered, and possibly outpowered with the full force of a Warrior Prime.

Dave grasped her shoulders. "That's your bond mate out there, Mel. You can do this."

She nodded. She could. Or she'd die trying.

Hunter stiffened, waiting for the hot poker to again burn through him. He glared at his father. The man was sick, and if anything, Hunter was so appalled by his actions, so disgusted, he took a small measure of comfort knowing he could never do what his father did, could never be his father's son. His body ached, but Arthur had healed his wounds so that he could start the torture all over again. He didn't know how long this would last for, but he was determined not to show his father his pain, or his worry for his mate. He'd left Melissa alone. He smiled bitterly. Based on his experience, he'd been so worried that she would walk out on him. He'd never once thought he'd be the one to walk out on her.

His gaze dropped to the curling, ethereal ribbons waving and fluttering from his chest. His father hadn't noticed it, couldn't see it. His father had no idea Melissa had become his bonded mate. Thank God. If Arthur knew, he'd go after Melissa in order to discourage any claim to his fortune. At least he would die knowing that she'd be protected from his father's cruel attention.

As though responding to his thoughts, the ribbons brightened a little. He saw them shift direction. They wavered, rising at an angle, then falling, but all the time transferring from his right side to his left. Uh, what was going on?

"Now, where were we?" Arthur said conversationally, the rod with the glowing tip in his gloved hand. "Ah, yes. I was telling you what a colossal failure you were." His features hardened. "How dare you think you can box me up?"

"Well, you boxed me up, I'd call that fair."

Hunter's head swiveled at the sound of the feminine voice, his eyes widening as he watched his mother walk down the alley behind the tavern's outdoor area. She wore that leather coat, the one that flared out like a long dress, her booted heels clicking on the surface of the road.

Arthur turned, his expression surprised for a moment. "Amelie."

She smiled, arms out to the side as she inclined her head in a courtly manner. "In the flesh, so to speak."

Arthur's eyes narrowed, and he scanned the area. "Where is that white freak of yours?"

Amelie's expression hardened. "My son doesn't share my consideration for Hunter," she admitted. "It's just me."

Arthur rolled his eyes, lowering the iron poker to lean on it like a walking stick. "Come, Amelie, do you honestly think I'd believe you'd come here alone, to face me?"

Her lips curled in contempt. "Oh, you don't scare me, you pathetic little man. Always using others to do your dirty work for you." She gestured to the men she passed as she entered the dead garden area. "Look around you. None of these men are loyal to you. None of these men care whether you live or die. You've had to compel them to follow you, to do your bidding. A true leader doesn't lead by trickery, Arthur—but that's something your tiny little brain couldn't quite grasp, isn't it? Seeing as you can't get your way by any other method…"

Arthur's lips tightened, and his eyes narrowed. "Why are you here?"

"I'm here to save my son," Amelie said, as though it was obvious.

Hunter turned his fists in the cuffs. He had no idea what the hell was going on, but this— His brain was grappling to process his mother and father, in the same spot, after all these years.

Arthur chuckled. "And how exactly do you plan to do that? You—against all of us, against *me*?" He shook his head, incredulous. "It hardly seems fair."

"I'm offering a trade," Amelie said, her hands on her hips. She glanced around at the men, shifted a little as they started to edge closer. "Let my son go, and you can have me."

Arthur set the iron poker against the wall, and folded his arms. "And why would I do that?"

"Because you can't stand the fact that I walked away," Amelie said, her voice succinct. "I left you. Can you imagine what your peers would say to that if they knew? How would that affect your standing with them, Arty?"

"Don't call me that," Arthur growled.

Amelie lowered her head to glare at her former husband. "Let my son go, *Arty*. Take me instead. I'm sure there are some lessons you think you can teach me."

"Why would I let him go, when I now have both of you?"

Amelie smiled derisively. "You never really had me, Arty."

Arthur sneered, and Hunter noticed the bond link move again. It fluttered, it writhed and it moved. Arthur held up his hands, and Hunter grasped hold of the chains above his wrists, gritting his teeth against the burn.

"No," he yelled.

Fireballs appeared on Arthur's palms, growing, expanding, roiling. The older man smirked. "This is going to be such fun." He threw the balls at Amelie, and Hunter roared in panic.

The fireballs smashed against some invisible barrier, roiling back in a wall of flame that flung Arthur back against the wall.

Hunter reacted, entwining his legs around Arthur's neck. He heard cries and grunts, registered the flare of fire, but concentrated on keeping his legs—and his father—exactly in the position they were. He glanced up briefly.

His mother was moving in a blur, her dark coat whirling as she dodged the men. She went after all the vampires, snapping their necks in lightning-fast moves that would put a light warrior to shame.

Arthur struggled against his legs, using his hands and twisting this way and that to try to break free. "Fight," he wheezed to his men. "Kill them."

Hunter tightened his hold, gritting his teeth against the searing pain in his wrists, fists and neck. Then he heard the chanting.

Melissa strode down the alley from the opposite direction, arms out, eyes focused on Arthur as she spoke some sort of spell. Meanwhile a tall, broad-shouldered man wearing biker leathers and sunglasses ran up to one of the homeless humans and jumped, landing with a heavy punch to the jaw.

Hunter froze, muscles clenched. *Melissa.* He'd thought never to see her again, and he had to blink to make sure he wasn't zoned out in some fantasy again. She was here, and she was coming for him. She'd had the opportunity to walk away, to leave, but here she was, facing off against his father and the shadow breeds who terrified her. For him.

God, he loved this woman.

One of the men snarled, his eyes beginning to glow as he stripped his shirt from his body and toed off his shoes. Even as he slid out of his jeans, he morphed into his werewolf form. With his teeth bared and a growl low in his throat, the wolf started running toward Melissa. Hunter yelled, and the man wearing sunglasses whirled, chanting something as his fist lashed out to punch the lycan off course. Hunter heard the whimper, then saw the lycan.

His mother cried out in pain as a vampire finally brought her down, his arm twining around her neck as he curled his hand over, ready to strike at her chest.

"No," Hunter yelled, then bellowed as Arthur finally managed to free himself. The Warrior Prime fired off a fireball at Amelie, and started running toward Melissa. Melissa's eyes widened, and she turned to Hunter, flinging her hand up as she muttered a chant. The restraints that held Hunter in place snapped open. Hunter dropped to the ground, crashing hard against the concrete.

He heard screams and glanced up. His mother had managed to turn and use the vampire as a shield. The vampire who held her was now on fire. His mother was trying to struggle free. His head whipped around to look after Melissa. She'd started running, and was dodging the flaming spears his father was throwing her way. She burst into an open doorway and ducked as a fireball crashed against the timber, setting the door alight. Then she disappeared into the dark opening, his father in pursuit.

Hunter rose to his feet and stumbled toward the alley. He would not stand by and watch his father kill the woman he loved, the woman he intended to spend the rest of his life with.

Chapter 22

Melissa raced up the interior stairwell, heart pounding as she heard Arthur burst into the foyer below. She'd made it to the second floor when she heard his steps on the stairs below. She glanced down into the stairwell, then jerked back as a fireball landed above her. She dived for the door on the second-floor landing, yanking it open, hurtling into the hallway and slamming the door behind her.

She glanced first in one direction, then the other, trying to catch her breath. It looked like some sort of old apartment building. There was a window at the end of the hall, and despite the grime and dust that covered it, she could make out the murky frame of a fire escape. She started running down the hall.

This wasn't part of Dave's plan. Well, not quite. The plan was to create a distraction, draw Arthur's attention away from Hunter long enough, distract the rest of the men for long enough, so that she could create a release spell for his chains. She'd used her reflection spell to protect Amelie, but didn't have enough to protect herself as well as free Hunter. She made it to the window and tried to lift it open, but centuries of disuse and grime had sealed it shut. She heard the door clang open back down the hall, and cast about wildly. There was a fire extinguisher strapped to the wall. She grabbed it. It was so old, it was highly unlikely it would work, and the irony didn't escape her as she lifted it to smash the glass as she tried to escape the enraged light warrior behind her.

She heard the roar behind her, and she dived out of the window, landing roughly on the grate outside, below the windowsill. A cloud of flame billowed out of the window above her, and she screamed as the explosion curled over her, then rose above to billow out over the alley. She crawled to the ladder, but screeched when a hand pulled at her hair, yanking her away from the escape route.

"You meddling bitch," Arthur seethed as he pulled her to her feet. He grasped her shoulders, twisting her around to face him. "You should have learned the first time, it takes more than just a weaselly little mirror spell to best me. I'm a—"

Melissa rolled her eyes. "Yeah, we all know. You're a Warrior Prime." She kicked him swiftly between the legs. His eyes rounded, his breath wheezed out in a high-pitched squeak and his fingers clenched on her shoulders. "You have to learn that doesn't give you a hall pass to be a dick."

His face became mottled, and Melissa felt the heat building on her shoulders. She tried to beat him off, but the searing heat singed her skin where his hands touched her. She muttered her dampening spell, concentrating on using the light force as an element to build on her incantation. The more he tried to burn her, the more effective her dampening spell became.

"Leave her alone," Hunter yelled from beneath them, but Melissa didn't take her eyes off Arthur's face, muttering her spell over and over as he tried to burn her.

Arthur growled in frustration, backing her up against the railing. Her eyes rounded as she felt the pressure against her. Arthur pushing against her shoulders, the railing at her waist. She tried to kick out, but Arthur dodged her feet, the whites of his eyes visible as he shoved at her, and then her feet left the ground, and she felt herself falling.

"No!" Hunter yelled. She reached for him, panic rising inside as she briefly saw his face as she fell toward him. The ground raced toward her. Hunter stretched out his hand, leaning out over the fire escape, and then a black cloud raced up and billowed over her.

Time seemed to slow—or at least, the speed of her fall did.

She screamed as she felt something hard grip her hand, and the muscles in her shoulder tore. Her other senses were ripped away from her. Sight, sound—she couldn't even tell which way was up or down. Slowly the black fog drifted away.

Hunter was half-over the railing, and he gasped with relief when he met her gaze, his hand holding hers tight. She hung suspended, caught by Hunter's death-defying grip, the ground still some twelve feet below.

Arthur screamed with rage as Hunter slowly pulled her up to him, the muscles in his arm bulging as, hand over hand, he transferred his grip from her hand to her wrist, her forearm, her upper arm, until he could finally clasp her under the shoulder and pull her over the railing to him. He enfolded her in his arms, and she collapsed against his chest, wincing at the awkward, heaving feel of her arm hanging by her side.

Arthur raised both hands, fireballs sparking on his palms as he took aim at them both. Hunter shifted Melissa behind him, facing his father.

"You're not going to win this time, Arty."

Arthur's eyes narrowed. "Watch me." He hurled the two fireballs at them, and Melissa even dodged behind Hunter, then frowned when nothing happened. She peered over Hunter's shoulder.

Arthur stood on the fire escape above them, and the confused expression on his face was comical. Sparks flared again, and he aimed them at the couple below. Melissa watched as little dark clouds danced over and swallowed them up.

Hunter chuckled. "Have you met my brother?" He pointed to the alley below.

Melissa glanced down. Griffin stood calmly below, arms folded, muscles bulging, his pale blue gaze trained on the scene above him.

"The white brat," Arthur seethed, and flung a fireball down at the albino. Griffin gave a flick of his fingers, and the ball of flame disappeared in a puff of black. Arthur frowned and clasped his hands together, a small explosion that fired down at Griffin with breathtaking speed.

Griffin curled his fingers, and black tendrils caught at the fireball, ripping it apart and consuming the flame. Griffin chuckled. "This is fun. I could do this all day."

Arthur growled, spreading his arms out, and Griffin sighed. "You really don't learn, do you?" Griffin raised his arms, and the tendrils of black fog leaped from his hands, spearing into Arthur's palms and slamming him back against the side of the building.

Arthur grunted, trying to free himself from the dark power that now trapped his hands against the side of the brick wall.

Griffin gave a swift yank, and Arthur flew from the landing, tumbling to the street below.

Hunter climbed down the fire escape as fast as he could, running over to where his father lay in the middle of the alley, his limbs bent at unnatural angles. Arthur blinked, as though trying to figure out, as much as his damaged brain would allow, what had just happened.

Hunter skidded to a stop as Griffin approached Arthur. The strange man who had knocked out a werewolf approached from the tavern garden, his arm around Amelie's waist as he helped her hobble along beside him. Melissa came up behind him, and her hand touched his shoulder. They all stared as the albino stood over the broken man on the ground, his expression harsh.

"You came into my home, and you killed my people," Griffin spoke quietly, calmly. "Your first mistake was entering Old Irondell and thinking you could do whatever you wanted. Your second mistake was compelling my man to betray me. Your final mistake was to attack my family."

Arthur's gaze shifted to Hunter, and Griffin nodded. "Yeah, he's my family, too." Griffin knelt on one knee by Arthur's side, his elbow resting on his other bent knee. "You see, we do things differently down here in Old Irondell. There is no Reform law, there is no tribal law. There is just me. My judgment is sound, my punishment is swift." He leaned closer, those pale blue eyes staring blindly at the man on the ground. "It's time for you to go."

Griffin placed his hand above Arthur's chest, and a dark blade, glistening in the fire from the distant braziers, emerged from his palm and speared through Arthur Armstrong's heart.

Arthur flinched, his expression stunned, before his mouth sagged open and his eyes glazed over as his skin turned to black. His head lolled to the side.

The man with the sunglasses grimaced. "Effective," he commented, his tone dry. Amelie stared down at the man who was once her husband, and shook her head, but said nothing.

Hunter stared for a moment, shocked, as his half brother rose to his feet. "You killed him," Hunter said, his voice low.

Griffin turned to him. "Did you want that privilege for yourself?" The albino's pale blue gaze flicked between the man at his side, and the corpse in the alley, and he finally placed a hand on Hunter's shoulder. "I have no doubt you would have killed him, brother, but hear me when I tell you this—no man should have to kill his father." Griffin raised his finger. "Trust me. You may feel the hate, and you may feel the justification, but killing a parent—that haunts you forever." He patted Hunter's shoulder, and Hunter stared at his younger half brother. He spoke with a weary wisdom beyond his years.

Griffin lifted a hand to Amelie. "You weren't supposed to be here."

"Well, you weren't going to do anything," Amelie retorted. "I had to do something."

"I told you to trust me to know what I was doing."

"You told me you weren't going to help your brother."

"No, I told you *we* weren't going to help my brother,"

Griffin corrected her. "You were supposed to stay back at the hall, all grumpy and righteous." He pointed to the Darkken who had lured Hunter away, and Hunter grimaced. His neck was twisted at an awkward angle. He felt no pity, though. The guy was a vampire. He'd regenerate, and awaken with a sore neck, but at least he'd still live. As much as the undead could live. Hunter took some comfort knowing his father's compulsions died with him.

"Knowing that one of my men had removed one of my guests without my say-so—I had to remove Hunter's protection so whoever was responsible would bear the news to Armstrong." Griffin shrugged. "And we followed."

Hunter arched an eyebrow. "Sneaky." He tilted his head. "I like you."

Griffin's lips twitched, and he indicated Amelie. "And you can heal my mom. I like you." Then he frowned. "Is that my shirt?"

Hunter glanced down at the bloodstained, ripped shirt. "Don't know, but I don't have a good track record with borrowed shirts." Then he frowned as he gazed across at his mother. "You're hurt?"

She waved a hand. "I'm fine, just got a little singed on my back."

The big man with the sunglasses shook his head slightly, and Hunter nodded, interpreting the man's silent signal. His mother was hurt more than she let on. He turned back to look at Melissa. Her complexion was drawn and pale, and one shoulder sat lower than the other. She'd dislocated her arm in the fall. She needed his care, too. He gathered his mate close. "Well, let's get everyone back to the hall. I'm going to need fire. Lots of fire."

"And beer," the man wearing the sunglasses suggested. "Lots of beer." He turned to help Amelie, but Griffin lifted his mother into his arms and strode down the alley in the direction of the hall.

"Who *are* you?" Hunter asked as he lifted Melissa into his arms, ignoring her halfhearted protests. "Shh, each step you take will jolt that shoulder."

Melissa sighed, then lifted her chin to the man who fell into step alongside them. "Hunter, this is my brother, Dave. Dave, meet Hunter."

Hunter nodded. "Ah, you're the witch brother."

Dave slapped a hand hard on Hunter's shoulder, and Hunter winced. "And you're the pyromaniac who nearly killed my sister and has now bonded with her." Dave jerked him closer. "Hurt my sister again and I'll kill you." Melissa's brother gave him another friendly pat on the shoulder that could have flattened a lesser man. "Welcome to the family."

Hunter halted, his gaze dropping to Melissa's face. She stared up at him, an eyebrow arched in challenge. Oh, hell. She knew. What's worse, her brother with a fist that could knock out a werewolf knew.

"I was going to tell you," he said quickly. "I just— I just—"

"Spit it out, hot pants," Dave muttered, and Hunter gave her brother an exasperated look, before turning back to the precious woman in his arms.

"Every woman I've ever loved has left me," he told her quietly, and her eyes filled with understanding.

Melissa sighed. She stared up at him, her smile gentle. "I promise you, I will never, ever leave you." She looked at him meaningfully. "And you know me—a promise is a promise."

She'd used those same words when she'd used her

energy to remove her wards instead of fighting off the werewolves. Hunter halted. This woman would literally die before she left him. She cupped his cheek. "I love you, Hunter. I'm not going anywhere."

"Likewise," Hunter breathed, and dipped his head to kiss his mate. "Let's get married."

Melissa nodded. "Let's," she said, just before his lips took hers.

Dave groaned and started walking. "Get a room, you two."

Epilogue

"Can I look now?" Melissa asked, arms outstretched. She wriggled her nose, trying to dislodge the blindfold. Chill wind tousled her hair and danced with her skirt. They were outside, but she had no idea where.

"No." Hunter guided her, his hands on her shoulders.

"What about now?"

He sighed, and his breath gusted past her ear. "Patience, wife."

She smiled. "I love it when you say that."

"What? Patience? Yeah, I feel like I say that a lot with you."

She elbowed him in his muscled stomach behind her. "I meant *wife*."

His hands slid down her back and around her waist, pulling her back against his broad chest. "I love it, too," he said as he nipped her neck. They'd been married for nearly three weeks. Her mother had been overjoyed to hear her daughter was marrying the light warrior, until Hunter had insisted she tear up any agreement she'd negotiated as recompense with the pack who had attacked his mate in her bookstore. Eleanor had discovered she had as much influence over the new family asset as she did over her daughter.

Which was zilch.

Hunter's breath gusted past her ear. She trembled, and he nipped her again, trailing his lips up to the sensitive spot behind her ear. She tilted her head to the side, giving him better access, and her breath hitched as his hands slid under her jacket to cup her breasts.

"Is this what you wanted to show me?" she said breathlessly, rubbing herself against his arousal pressed against her butt. He'd made her put on the blindfold as soon as he got her into his car, and she had no idea where they were, or who could possibly see them. It was Sunday, it was chilly, and she'd rather be back at their home, heating up the bedsheets with her sexy husband.

"Oh, I've got something to show you, Red," he whispered in her ear, then growled in frustration. He flicked her nipples with his thumbs, just once, then drew his hands away. "But I've got something else first."

He guided her along, her booted heels clicking on the pavement. She sighed. It had been a busy three weeks. Hunter, with Ryder's agreement, had sought and successfully petitioned Reform Court for a family status. It had caused quite the sensation when the public learned that light warriors weren't an extinct breed, after all.

And now she was Consort to the Galen Warrior Prime. An impatient, blindfolded Consort.

She heard the rattle of chains, the clink and groan of something that sounded like a gate, and then Hunter guided her farther. "Careful," he told her, "it's a little messy." She could feel the dirt and rocks under her feet, and her heel sank into soft earth.

"Okay, stand still." Hunter's hands untied the blindfold, and he pulled it away. Melissa blinked in the light. Christmas had come and gone, but gray snow was still on the ground in some parts. She looked down into the great big hole. She could clearly see the neatly poured concrete foundations, the spray-painted markings that delineated zones, the pipes that protruded from the slab. She glanced around in surprise. It was her building. Well, the place where her apothecary and bookstore had once stood.

"What's going on?" she asked, confused.

Hunter stepped beside her to gesture to the staked-out markings. "That's your wedding present."

She arched an eyebrow. "A slab of concrete?" A chill breeze drifted through the chain-link fence and scaffolding that edged the lot. A tattered cover lined the fence, blocking the view of the site from the street. She folded her arms, hugging herself.

"No, this is your new store," Hunter stated. He folded his arms, his navy blue sweater pulling taut across his chest.

"Okay," she said slowly. He'd been working on expanding his clinic since their return above—or so she'd thought. It was as though his time away from tending people had renewed an energy, creating a drive in him to work. He worked hard—and then he came home and played hard. He reached for her hand, and dragged her over to the site office. He unlocked the door, pulled her in and shut out the wind behind her. In minutes he had lights on and the heater going. She glanced around. The desk was surprisingly neat for a construction zone. Plans were pinned to the wall, and Hunter gestured to it.

"Here it is," he said huskily. "Your new store and apothecary."

Her eyes rounded. "What?"

He clasped her one hand in two of his. "You lost your apothecary because of me and my family." He nodded to the plans. "I wanted to give it back."

"Are you serious?" she gasped, glancing between her husband and the schematics drawn on the wall. She was still trying to get her insurance claim completed for her building. This—this was—wow.

Hunter nodded. "Uh-huh." He stepped up to the drawing. "See, you have a separate area here, on the lower level, for you to mix all your witchy-woo potions and lotions, and a separate consulting room here if you want it. I've added some storage there, for your supplies," he said, gesturing to some markings. "And the stairs are wider, but you also have an elevator if you need to move supplies between the floors. Your apothecary will be made from reinforced concrete—it's going to be a bunker that can withstand the end of the world, if need be," he muttered, waving his hands casually. "And here are the plans for the bookstore, with some event space if you wanted to get authors in for a talk or signing, or something…" He turned to her, and for the first time his expression was unsure. "And if you want, you can change anything you like."

"Hunter, this is so generous," she gasped.

He rolled his eyes. "Well, not quite. My family destroyed your clinic twice, so it seems only fair we should rebuild it, and—" He grimaced. "This makes me feel better after what I did to you, so it's completely selfish." He leaned down and kissed her quickly on the lips, before drawing back and holding up his hand. "I was going to attach your apothecary to my clinic, but then realized your patients wouldn't want to be anywhere near mine, but really, if you want to build somewhere else, that's fine, too—whatever you want." He drew her closer. "I just want you to be happy," he murmured. He lifted his gaze from her lips to her eyes. "What do you think?"

She smiled. "I think it's wonderful. Thank you."

Hunter closed his eyes in relief and tilted his forehead against hers. "Thank God. I wasn't sure if I was over-stepping the mark, or—"

She rose on the tips of her toes and kissed him. "It's wonderful," she reassured him. He nodded, pleased.

"I find I like making my family happy," he said huskily, and despite the warmth in his gaze, she also saw the fleeting concern.

Melissa squeezed his hand. "We'll find her, Hunter. Soon."

Ever since Arthur had mentioned the missing sister, Hunter and Ryder had been searching for her. They were slowly wading through Arthur's papers in an effort to discover the name of the woman who had birthed him a daughter. Griff was helping, too, and Lance. With so many searching, it was only a matter of time before they located their unknown sister.

He nodded and winked. "We'll find her," he repeated, his expression grim with determination.

She looked at him in inquiry. "Wasn't there something else you wanted to show me?" she said suggestively.

His lips curled in that wicked, sexy way of his, and those golden flecks in his eyes flared. "Why yes, yes there is."

He leaned over and flicked the lock on the site office door, and stepped closer to her.

"You know what they say about a new office, though, right?"

"This isn't my new office," she pointed out.

He nodded. "True, but we can practice."

The golden flecks glimmered in his eyes as he stopped in front of her.

Melissa shook her head. "Practice what, Hunter? What do they say about a new office?"

"That you should christen it at the very first opportunity," he murmured as he dipped his head. He took her lips in a scorching kiss as he slid the jacket down off her shoulders. She shrugged out of the garment, then slid her hands up his arms, enjoying the dip and flex of muscle as he started to unbutton her blouse.

His lips drifted across her jaw to her neck. "I hadn't heard that one," she admitted breathlessly as he opened her shirt, kissing his way over her collarbone and down to the lacy edge of her bra.

"Oh, yeah. It's a tradition." His hands caressed her back, unsnapping her bra strap and drawing the garment down her arms. He turned briefly and fired it like a slingshot at the top of a filing cabinet set against a wall. "You have to christen the desk, the chair—the floor."

He dipped his head to take a rosy peak in his mouth, and she trembled, heat flooding her as arousal built. "Oh, I had no idea," she murmured, then moaned as he drew down on her nipple, nipping gently with his teeth before laving it with his tongue. He cupped her other breast, alternating his attention between the two.

"Oh, yeah," he said huskily. "Then we have to christen my office."

"We do?"

He rose up and kissed her, bearing her back down on the surface of the desk. "Uh-huh." He pulled his sweater over his head, and she sighed as his muscled chest came into view.

"I like your traditions," she said, trailing her hands over his pectoral muscles. He grasped her hands, kissing each before placing them over her head so that she clasped the rim.

"You're going to need to hold on," he whispered, and she shuddered. He drew the palm of his hand down from her neck to the waistband of her skirt. He waggled his eyebrows.

"There are lots of them," he told her, and she frowned, trying to keep track of the conversation and not drown in sensation.

"Lots of what?" she asked as he rolled her hips to the side so he could access the zipper of her skirt. The sound of her zipper in the small office was loud and full of carnal promise. Her nipples tightened, and she could feel herself getting damp.

"Traditions," he told her as he slid her skirt down her legs and off, along with her panties. His eyes flared when he saw her garter belt and stockings. "Holy smoke."

She smiled at his appreciation. "What other traditions?" she prodded him as she turned back to face him.

"Oh, we have to christen each new moon," he said, dipping low to kiss her navel. She heard the slide of his zipper, heard the soft thump as his jeans hit the floor. "We have to christen each sunrise," he murmured as he kissed his way farther down her body. "Oh, and every time we open a new cereal box. Lots of traditions."

She shuddered as she felt his breath against her and her head arched back. She had to remind herself they were in a site office of a construction zone. What if one of the builders turned up? "Uh, Hunter, should we be doing this?" she murmured, eyeing the door. It was locked, but still, if the site supervisor turned up for any reason... She had no idea how busy a construction site could be on a Sunday, or whether people were likely to walk in and interrupt what was going on in the about-to-be-christened practice office.

She glanced down, and Hunter met her stare, his brown gaze wicked with promise.

"Trust me," he murmured. "I'm a doctor."

He dipped his head, and then she didn't care who saw or heard what as her husband showed her just how much he knew about the female anatomy. All she knew was that she loved this man, loved his sexy traditions, as well as the quirky little fireworks he set off each time they made love. He challenged her, he protected her—but more than anything, they were true partners. Mates for life. Her orgasm swept over her, and she cried out her release as Hunter entered her, and then it was starbursts and sparkles everywhere.

* * * * *

MILLS & BOON®
n o c t u r n e ™

AN EXHILARATING UNDERWORLD OF DARK DESIRES

A sneak peek at next month's titles...

In stores from 15th December 2016:

- **A Venetian Vampire** – Michele Hauf
- **Bayou Wolf** – Debbie Herbert

Just can't wait?
Buy our books online a month before they hit the shops!
www.millsandboon.co.uk

Also available as eBooks.